$\mathcal{A}$BSENT
. . . ONE FROM ANOTHER

Cheryl J. McCullough

Order this book online at www.trafford.com
or email orders@trafford.com

Most Trafford titles are also available at major online book retailers.

Cover design by Ariana Farquharson. www.foxxwork.com

Printed in the United States of America.

ISBN: 978-1-4907-4893-1 (sc)
ISBN: 978-1-4907-4895-5 (hc)
ISBN: 978-1-4907-4894-8 (e)

Library of Congress Control Number: 2014918316

Trafford rev. 10/24/2014

www.trafford.com
North America & international
toll-free: 1 888 232 4444 (USA & Canada)
fax: 812 355 4082

May the Lord watch between you and me,
while we are absent one from another.
                                        —*Genesis 31:49*

THE WEDDING PARTY
Final Chapter

The rehearsal was set to start at 5:00 p.m., the same hour as the wedding. There would not be a traditional rehearsal dinner, and Leah and Grant decided to have a party. There had been no bachelor party or bachelorette party; one big wedding party with their family and friends was what they wanted.

The staff from Lola's, including Campbell, had been there since early afternoon decorating and preparing food. Campbell was grateful for the long day. He needed the distraction and the money. He and Chloe were going to meet the couple who were going to adopt their baby tonight. They would be at the party, and Kathy thought that would be less formal for their first meeting. Kathy invited Chloe to the party. Neither of their parents was invited.

Kathy, Jill, and Gretchen had things in order. They did such a good job that they were afraid they had forgotten something. Gretchen made arrangements for all of the ladies, plus Brittani, Brianna, and Leah, to have a spa day on Friday.

Raja would be arriving in time to see Jill before the rehearsal. Jill was looking forward to seeing him. Things were getting pretty serious between them. She was sad, though, that his parents were putting so much pressure on him. His mother was being totally unreasonable. She had gone so far as to tell him he had to choose between Jill and his family. Tara told Jill to be patient and supportive. It was hard, but she knew Raja would do the right thing. Jill hoped his parents would back off. She wanted him to have her in his life and still have a relationship with his family.

As he drove into Hattiesville, Raja played over and over in his mind how he would tell Jill.

How could he blatantly disrespect his parents? The scripture said, "Honor your father and mother."

He knew they had his best interest at heart. He just hoped he could make Jill understand. She was the most incredible woman he knew; his parents didn't give her a chance.

Kirby had been sick all morning and Enoch didn't know if she was going to make it to the rehearsal and the party. He thought the morning sickness would have passed by now, but the doctor assured them everything was fine. They were both a little nervous about meeting the young expectant couple. Enoch wasn't totally sold on the open adoption idea, but Kirby had been right about the in-vitro, so he trusted her on this.

There had been so much to do to get Brianna and Brittani ready for the wedding; Belinda hadn't spent much time with Ben. He told her he would pick her up for the rehearsal since the girls would arrive with the other attendants. Grammy and Auntie were not involved with the rehearsal, but Ben got permission from Leah to invite them.

Grace wanted Paul to skip the rehearsal and the party so he wouldn't be too tired to enjoy the wedding and the reception, but he wouldn't hear it. "My only son is getting married, and I intend to be there for the whole thing." She gave up the fight. Gretchen made all the arrangements, and things were in order, so Grace decided to relax and enjoy herself too. She was so worried that Leah wasn't going to be well enough to get married. She was immensely grateful to God that this day had come. And Grant being back in the States was icing on the cake.

Katherine couldn't believe Lee was working. He had a meeting he said couldn't be scheduled for another day. His flight was due in at 2:00 p.m. which would give him plenty of time if the meeting didn't run over and there were no flight delays. She just wouldn't let herself think about that. "If he was late . . ." Okay, she said, she wasn't going to think about it. His amour bearer would pick him up, and they would meet at the church.

Leah walked into the fellowship hall and literally jumped for joy. It was perfect. She and Kathy went over the last-minute arrangements, and the reception director told them what would be the same and what would be different for the reception. Leah stood there in awe. Tears rolled down her face.

"Don't cry, Lee. You are messing up your makeup!" Kathy said. She rolled her eyes at her sister who put her arms around her, and they hugged tightly for a long minute. Leah asked for a glass of water, but she didn't let Kathy see her take the pill. She had a headache all day.

Janis called in sick for the second day. Her plan was not coming together. She didn't know if Grant was in town or not. *But he's supposed to get married tomorrow, so he has to be.* She laughed to herself. There would be no wedding tomorrow. Not if she had anything to do with it. She hadn't seen him or any evidence of him. She checked the flight schedule from Frankfurt for the last two weeks and spent a considerable amount of time in the airport but to no avail. She had been by the barbershop twice today and past Lola's and the church. She had to find Clay because she knew if she found Clay, she would find Grant.

There was a lot going on at the church, but she had not spotted Grant or Leah for that matter. The only people she saw that she knew were the ladies from Lola's. It was going to be hard for her to hide in the parking lot, but she would have to figure it out. *Who can I switch with so they won't recognize my car?*

Ben and the wedding director talked previously, and things were in order. Grant and Clay arrived at the church early enough for Grant to have a few minutes alone with Leah. Clay dropped Grant at the door and went to park the car. Just as he got out, Delia approached him. *Where did she come from?* He thought.

"Clay, may I speak to you for a minute?"

"I don't have much time, Delia." He looked at his watch for emphasis.

"I don't need but a couple of minutes." They hadn't seen each other since the night he asked her to take the pregnancy test. They had spoken only once when he called to get her permission to pick up Jeremy from baseball practice. He and Jeremy talked, and he told Jeremy he was going to be assigned to a new big brother. Jeremy was okay with it. He just asked Clay if he could still call him sometime.

"Clay, I want to apologize for lying about being pregnant. I panicked when you said the relationship wasn't working for you. I needed a way to keep you around, keep you in my life."

"Dee . . . uh, Delia, we didn't have a relationship. We were not dating or courting, whatever you want to call it. We were having sex."

"But you had to have feelings for me, or do you just have sex with anybody?"

"My feelings for you were physical. You are beautiful. You have an amazing body, and the sex was great. It didn't go any further than that."

Tears were streaming down her face. She looked embarrassed by what Clay was saying.

"Do you remember me telling you our lack of having a relationship was your fault?"

"Yes. Why?"

"But you never figured it out, did you? The reason I said that is because men are only as faithful as their options. You allowed me to have options. You didn't hold me accountable, and I took advantage of that. You were good with me spending the night and not even calling you back." He looked at his watch. "I gotta go, but hear me on this. You need to step up your game. Have some pride, don't be so easy. Don't let anybody else do you like I did."

"So what about your friend? I guess she's not easy, and she has pride. If I was like her, I guess you would like me." She was being sarcastic.

Clay chuckled and shook his head. "She's a class act, and we have a real relationship. We talk, we laugh, we eat together—things you and I never did. She made it clear to me that we would not have sex until and unless we were married. And you know what, Delia, I'm fine with that."

He walked away.

Ben suggested to the wedding director that since Leah would be seated during the rehearsal that Belinda could be the one to stand in for the bride. She was a little surprised when the director asked her, but she accepted. She blushed when Ben gave her a single long-stem pink rose to use as the bridal bouquet. They hadn't been very public about their relationship, so this was a major statement.

The rehearsal went like clockwork. Grant clowned a bit, teasing Belinda about being the bride. When the wedding director asked at the end if anybody had any questions, Ben stepped up and said he had one.

He took Belinda by the hand and got down on one knee. Grant stepped out of the way. A collective gasp went through the group. The sanctuary was completely quiet.

"Belinda." His voice cracked; he cleared his throat. "Belinda, I love you very much, and I want to spend the rest of my life with you."

Belinda knew everybody could hear her heart beating. She was looking down at Ben, and he was looking directly into her eyes. "You are my best friend and my soul mate. I praise God every day for finding you. Will you bless me forever by being my wife?"

With a big smile, she said, "Yes."

And he slipped the ring on her finger.

The party was off to a great start. There was plenty of food and great music. Leah's headache had eased considerably, and she was having the time of her life. It was like a fairytale come true. All the people she loved were there, and she was marrying Prince Charming. God had smiled on her, and she was eternally grateful.

Ben's proposal to Belinda exasperated the celebration. The twins ran to Belinda screaming. Grammy and Auntie were wiping tears, and everybody else was surprised. Belinda was totally and genuinely shocked. Enoch wanted to know what Ben would have done if she had said no.

When Raja arrived at the church, the rehearsal had already started. Jill was standing in her place at the altar. He let his imagination run away with him for a minute. He imagined her standing there in a wedding gown.

With all the excitement, the party was going well. Raja hated to pull Jill away, but he was prolonging the inevitable. He finally asked her if they could go somewhere and talk for a few minutes. He looked so serious. Jill got up immediately, took his hand, and walked out of the fellowship hall. They went outside into the courtyard.

"Raja, are you okay?"

"Yeah, I'm okay. I apologize for pulling you away from the party, but I need to tell you something, and I didn't want it to wait.

Jill's heart was beating fast. "What is it?"

She sat down on the bench, and he sat down beside her.

"You know, my parents and I have been at odds since we went to London for Yash's wedding. There is a lot more to it than what I have shared with you. They gave me an ultimatum: to choose between you and my family. Jill, I love my parents, and I am their only child. I can't imagine life without them. Sure, they—well, my mother drives me crazy, but they're my parents. I know you understand because you love your family too, and you understand how important family is."

Jill was getting angry. But she didn't say anything. She couldn't believe he was letting them control him and his life.

He continued. "I had a long talk with Tara, and of course, she told me to cut my ties with them and go on with my life. But how can I? Even the scriptures address how we are to treat our parents."

As he continued to talk, Jill was thinking to herself that she would not let him ruin this occasion for her. Leah had fought her way back, and she was getting married tomorrow. Raja could go back to Chapel Hill and out of her life. Tears were stinging the back of her eyes.

"Jill, you are so important to me, and I don't want you out of my life either."

She was thinking, *Okay, here it comes—"Can we still be friends?"* She was going to say no.

As if Raja was reading her mind, he said, "And I don't want us to be just friends. I want more than that. So I have made a major decision, but I have to know that you are with me, that you want what I want. Once I tell my parents, you and Tara will be my family."

Jill took a deep breath.

"I don't want you to think I am a terrible person or an ungrateful child. Jill, I am committed to making our relationship work, and if that means I have to cut my ties with my parents, so be it. For my whole life, I have done everything my parents asked but not this time. I want you, Jill, more than I want their approval."

Her heart was melting. She wanted Raja too, but how could she let him sever his ties with his parents? This was very serious. What if he resented her for that one day? *God, please tell me what to say*, she thought to herself.

"Raja, you are very important to me too, and I don't want to be out of your life. Yes, Raja, I am with you. I will be your family. I will be who you need me to be. Family is who loves you when you need them."

He stood and pulled her into his arms. They held each other without saying anything.

The door to the patio opened, and Jill looked up to see Clay and Cicely hand in hand. Clay winked at her. She smiled and realized that they had been gone for a while and needed to get back inside.

"Clay Sturdivant, why did you take me away from my shrimp, bring me out here, interrupt Jill and Dr. Raja, and you're just standing here grinning?"

He put his arms around her, kissed her forehead, and stepped back. He looked into her eyes and said it: "I love you, Cicely." Before she could say anything, he went on. "I have had a good run, but I'm done with the lying, the deception, and the games. I will tell you my story later, but I just want to say to you right here, right now, that I have asked God to forgive me for my foolishness, and I hope you will find me worthy of you and your heart."

Janis switched cars with her brother and parked his truck at the back of the parking lot. A few people left, and she saw someone come out and put trash in the dumpster, but she sat there for what seemed like hours. She spotted Clay's car, and that's what she needed to keep an eye on. People started to come out, and eventually, she saw Clay walking a lady to her car but no Grant. A few minutes later, Grant and Leah walked out arm in arm, her sister and a couple of other people behind them. Grant walked her to the car. They stood and held each other for a long while. Janis closed her eyes. She had to stay focused.

She reached in her pocketbook to make sure the gun was on top. She hadn't ever fired a gun before, and she hoped Grant would cooperate tonight and she wouldn't have to. She also hoped she wouldn't have to hurt Clay in the process. All she wanted Grant to do was call off the wedding and take the time to establish a relationship with her. She knew that if he just gave her a chance, she could make him happy and be a good wife to him. Once she and Grant were married, she would be well respected in the community, and Leah would be the second-class citizen.

Clay walked over and said something to Grant. They laughed and shook hands. Clay got in the car with the lady, and Grant got in Clay's car on the driver's side. This was working better than she planned.

Janis pulled out of the parking lot behind Grant but kept her distance. When he turned toward the interstate, she knew it would be hard to keep up with him, but she had to. Where was he going? This wasn't the way to his parents' home or his sister's home. Did he know she was following him and was trying to jerk her around?

When Grant got off the exit, Janis didn't know where she was. She looked for a couple of landmarks so she could get back to the interstate.

This had to be a new subdivision, she thought, *because there weren't many streetlights.*

She slowed down to see what he was doing. He turned onto a driveway, so she turned in behind him and blew the horn. Grant was puzzled about who was in the truck. Janis reached for her purse and put it on her shoulder, her hand on the gun.

He couldn't believe his eyes when he saw her standing there. "Janis, go home. I am not going to deal with you tonight." He reached for his phone.

She pulled out the gun. "Give me the phone, Grant."

"I'm not giving you anything. Janis, what do you want?"

"We need to talk, Grant. You are going to hear me out. You are going to call off the wedding, and you and I are going to get married."

Grant laughed, and that infuriated Janis. "Are you going to say anything I haven't heard before? He started to dial the phone, and she made sure he knew she had the gun.

"Give me the phone, Grant."

"Give me the gun, Janis."

Grant knew he could physically overpower her, but he had to figure out how to get the gun away from her without either of them getting hurt. Janis had cracked up; she had really lost it. Grant knew Clay was on his way, but he couldn't wait. He had to manage the situation then.

"Janis, what do you want from me? I have told you, over and over, I don't want you. I don't love you. I love Leah, and I am going to marry her tomorrow."

"You *will not* marry Leah Robinson. Not tomorrow, not any day!" She was screaming. "Grant I will kill you before I let you marry her!"

"Janis, if you kill me, then I can't marry you either." She was standing close and waving the gun in his face. He had her attention with the word *marry.*

"Okay. Okay, Janis. I'll call her. I'll call Leah and tell her the wedding is off, but you have to give me the gun."

"Let me hear you tell her you love me and not her, and you want me to be your wife. Do it, Grant!"

Grant dialed Clay's number. "What's up, G?"

"Leah, this is Grant. I'm here with Janis, and I'm calling to tell you the wedding is off. I am going to marry Janis."

"Oh, man, is she at my house with you?"

"Yeah."

"I'm on my way, G. I'll call the police." Clay hung up.

"Let me speak to her."

"She hung up, Janis."

Clay called 911, and he and Cicely headed to his house. They were about twenty minutes away. The police should get there quickly. There wasn't a whole lot going on in Wyndham. Clay sped up, and he dialed Grant's number. It went straight to voice mail.

"Call her back, Grant. I want to speak to her."

"Janis, you said if I called Leah you would give me the gun."

"Not yet. I won't give it to you yet."

"How can I marry you, Janis, if I can't trust you to keep your word?"

Janis was sweating and wide eyed. Grant had to get the gun from her. He grabbed her, and they both fell.

"This is 911. What is your emergency?"

"I heard what sounded like a gunshot at my next-door neighbor's house.

Epilogue

Leah went to her room took two more pills for her headache. She lay across the bed and recounted the events of the day. The sanctuary and reception hall were beautifully decorated. She looked across the room. Her wedding gown was absolutely gorgeous. She thought about Grant. He was the most wonderful man in the world, and he loved her. How cool was that? At that moment, there could not be anybody in the world happier. She closed her eyes and prayed, *if I should die before I wake, I pray, dear Lord, my soul you'll take.* And He did.

PROLOGUE

He heard the phone. It was the second time it rang. He wouldn't answer it. They planned to be together this weekend for months. Birthdays are special. This relationship had no demands, no expectations. He appreciated that. He turned over, snuggled closer, closed his eyes, and ignored the ring. Whatever it was would have to wait. Being here was his priority at the moment. There was a lot of maneuvering to make this work. He dozed off. There would be no way to explain suddenly having to leave. He promised nothing would come between them, not this time. Plus, there was a lot to lose if he made a bad decision. Too many lives were entangled. Too many.

CHAPTER ONE

It had been three years since Kathy Robinson's older sister Leah passed from an aneurysm the night before her wedding. But for Kathy, it was still so fresh. As she reconnected with Sterling, she found herself talking a lot about Leah and the last year of her life. Sterling was the only person in her circle who wasn't around when Leah passed. It was actually kind of refreshing. Her parents, their extended family, the church family, and friends were all still reeling from what happened.

Kathy's father, Bishop Lee Robinson, was the pastor of the very progressive Hattiesville Community Church. He was so devastated by his daughter's death that it took him months to return to his pulpit. His wife Katherine finally put her own grief aside and convinced him to go back. She knew the church couldn't begin to heal until he returned. They were all in a tough place—that place where you know God is but you can't hear Him or feel Him. That space where you can't pray because you can only cry.

During the months that the bishop was away, Minister Benjamin Coffey took the reigns and led the staff and other church leaders in keeping the ministry moving. In taking over for Bishop Robinson, Ben had to put on hold the plans for the first church plant in the Atlanta area, marrying Belinda Stewart, and adopting her twin daughters Brittani and Brianna. But a year later, they were married in a small ceremony which Bishop Robinson officiated. Belinda's sister Kirby was her matron of honor and Kirby's husband Enoch was Ben's best man.

When Kathy saw the friend request from Sterling Chance on Facebook, she was surprised but not shocked. They met originally in college, dated briefly, had a misunderstanding and didn't see each other again until a year ago when they met at a conference, and he talked her into having dinner with him. He was now the head football coach at DavisTown College, and they resumed their friendship.

She was a big football fan, so he knew that was a good way for him to spend some time getting to know her better. He really liked her, but she seemed so distracted. He took the team to worship at Hattiesville Community Church occasionally, and he would come pretty regularly during the off season. When she asked why he didn't join, he told her that he knew they had a high level of accountability, and he couldn't serve at that level because of the demands of his job. Kathy didn't accept that as an excuse, but he knew that was a stipulation of them moving from friendship to courtship.

Sterling Chance had been a standout college football player— an All-American—at DavisTown. He was drafted by the NFL and played five seasons for the Dallas Cowboys. An injury sidelined him for an entire season, and his comeback season was not without its challenges. He retired from the league, and the timing was perfect. The DavisTown coach was retiring, and they hired Sterling immediately.

Clay had been true to his word when he told Cicely the night before Leah and Grant were supposed to get married that he loved her and wanted to be in an exclusive relationship with her. He asked her to move in with him but she refused. She was true to her word about doing things the right way. He did get her to rearrange some things financially so that she could quit the part-time job. Her being more available had definitely enhanced their relationship.

Clay was still concerned about Grant. He had gone through with the transfer to Walter Reed Hospital in Washington DC, but for the first year after Leah passed, he did not adjust well. His family encouraged him to get some counseling, but it didn't seem to help. He was angry with God for allowing Janis to live and Leah to die.

The night before the wedding Grant and Janis struggled over a gun that she intended to use to keep him from marrying Leah. She was shot and the bullet was lodged in her spine. She had surgery and was hospitalized for weeks but survived. Leah had unknowingly developed another cerebral aneurysm. Her blood pressure went up and the aneurysm ruptured, causing her death the night before her wedding.

CHAPTER TWO

"What kind of name is Jacksa?" he asked.

She laughed. "When my parents met in Korea, my mom didn't speak much English. My dad told her his name was Jackson. She pronounced it 'Jacksa.' That became her nickname for him, and after they were married, they decided Jacksa would be the name of their first child. So here I am!"

Anderson Thorn had recently met Jacksa Baye at the birthday party of a mutual friend. He thought she was fascinating, she thought he was mysterious. She asked about his name.

"My mother's maiden name is Anderson, and since I am the only male in the family, my grandmother wanted me to have the name."

"You don't have any brothers?"

"No, I am the youngest of three. I have two older sisters, and my mother had only one sibling—a sister."

"I bet you are really spoiled."

"Well, I admit to being grandma's baby, a mama's boy, and the apple of my sisters and my aunt's eye!"

Jacksa just rolled her eyes. His dimples were so cute when he smiled.

Anderson grew up in South Carolina, along the Catawba River, on the reservation of the Catawba Indian Nation with his paternal family. His mother was half-Catawba, but his father was full-blooded Catawba Indian. His father died when he was young, but the community rallied around him, his mother and sisters. When he moved away to attend college, it was a success story for everyone on the reservation.

Jacksa Baye had been hired as a paralegal in the law offices of Sandra and Roderick Matthews. She didn't intend to come home to Charlotte, DavisTown, actually. But her mother's illness compelled her to be close. Jacksa and her brother Jackson Jr., JJ, always thought their mother would be better had the multiple sclerosis been diagnosed earlier. For six years, her condition was misdiagnosed, and now Min Baye was getting progressively worse. She was using a walker all the time, and her vision was worsening. The dark spot in her eye had become a blind spot. She still insisted on working a few days a week, teaching an online class for DavisTown College.

Jacksa's parents, Jackson and Min met as children. His father was in the military and stationed in Korea. Min's mother and father worked on the base. Min and Jackson went to school together, and their families lived in the same complex. He had always loved her. But she couldn't stand him! He used to throw rocks at her and tell her he was going to marry her when she grew up.

After Jackson and his family left Korea, they communicated occasionally if he initiated the contact. But when she came to the States to attend college, she wrote him to let him know. He was a senior at Howard University when Min arrived as a freshman at Georgetown University. Because Jackson was the only person Min knew in the States, she depended on him a lot and he liked that. They married shortly after she graduated.

Jackson Baye usually got a haircut on Thursday after work and then had a drink with his barber. Min didn't expect him until around nine o'clock and during basketball season later after the game. Since JJ was away in school, Jacksa made a point of seeing her mother on Thursday. Min didn't like Jacksa fussing over her, but she enjoyed the company. They decided to eat out. Min was feeling particularly strong that day. They had a good visit and, like clockwork, Jackson came in a little after nine. Min sat and chatted with them for a few minutes and then excused herself to get ready for bed. Jackson remarked to his daughter that it was taking Min longer now to dress and undress, actually longer to do everything. He insisted that she not shower unless someone else was there with her. He also didn't like for her to cook. She had gotten burned because she couldn't feel her hand on the hot toaster oven. The burn wasn't bad, but it could have been worse.

As her father was talking, Jacksa looked at him closely. He was a fifty-six-year-old man who was aging gracefully. He worked out regularly, and it showed. Her mother was a fifty-one-year-old woman with a debilitating disease that was aging her rapidly. She knew they were still very much in love, and Jackson was super attentive to Min, but Jacksa couldn't help but wonder about their relationship.

She left her parents' home a little down, but a call from her brother lifted her spirits. JJ, as she called him, always had a story to tell. He was a junior basketball player at Duke University. He asked her about her visit with their mom. She was always honest with him, and she was glad today to have a good report. JJ was a good player, and he earned a full scholarship. Going to "the league" was a dream, but he knew the reality was he needed to make the best of his free education. His major was broadcast journalism. He wanted to be a sportscaster.

Jacksa was JJ's biggest fan. When their mother got sick, she took care of him. She cooked for him, made sure he went to all his practices, and taught him how to do laundry. When she went to college, she was confident he could manage with minimum assistance from their mother.

The feeling was mutual. JJ adored Jacksa. Their parents teased him that what Jacksa said was "gospel" to him. When she was in college, he visited as much as he could. And now that he was playing at the college level, she went to as many games as possible. Jackson would usually go to his games too. Min attended all the home games his freshman year, fewer the sophomore year, and even fewer this past season.

Jackson sent a text message as soon as Jacksa left. *"Home. Daughter was here. Talk tmrw. Good nite."*

While JJ and Jacksa were talking, Anderson sent a text message to confirm he would see her the next day; he had some news. Jacksa and Anderson were settled into a routine of having lunch on Fridays. Things were usually slow in the office, and that was his day off. Today, Anderson was excited. He shared with her that his application for the promotion had been accepted. He was going the following week for the first round interview. So if all went well, he would be promoted to detective. Anderson told Jacksa that ultimately he wanted to be an FBI agent, and this was a step in that direction. Jacksa wasn't sure how she felt about that, but she was excited for him.

"Have you told your family? She asked.

He laughed. "Yeah, I told my sisters, and they told my mom and my aunt, but we all agreed not to tell my grandma yet. I'll tell her in person once everything is solidified. No need to worry her unnecessarily."

"Do you think she's going to be worried?"

"No doubt. She hates that I have a job where I carry a gun everyday." They continued to talk, and Jacksa was surprised at how open he was with her. They were friends, but she didn't feel as at ease with him as he obviously felt with her. He told her about the training and that the job may require him to go undercover at some point.

CHAPTER THREE

Kirby and Enoch Casebier tried for over a year for her to become pregnant. They finally went through the in-vitro process and had a baby boy whom they named Blake. Blake was born exactly two months before his brother Nicholas, the baby Enoch and Kirby adopted from a teenage couple. Having two infants was more work than Kirby imagined, but she loved every minute of it. Because Ben and Belinda did not move right away, Ben's grandmother Victoria Coffey and his great-aunt Avis Johnson were still in Hattiesville too. Grammy and Auntie were a tremendous help to Kirby and Enoch. The boys were three years old and getting ready to go to Montessori school, so Kirby was going back to work full time. She and Enoch owned Casebier Collection, a trash and recyclables pick-up company. Business was good, and they were glad.

Campbell did all he could to keep his relationship with Chloe going, but she had changed. The baby they gave up for adoption was now three years old. It was a son they named Nicholas, named after Chloe's middle name, Nichole. That was Campbell's idea. He thought it would help to heal her heart. They had agreed to give the baby up. They were sixteen years old, and still in high school. They also agreed to an open adoption and the Casebier's agreed to let them check up on Nicholas from time to time. Campbell called at least once a month, and he knew in his heart of hearts that they made a good decision. Chloe started off doing the same, but her contacts with Nicholas became less and less. Now she wasn't responding to Campbell either. He was in college at DavisTown, and Chloe was in Atlanta at Spelman.

Ben, Belinda, and the twins had settled into their life in Landridge, Georgia. The Landridge Community Church had celebrated its first anniversary. Ben settled into his life as father, husband, and pastor. Brittani and Brianna were attending the International School and were "majoring" in the arts. Brittani chose ballet and the violin; Brianna chose ballet and drama. Everybody who knew Brianna knew drama was a good choice for her. They were both also in creative writing. Belinda and Ben were particularly impressed with the school. Though it was not a Christian school and that was their first choice, they found the student body, faculty, and staff of the International School to be diverse and the school to have a broad curriculum.

Belinda was working as an operating room nurse at Emory Hospital. Ben didn't particularly want Belinda working. They could live comfortably without her salary, but he knew how hard she had worked to earn her nursing credentials and how much she wanted to work. So their agreement was that her salary would go toward savings, mainly for their children's college education. She did a good job of balancing her responsibility as first lady, wife, mother, and nurse. Life for the Coffey family was good.

"Brittani, you have to tell Mommy or Daddy."

"I can't, Brianna. She made me promise not to tell anybody. I'll just take some extra snacks and give them to her."

"Do you think Mommy won't know?"

Brittani let out a big sigh. She knew her sister was right. Her friend, Carlotta, had confided to her that her family didn't have much food, and lunch at school was her only meal most days. But Brittani was determined not to break her friend's confidence. She put an apple, peanut butter crackers, and a bagel in another bag and hurriedly hid it in her backpack. When Ben walked into the kitchen, he knew they were up to something, but he didn't ask.

He knew Belinda would figure it out. She always did. He called her the holy ghost of their home. She knew everything.

On the ride to school each morning, one of them would pray. Today it was Brianna's turn. She prayed that they would make their day great and thanked God for their family having enough food. When she prayed for Carlotta, Brittani drew in her breath. Ben didn't miss any of it, nor did he miss Brittani stomping her foot at Brianna when they got out of the car. He made a mental note to tell Belinda when she called him on her morning break.

When Brittani saw Carlotta during the first block, she gave her the bag. Carlotta was very grateful and ate the bagel immediately. But she made sure Brittani had not told anybody. Brittani was honest that she told Brianna, but she told Carlotta they could trust Brianna.

"Thank you, Brittani. If any of the teachers or adults find out, they may take us from our parents."

"What do you mean take you from your parents?"

Carlotta whispered to Brittani, "My mama said my daddy lost his job because he didn't have a security number."

Neither of them knew what that meant, but it sounded important, and Brittani knew it was keeping her friend's family from having enough to eat.

Days went by, and Brittani continued to take snacks to Carlotta. She knew Carlotta was sharing the snacks with her younger brother who was in the third grade. One morning, while Belinda was preparing the girls' lunches and snacks for an all-day field trip, she made an arbitrary comment to Ben about replacing snacks so often. He remembered he hadn't mentioned the incident to her that he intended to. He told her about Brianna's prayer and Brittani's response to it. He went on to tell her about them adding snacks to their bags one morning after Belinda prepared them. But they didn't know he saw them. Belinda's response was to ask Ben if he would make a point to be home for dinner that evening. He said he would. He laughed. He loved his wife and her way of getting things done.

That evening at dinner, everybody reviewed their day by using a technique Belinda read that First Lady Michelle

Obama said her family used at dinner: "Roses and Thorns." Ben started and said his day had been more roses than thorns. He had been looking for another building for the church to move into. They were experiencing steady growth, and Ben wanted to be proactive. He and Bishop Robinson talked, and Ben would be going back to Hattiesville for a few days. He also talked to Grammy and she was going to come back with him for a while. That also usually meant Ben would be accompanying Bishop Robinson on a trip. Brianna said all roses, as did Brittani. Brittani went on to explain that someone had challenged her for her first chair violin status in the orchestra, but she was able to maintain it.

When it was Belinda's turn, she said more thorns. "Oh, Mommy, why?" Brianna asked. She told them that she was really tired from her surgeries that day, and she had to stop at the store to get more fruit, snacks, and juice boxes. She continued to talk about the grocery getting gone so fast and how much money they were spending on food. She and Ben made eye contact, but the girls didn't look up. When she finished, Brittani said she hoped the next day would have more roses. Brianna agreed then wanted to know exactly when Grammy was coming.

Campbell was surprised to get Chloe's call. They hadn't talked in days. She told him she wanted to see him and she would be home for the weekend. He was working at Sheldon's, an exclusive lakefront restaurant. He only worked two or three days per week. As much as he wanted to see her, he had to work his shifts. He was also afraid that if he didn't agree to see her she wouldn't come home. He agreed to see her. He would just have to make it work. Campbell loved Chloe. He wanted to marry her and have a family with her when they were more established. For a year after the baby was born, even during the pregnancy, they were so close. He took care of her and she let him. Then something happened. Everything changed. Campbell didn't see it coming, and he really couldn't explain it. One day everything just changed.

Campbell was able to work out his schedule so that he and Chloe could spend Saturday evening together. They were really glad to see each other. She looked fantastic. She had colored her hair, and it was longer. As always, she was dressed immaculately. She was wearing the gold heart necklace he gave her for graduation. They talked openly and candidly. She confided in Campbell that she took her mother's advice and sought counseling. She told him that during that time she couldn't talk to him or anybody else. They ate, laughed, and walked holding hands. Toward the end of the evening, she asked him if he had been in touch with Kirby or Enoch about Nicholas. Campbell looked at Chloe and smiled. He took both her hands in his. "Yeah babe, I have, and he's fine. I asked them for a picture, but I haven't gotten it."

"I know it's weird that I haven't called, but I couldn't. I was just feeling too sad and so guilty."

"Chloe, we've been through all that. We made the best decision we could make at that time. Nicholas is doing well; he has great parents and a brother." Campbell put one arm around her. "When we get out of school . . ." He kissed her cheek. "We will get married . . ." He kissed her hand. "And then we will have more kids that we can raise together . . ." He kissed her lips. She laid her head on his shoulder, and he put both arms around her. This was a full circle moment for them.

They talked about school and their plans for the summer. Chloe said she was looking forward to being back in Hattiesville with Campbell and her parents. She would be working for her parents in their law office. Campbell would keep his job at Sheldon's but he was also going to work as an intern in sports information at DavisTown College. He hoped his two jobs wouldn't interfere with their summer.

CHAPTER FOUR

For the first two years after Clay and Delia ended their "relationship," she didn't seriously date. She was so undone with the way things ended between her and Clay, how he dismissed her, telling her their relationship was purely physical. Delia knew she had to do better. Clay was right. He took advantage of her because she allowed him to.

First things first, Delia knew she and her children, Jeremy and Crystal, needed to start going to church. Jeremy wanted to go to Hattiesville Community Church, but Delia knew she couldn't be there with Clay and Cicely. A coworker of Delia's invited her to his church. There was a good mix of people and more of a Hispanic contingent than Hattiesville Community Church. Delia joined after visiting a few months, and during new members' orientation, Delia met Javier Salvatore. They hit it off immediately.

Javier was the general manager of a family of movie theaters, so Jeremy and Crystal liked being able to see all the movies and most of them before any of their friends. Delia liked the fact that Javier treated her like a lady. He was different from any man who had ever been in her life. Maybe it was the fact that he was a little older, or maybe it was the fact that he was a Christian. Delia wanted to believe he treated her better because she treated herself better. She expected more and received more. One thing she took to heart was a statement the pastor made. She posted it on her desk at work and on her bathroom mirror: "If you want something different, do something different."

Kirby watched her boys as they finished breakfast. Blake was more like Enoch, quiet, very independent, and thoughtful. Nicholas was more rambunctious, more playful, and loved to be the center of attention. Kirby imagined his personality to be more like Chloe's, his biological mother. Campbell was more quiet and reserved. Chloe was bubbly. Kirby had gotten an e-mail from Sandra Matthews, asking about Nicholas. She replied that he was well and that she would send a picture soon. Sandra, Nicholas's biological grandmother, was only interested in his well-being, but Kirby didn't want to encourage Sandra. All of them gave up their rights to Nicholas when he was adopted, and although they agreed to the open adoption, she was adamant about not letting them interfere with her family.

Kirby had the life she prayed for: a wonderful husband, two great kids—one she had birthed from her own body—a job she loved, managing her husband's business, and to top it all off, her sister was happy too. For two girls who grew up in foster care, they were doing well.

Blake interrupted her daydream. "Look, Mama!" She looked up to see Nicholas drinking his milk holding the cup with his teeth and no hands. Blake was laughing, which encouraged Nicholas. Before Kirby could reach him, the cup dropped to the table splashing milk all over his shirt. Kirby loved her life.

Carlotta was out of school for two days, and Brittani was worried. She casually asked one of their teachers if Carlotta was sick. The teacher didn't know. Brittani saw Brianna in the library and told her Carlotta was out again. Brianna asked to be excused and ran to the cafeteria to see if Carlotta's brother was there with the other third graders. He was not. At the last block of the day, Brianna and Brittani met in ballet. Brianna tried to convince

Brittani she should share her concern with their parents. Brittani said she would if Carlotta wasn't in school the next day.

Many days the girls didn't know who would be picking them up. Belinda worked twelve-hour shifts, and Ben's schedule was somewhat unpredictable. The backup person was Thelma, the lady from church who helped Belinda around the house. Belinda didn't like referring to Thelma as the housekeeper, and the twins didn't like saying she was their sitter. They were eleven years old; they didn't need a sitter! Ben didn't care what they called her. He liked her because she handled business, and she reminded him of his aunt Avis. They were the same age and had a lot in common. Brittani and Brianna decided she should be referred to as the family helper. But today it wasn't Mommy, Daddy, or Thelma. Much to Brianna and Brittani's surprise, Grammy was there to pick them up. She walked the half mile to their school as she usually did if the weather permitted. They were ecstatic. Both of them fired questions at the same time. As they walked home, she told them she decided to come a few days early so their parents could have some private time before their dad left to go out of town with Bishop Robinson. Grammy loved referring to Ben as their dad. The truth was he couldn't have loved them more if they were his biological children.

When Grammy was in town, things in the Coffey household had a different energy. She would be up when the girls got up and still be up when they went to bed at night. Belinda said Grammy did too much, especially for the girls, but Grammy said the whole point in the being there was to help.

By sheer observation, Grammy figured out the basic issue with Brittani and her friend Carlotta. Grammy didn't know the details, but she would give Brittani a chance to fill in the blanks. On the walk home the third day, Grammy was there. She asked Brittani about the extra snacks in her book bag.

Brianna looked at Brittani with the I-told-you-so look. Brittani didn't immediately answer. Grammy walked a little further and repeated the question. "Can we please talk when we get home?" Brittani asked. Grammy agreed.

At the kitchen table over a bowl of popcorn, Brittani explained to Grammy that she had been taking snacks to her classmate and why. Brianna jumped in from time to time, and finally, Grammy asked her to let Brittani tell the story. Grammy was concerned about Carlotta and her family, but first things first.

"You know you will have to tell your mama and daddy when they get back."

"Yes, ma'am."

"So what do you think your punishment should be for taking the food and not telling the truth about it?" Brittani thought briefly, but Brianna spoke up.

"Gram, I don't think Brianna should be punished. She was trying to help her friend."

"Can we talk to Daddy about it when they call tonight?" Brittani asked.

Grammy knew the girls would get Ben to see their rationale. Grammy wasn't really interested in punishing Brittani; she just wanted her to make better decisions.

CHAPTER FIVE

"Clay, what's up, man?"

Clay looked back surprised to see Jeremy, the young man he mentored through the Big Brothers program. He resigned from being Jeremy's big brother and from the program after being in a relationship with Delia, Jeremy's mom. It was a relationship that went terribly wrong. Jeremy and a couple of his friends were coming out of the theater at the mall and headed for the food court. Clay couldn't believe how tall Jeremy was, but he hadn't seen him in at least two years.

"What you been up to, Jeremy?"

"I'm doin' good. Grades good, made the varsity team, and playin' AAU!"

"That's what's up. Proud of you. You still in the program?"

"Naw, my mom took me out. I been doin' all right in school and stuff. Plus, hangin' out with Javier gives me somebody to talk to."

"Who is Javier?"

"My mom's boyfriend, fiancé, whatever you call it."

Clay didn't respond to that comment. He changed the subject, asked about Jeremy's next game. He asked Jeremy to send him a schedule. "I'll tell my mom to e-mail it to you. I'm off the computer, except for school stuff. I was spending too much time on there, so Javier put me on restriction." Clay wanted to ask if Javier was living with them, but he didn't.

They parted. Clay got his food and sat down. He hadn't really thought about Delia in a long time. She had told him she was pregnant after he told her their relationship was not working for him anymore. When he forced her hand to prove she was pregnant, she couldn't. He hadn't seen her since the night before Grant and Leah were supposed to get married. She showed up at the rehearsal to apologize. Clay allowed his mind to go back to those days, to all the women who were in his life then, including Cicely. To all the nights he spent with Delia knowing their relationship was against the agency rules and knowing that for him it was purely physical. He recalled how frightened he was when he considered she may have been pregnant. He knew he didn't want a baby with Delia. He wanted to be with Cicely.

That situation shocked him into reality, and at the wedding party he told Cicely he wanted to be in an exclusive relationship with her. He eventually told her everything about the other women and about Delia. Things were uneasy with them for a bit, but they worked through it. Cicely insisted he be tested for HIV and STDs. He was given a clean bill of health. She forgave him, and they were able to move on.

That seemed like such a long time ago and yet not so long at all. Clay hadn't formally proposed to Cicely, but his mind was there. He was processing it all. He loved her for real. Thinking about getting married always made him think about Grant. So he called him.

"What's up, G?" Clay made a point of sounding upbeat. He didn't know what to expect from one conversation to the next.

"Clay, how ya doin'?" Grant sounded good; today must have been a good day. They talked, and Grant told Clay he would be home for the weekend.

"Need to see everybody," Grant told Clay.

"That's what's up. You gettin' in time to play Friday night?" Clay asked.

"You really don't want none'a this!" Clay, Grant, and Enoch had an ongoing Xbox and PlayStation competition. Ben would play with them before he moved.

Clay laughed. "Okay, I'll see whatcha got. I'll set it up. You want me to pick you up?"

"No I'm drivin' in. Be there early afternoon." Clay called Gretchen, Grant's twin sister, and asked her to prepare some food for Friday night. Then he called Cicely to tell her his plans.

CHAPTER SIX

Grammy inquired at the school and found out that Carlotta and her brother had not officially withdrawn, but they had not returned. The lower school administrator shared Grammy's concern. She promised Grammy she would follow up, and Grammy told her she would talk to Ben to see what the church could do to help. He and Belinda would be back the next day.

Among all that Brittani and Brianna had to tell their parents, Brittani told them about the situation with Carlotta and the snacks. Brianna defended her. Grammy added what she found out. Ben spoke first because he knew Belinda would want to deal with them not telling her the truth. As far as he was concerned, that was minor to getting the situation resolved.

"I'll make some calls in a few minutes, see what I can do. But, Brittani, you owe us an apology. You know we don't keep secrets." Brittani and Brianna dropped their heads. "We won't punish you this time because you were doing a good thing, but you should have been upfront with us," Ben continued. Brittani had tears in her eyes.

"I'm sorry, Mommy and Daddy. I didn't mean to break the rules." The tears rolled down her face. "Bree, I'm sorry for getting you to help me and not telling Mommy like you told me to."

"It's okay, Britt. I could have told too."

Grammy was satisfied. Ben knew he would have to square the "no punishment" decision with Belinda. The girls cleaned the kitchen with Grammy's supervision while Belinda unpacked, and Ben got on the phone. As he was headed to his office, Grammy told him they needed to talk.

The next morning, Ben and Grammy walked the girls to school. Ben told the lower school administrator he wanted to talk with Carlotta's parents. He wanted to help them get situated and get the children back in school. She knew she wasn't supposed to give anyone the information, but Ben was her pastor, and she trusted him. The only information she had was the phone number of a restaurant where the mother worked part time. Ben was familiar with the restaurant, so he would start there.

On the walk back home, Grammy told Ben she wanted to give him the money to buy his family a house. "I want you to buy or build a house, make a home for you and Belinda and the children. Ben was holding his grandmother's hand. He looked over at her. She was seventy-nine years old and in good health, and her mind was still good. But he wondered where this was coming from all of a sudden. She was still talking. "I made arrangements for the bank to transfer one hundred thousand dollars to your savings account. That should get you started."

"Gram, where is this coming from? Why are you doing this now? A hundred thousand dollars is a lot of money." Grammy stopped walking and looked up at Ben.

"Benji, I have more money than I can or want to do anything with. What else can I do with it except give it to you? You have two children already to educate, and I know you and Belinda will have more. Why wouldn't I give it to you now? What good will it be if I live another twenty years? If you are asking me if I'm sick or something now, no, I am just fine." She started to walk again and neither of them said anything for a few minutes. As they reached home Ben told her they would complete the transaction when he took her back to Hattiesville.

"Thank you, Grammy. Thank you." His voice choked. For a split second, he was sad. He knew his late grandfather had worked hard, invested soundly, and left that money for his grandmother. He put his arm around her, and they lingered there for a moment. Ben still wanted to know why now, why so suddenly without them even having a conversation about it. He was anxious to tell Belinda. Maybe Grammy would confide in her.

CHAPTER SEVEN

Natalia Durand was a sixteen-year-old high school sophomore from Haiti who was in the United States at the time of the earthquake. She and three other students were visiting colleges. Natalia could not go back home to Port-au-Prince. She had no home to go back to.

Sandra Matthews and her husband Roderick had a very successful law firm in Hattiesville, and they were members of Hattiesville Community Church. Sandra read an article in the local newspaper about Natalia and the other students who were traveling with her. It didn't take much for her to convince Katherine Robinson, the bishop's wife, to bring a project before the women of the church to care for these children. The two boys moved in with a couple who already had two sons. The two girls moved into the home of a retired couple whose children no longer lived at home. Sandra and Roderick helped all of them find part-time jobs. Natalia worked in their office. She had only met Chloe once, but she was intrigued with her. Sandra gave Natalia some of Chloe's clothes, but the weekend they met, Chloe gave her shoes and accessories and took her to the hairdresser. Chloe became Natalia's "hero" and was Natalia's standard that everything else was measured by. Natalia was looking forward to working with Chloe for the summer. Chloe seemed to take it all in stride.

Kathy and Sterling spent enough time together that she decided to formally introduce him to her parents. They met at Lola's for dessert. She thought a full meal would be too much. Her parents and Sterling hit it off. The conversation was easy. Sterling and Bishop Robinson did most of the talking, but it was obvious Katherine was totally smitten. As they were ending the evening, Bishop Robinson told Sterling he would look forward to seeing him at church on Sunday; Katherine invited him to dinner "anytime."

Sterling was feeling pretty good. He felt his position was solidified. Although Kathy still wasn't "all in," she was glad her parents liked him; so did her friends and her cousin and best friend Michelle. Kathy hadn't ever been in a serious relationship. She wasn't sure she wanted to be a wife and a mother.

"Kathy, what are you afraid of?" Michelle asked. She and Kathy were having one of their late night phone calls.

"I don't know, Chelle. I know the right thing to do is move from here to full-fledged courtship and from courtship to marriage, but I'm just not sure I want to share my personal space with anybody else."

Michelle was laughing. "Kathy, the man has not asked you to marry him. Relax! Enjoy his company, have some fun."

"You know Leah was the one who was supposed to have the husband and supply the grandchildren. That was never my role. I'm headed to grad school and to get my doctorate. I don't have a domestic bone in my body."

"You're really taking this too seriously. If that's the way you really feel, why did you introduce him to your parents?"

They talked awhile longer, and Michelle asked Kathy again what she was so afraid of. She went to bed thinking about that question with no real answer.

Campbell and Chloe were talking every day. She decided to get him a new phone for his birthday so they could have "face time." They did see each other on Skype from time to time. *Maybe I will have a party for him too. I will talk to Natalia about it. I know*

she will do a lot of the work. It will have to be a small party. Campbell doesn't have many friends, she thought to herself.

Natalia and Chloe talked pretty regularly. Natalia usually initiated the calls. The questions of the students' legal status were still unanswered, but Sandra was working on it. Chloe assured Natalia her mom would take care of everything. Natalia was at peace about the whole situation. She trusted Chloe completely.

CHAPTER EIGHT

Ben went to the restaurant and introduced himself to Liliana Marcos, Carlotta's mother. He explained to her why he was there. It was obvious by her body language that she was embarrassed and nervous. Ben assured her that he and his family only wanted to help.

In broken English, she explained the situation. They were illegal, including Carlotta. Only Jorge, the eight-year-old son, was born in the United States. At the moment, they were living in their car. Ben knew the legal part was over his head, but he knew an attorney he could call. What he could do was get them a hotel room for a week until they could figure out what to do next.

Brittani was delighted when Ben told them at dinner that he found Carlotta and her family; that they were safe and Carlotta and Jorge would be back in school the next day. Brianna told Ben that he was her hero. Belinda sat and watched the exchange between her daughters and their "dad," her husband, the man God sent to find her.

After dinner, Ben checked his messages. The realtor had left a message that there was a property she wanted to show him that the church may be interested in. He thought about the gift from Grammy. He could let her know they would soon be interested in looking at some residential properties too. The next day was Belinda's day off and their date day. He asked her to go with him to look at the property.

Carlotta was waiting for Brittani and Brianna when they arrived at school the next morning. They hugged, and Carlotta immediately proceeded to tell Brittani about everything that had happened. Brittani reminded Carlotta she had a lot of school work to catch up on, and promised that she and Brianna would help her.

Ben and Belinda had breakfast at their favorite restaurant and then drove across town to meet April Josephs, the realtor. She was already there when they arrived, and there was an older gentleman with her. Ben thought he must be the current owner of the building. But he didn't necessarily want to deal with the owner yet.

"Good morning, Pastor Coffey," April extended her hand. "And, Mrs. Coffey, how are you? It's good to see you." She hugged Belinda. "I would like you to meet Hampton Josephs, my business partner . . . and, oh yeah, my dad!" Ben and Hampton shook hands as they laughed at April, but he was staring at Belinda. When Hampton shook hands with Belinda, she thought he held her hand too long, and she didn't like the way he looked at her. She felt very uncomfortable.

"This was the original International School building when I was a student there," April was explaining to Ben. Belinda walked away from Hampton to stand closer to Ben. "Another school moved in when the 'I' School added high school and moved to the current location." She continued. Hampton joined the conversation.

"A little over a year ago, they ran into some financial problems, so I bought the building. They didn't recover, so they closed the school. I am ready to sell it, and April thought you may be interested."

"I am definitely interested in taking a look at it." Ben said.

"It's pretty dirty; it has been vacant for a few months," Hampton told them as he unlocked the door. They went in and looked around. Ben was totally intrigued. There was more than adequate office space, plenty of classrooms, a full-service kitchen and cafeteria, and a gym. What Ben wanted to see more than anything was the auditorium. April saved that for last.

Hampton opened the door from the lobby area to the auditorium as he explained to Ben what he thought they could do to make that area look less like a school and more like a church.

As they walked around the building, Belinda noticed how Hampton kept staring at her. She was going to tell Ben she didn't like this Mr. Josephs, and she didn't recommend that Ben do business with him.

$\mathcal{C}$HAPTER NINE

Jackson and Jacksa went to Durham to see JJ play basketball on Thursday night, so he got his hair cut on Friday. He came in a little after ten o'clock. Before he came into the house, he sent a text message: *Home safely. Njoyd u tonite.*

Before he could get out of the car, the phone rang. "I miss you," the caller said.

"I miss you too. I will call you tomorrow," Jackson replied.

When he reached the door to enter the house, he took a deep breath and went in. He pressed the button on the top of the monitor that sat on the kitchen counter.

"Hey, sweetie, do you need anything?"

"May I have some juice please?" Min answered into the monitor beside the bed.

Jackson had placed the monitors throughout the house, in case Min fell or got sick. He took the juice into the bedroom. He held the straw for her, and she took a long sip. She didn't need his assistance, but he did it anyway. They chatted while he undressed. He told her more about JJ's game. She laughed at some of what he said because JJ had called earlier and told her about the game. He showered quickly and got into bed beside her. He pulled her into his arms, gave her a kiss, and closed his eyes. Min looked up at him after a few minutes. He was dozing off with a slight smile on his face. She looked at him and became really sad.

Saturday morning, Jackson got up first. He cooked breakfast for Min and served it to her in bed. They talked and started to plan their day. Jackson talked her into riding to the mountains to their favorite bed and breakfast in Lake Lure for the night. She protested but he insisted. He put her power chair in the car just in case.

They rode up the mountain singing old Motown hits. "You know I turned you on to Motown," Jackson told her.

Min laughed. "I was a college student. I knew about all types of music."

"No, you didn't. You were listening to Bach and Beethoven!"

He was singing The Temptations' "My Girl" and twisting her hair around his finger. They stopped for Min to use the bathroom after about an hour on the road. It took her about fifteen minutes. In the meantime, Jackson sent a text simply saying he was away until the next day. Then he called Jacksa to tell her where they were going.

Jacksa missed her dad's call. She was in the mountains too, on a bicycle ride with Anderson. She liked to ride but hadn't been on her bike in a long time. After the first leg of the ride, they sat and talked over lunch before riding the second leg. He told her about his training for the new position as a detective. She told him about preparing to study for the bar exam. He also told her that his family—mother, sisters, aunt, and grandmother—were coming to Charlotte the following week to see the Alvin Ailey dancers at Blumenthal. He wanted her to meet them. Jacksa was a little stunned.

"Wow, Anderson! How appropriate is that now?"

"I think it's time. They know all about you."

"Are you serious?" she asked frowning. "Let me think about it," she said.

Anderson laughed, took the final gulp of his drink, and put his gloves back on. "Let's ride" was all he said.

They rode back down the mountain, and by the time they reached the bottom, Jacksa had decided she didn't want to meet his family. She told him while he was putting the bikes in the back of the SUV. He didn't respond until they were in the car.

"Jack, I always win, if not in this trip, the next one." He changed the subject. She didn't know if that was confidence or arrogance.

CHAPTER TEN

It was Sunday morning, and Belinda and the girls were seated in the front row. Ben made a few comments, and then he asked the congregation to greet their neighbors with a hug. Belinda turned around to hug the people in the row behind her. In the row behind them was April Josephs. Sitting beside April was Hampton Josephs, her father, and again, he was staring at Belinda.

Belinda hadn't told Ben about how uncomfortable Hampton made her the day they met. He was so excited about the building that she didn't want to squash his mood. She would tell him before the board meeting this week. Ben mentioned to her that he asked April and Hampton to come to the meeting to present the building proposal. Or maybe she just wouldn't go to the meeting. She had to go. The board only met quarterly, and Ben knew it was on her calendar. Plus, Bishop and First Lady Robinson were going to be there.

April smiled at Belinda and she smiled back. She couldn't ignore Hampton so she looked at him and nodded. He didn't take his eyes off her. The way he looked at her when they met was flirty. The way he looked at her today was more like he was studying her. He wasn't smiling; he was just staring at her.

Belinda was engrossed in the worship service and in Ben's message, so she forgot about Hampton. At dismissal she didn't look back; she headed straight for the office area. When she walked out to leave April was waiting to see Ben. Fortunately, Hampton wasn't with her. "Mrs. Coffey, Pastor told me you all will be interested in looking at some houses pretty soon! Let's have lunch so you can tell me what you're looking for." Belinda wanted to tell April she would meet with her as long as she didn't bring her father. "April, my husband is excited. Let me talk with him, and I'll call you."

She was going to have to talk with Ben. She knew he wasn't going to use another realtor. He had full trust in April, but Belinda didn't want to deal with Hampton.

As usual on Sunday, Thelma cooked dinner for Ben and his family and even got to the house ahead of them to set the table. Belinda was still unaccustomed to all the attention her family received. After she cleaned the kitchen, she walked through the house. Ben was in the den watching the basketball game, and Briana was there working on a science project. Brittani was upstairs in her room practicing her violin. This was a good time for her to call Kirby. She wanted to talk to her about Hampton.

"Hello, Aunt Belinda!" It was Blake and Nicholas on the speaker phone.

"Hey, Nick. Hey, Blake. How are you?" One said fine, one said good. She couldn't tell who said what. "What are you guys up to?"

"Up to nothing."

She still didn't know which one it was. There was a lot of movement in the background.

"Aunt Belinda, Blake is standing on the table." Nick was laughing.

Belinda wanted to know where their mommy was.

"I'm right here."

"Sounds like you need me to call later."

"No, give me five seconds, and I can talk."

Belinda could hear Enoch saying something in the background, and then it was very quiet.

Kirby and Belinda caught up with what had happened since they talked three days before, and Belinda told her about Hampton Josephs.

"Belinda, I'm sure you are overreacting."

"I thought that too until I saw him staring at me this morning."

"Wait and see how he acts at the meeting. That will be the third encounter. Three strikes and you're out!" Kirby said.

"I thought maybe I would tell First Lady too so she can notice him during the meeting," Belinda said to Kirby.

"Oh no, don't do that!" Kirby laughed. "If she thinks something is wrong, she will tell Bishop, and he will shut it down!" They both laughed. "In all seriousness, don't let Bishop find out and have to deal with it. Ben will resent it if you don't tell him first." Belinda knew her sister was right.

As they continued to talk, Kirby told Belinda that she received an e-mail from Sandra Matthews asking about Nicholas a few weeks ago, an e-mail from Campbell a week ago, and then a call from Chloe the day before.

"But don't you usually hear from them quite regularly?" Belinda asked.

"Yes, but not all three of them within a month's time; especially not Chloe. I bet I hadn't heard from Chloe in six months. I hear from Sandra once in a while. Campbell is the one I hear from regularly. I don't know what they're up to . . ." Kirby said.

"Why do they have to be up to something?"

"Belinda, I don't believe this is a coincidence."

"Did you respond?" Belinda asked Kirby.

"Not to Sandra or Chloe. I did e-mail Campbell back. I simply said Nick is doing fine. You know Enoch didn't want to do the open adoption, but I thought it would be okay. Now I'm not so sure."

"K, don't over analyze it. Just keep in mind that you and Enoch are his parents. Chloe, Campbell, and even Sandra don't have any rights to anything, except what you allow them."

CHAPTER ELEVEN

"Jacksa, you are an adult, so I am going to tell you this. I have not been a wife to my husband for a long time—years. I know he loves me, and he's devoted to me, but I also know he has someone else in his life."

It was Thursday night. Jackson was out, and Jacksa was visiting her mother. She and Min were finishing dinner. Jacksa was staring wide-eyed at her mother. Min continued. "He has for some time now. I don't know who it is, and I don't want to know."

"Mom, what are you going to do about it?"

"Nothing, not one thing! Jackson is good to me. He is a great provider, and he takes good care of me. I don't want for anything."

Jacksa was crying as she listened to her mother talk. She started to say something, but Min interrupted her. "Let me finish. What I appreciate about your dad the most in this situation is he hasn't been disrespectful to me. He hasn't ever brought his other life into our home. He comes and goes at respectable times. He's accountable, and there hasn't ever been even a phone call."

Jacksa cleared her throat. "Mom, are you sure? How do you know you're right about this? Maybe it's your imagination."

"Sweetheart, I know your father. I know my husband. I have been married to him for thirty years. I know the other situation is physical. I know he is not emotionally attached."

"Mother, you are sitting there telling me my dad is in a relationship outside his marriage, and you are okay with it?" Jacksa was being very animated.

"It is not a relationship, Jacksa. It is a situation."

"You can call it whatever you want to, Mom! He is having an affair! Oh my god. I cannot believe you are okay with this!" Jacksa was screaming.

Min simply sat there looking at her daughter. She hated to have to tell her this about her father, but it was the truth. And it had been her truth for a long time. She couldn't pinpoint the day she came to the realization, but she remembered how sad she was. She knew her limitations sent him into another's arms.

"Mom, does he know that you know?"

"No darling. We have never talked about it. There is no need."

"What about your vows: in sickness and in health, forsaking all others?"

"We meant that when we said it, Jacksa, but neither of us expected this to happen." She looked down at her body."

"Mother, I cannot just accept this."

"Yes, you can, and you will. I shared this with you in confidence. You cannot break my trust. Do not mention this to Jackson, and do not mention this to JJ."

Jacksa looked at Min in total disbelief. It was obvious her mother had made peace with this. Min deliberately changed the subject, and when Jackson came in, he only saw his wife and their daughter enjoying each other's company.

Sterling and Kathy were seeing each other on a regular basis. Sterling was excited. Kathy wasn't. There was something about this "relationship" with Sterling that just didn't click for her. The Robinsons were delighted that Sterling was around. He joined Hattiesville Community Church though he still didn't attend regularly. He did, however, have dinner with them from time to time. Bishop Robinson and Sterling watched games together on television, and Sterling gave him two season tickets to DavisTown College basketball.

Kathy confided in Michelle that she thought her parents just wanted a son-in-law and of course, grandchildren. But she was moving forward with her plans for grad school. She hoped Sterling and her parents understood that and hoped Sterling knew he would have to adjust. What she hadn't told Michelle, her parents or Sterling was that she also applied for a job in Paris teaching English to French and African students. The truth was she needed a change of scenery. She couldn't fill Leah's place because, frankly, she didn't want to.

Kathy missed Leah too, but God had taken her, and there wasn't anything any of them could do. She just wanted to be able to move on. Everywhere she turned, there were reminders of Leah. Her dad insisted she continue to live in Leah's townhome. She redecorated some, but it still just looked like Leah.

CHAPTER TWELVE

Hampton was driving his new black Jaguar XJL. He laughed to himself because he still didn't know how to work everything. It was his birthday gift to himself. April suggested it, and thanks to her, he could well afford it. Hampton was very proud of his daughter and what she was doing with the business. He had done well in real estate, but April took the company to another level. She stayed in Atlanta, went to college at Georgia Tech, and earned a degree in architecture. She added real estate development to the business, and it proved very profitable. Simply put, April had raw talent and an eye for what worked.

"Damn it!" Hampton had missed his exit. He was distracted, thinking about Belinda Coffey. He couldn't stop thinking about her since they met a few weeks ago. She was stunningly beautiful. When he saw her at church on Sunday, he couldn't take his eyes off her. He was anxious to see her at their meeting this week. He thought about her smile and how gracious she was. He wanted to know more about her. He had to know more about her.

Once he was headed in the right direction, he engaged his phone and spoke a name out loud. The computer voice acknowledged his request and after two rings the private investigator answered.

"¡Hola! Señor Josephs, que pasa!"

Hampton laughed. "What's happening with you, Carlos?"

"Been pretty busy actually, but not too busy to offer you some assistance."

"I appreciate that."

They chatted briefly, and then Hampton told him the main reason for his call.

"I need you to get me some information on Belinda Coffey."

"Coffey, that's the name of that new pastor."

"Yes, she's his wife."

"You lookin' for anything particular?"

"I want anything you can find. And, Carlos, I know I don't have to say this to you, but please exercise extreme caution and discretion. This is not business, it's very personal."

"*Si, señor. Etiendo.* I understand."

A few days later, Carlos called Hampton Josephs's cell phone and left a message that he had some information and would be in his office after 3:00 p.m. Hampton showed up at 4:00 p.m., anxious to hear what he had to say.

"Señor, her full maiden name is Belinda Denise Craig, and she was put in foster care in Greenville, North Carolina, when she was four months old."

Carlos went on to tell Hampton about her foster parents and that she left college after her sophomore year. He told Hampton about her first husband, Canady Stewart, being killed in Iraq, and he ended by saying she and Ben had been married almost two years and moved to Landridge from Hattiesville, North Carolina. Hampton listened intently to everything he said.

When Carlos finished, he asked Hampton if he wanted the report in writing. "No, not now. I need two more things: a copy of her birth certificate and I want you to keep a soft eye on her for a few days."

"I'll take care of it."

"No need to spend any time on it Thursday evening. I know where she'll be," Hampton said not smiling.

Carlos trailed Belinda off and on for a week, but when he met with Hampton he had not been successful in getting the actual birth certificate. He told Hampton where she worked, what she drove, where she went to the hairdresser, where the girls went to school, and that she had a part-time housekeeper. "Because she was in foster care as an infant, her birth certificate is sealed. She was a ward of the state of North Carolina until she was eighteen years old. I do know her birthday is January 1, 1976, but I don't know where she was born or why she ended up in foster care." Hampton sat for a minute saying nothing. He was in deep thought. "What would it take for you to further investigate that situation?" he asked.

"I would need to go to North Carolina." Carlos answered.

"When can you get away?" Hampton asked with no hesitation. Carlos looked at his calendar.

"I can drive up early next week."

As he walked to his car, Hampton thought about Ben. He knew he would be ticked off if Ben Coffey was investigating his wife, but he wanted and needed to know everything about Belinda. As he drove away, he called Carlos back. "While you're in North Carolina, find out what you can about Ben Coffey too."

"Si, señor."

April hit a homerun at the board meeting. As expected, Bishop Robinson asked a lot of questions; some of them were pretty tough, but she handled it. Hampton did his part, but she was the star of the show. It was just as well, Hampton was distracted; he couldn't stop looking at Belinda. He watched her; paying attention to her mannerisms, her voice, and her laugh. He noticed her wedding rings. He noticed the pen she wrote with. She was obviously very well taken care of. Hampton watched Belinda interact with Ben. She was obviously very much in love with him; he could see it in her eyes. And he could see that Ben was very much in love with her.

Hampton also realized how much influence the bishop had on Ben and Belinda. He was a powerful man who demanded and received respect. Hampton knew he would have to be very careful with the information he was able to gather on Belinda and Ben. He would have to be careful how he used it and how he would eventually approach her. The bishop could be a tough opponent, and he would be if he thought Belinda needed his help.

Ben was excited about the presentation and excited that the bishop and first lady were staying for the weekend and the bishop agreed to deliver the Sunday message. Belinda was happy and very engaged in what Ben was doing. She managed to forget Hampton was in the room. She had taken Kirby's advice and not said anything to First Lady Robinson. She decided not to mention anything to Ben until after the weekend if she still felt uncomfortable.

Natalia was rearranging one of the offices on Roderick's side of the building. It was where Chloe and one of the other interns would work for the summer. She was excited that Chloe would be in town in two weeks. She was taking a week off, and then they would see each other every day. Chloe told Natalia she wanted to have the week off to spend some time with her boyfriend, Campbell. Natalia had seen a picture of him and she couldn't wait to meet him. She also couldn't wait to go to lunch and to the hairdresser with Chloe. The big discussion she wanted to have with her was about going to college. Natalia wanted to go to Spelman too. Sandra told her she should investigate and apply for scholarships, but she should also consider going to a local school. The two summer interns were students at Johnson C. Smith University, so maybe she would talk with them too.

The job at the Matthews Law Firm was working out good for Natalia. She was learning so much, but she was also making some money and had plenty of time to do homework. Her host parents were great people, and her roommate was easy to get along with. She missed Haiti, and she missed her family. The toughest part was not knowing where any of her family was—if they had survived the earthquake or not. As far as she knew, nobody had tried to contact her, so she suspected none of them lived. So she was making the best of her new life in the US. She had a wonderful role model in Chloe, and she intended to spend as much time with her as she could. Her big project for the summer was to save enough money to get a car and pay the insurance.

"Babe, will you get that for me?" Ben was asking Belinda to answer his cell phone.

When she picked it up and saw Hampton Josephs's name on the screen, she wished he hadn't asked her to answer it.

"Good morning." There was silence on the other end.

"Hello," she said.

Hampton finally spoke. He was a little startled that she was answering. "Good morning, Mrs. Coffey. This is Hampton Josephs. How are you this morning?"

"I am well, Hampton. How are you?"

"Great, thanks for asking."

By that time, Ben was close by, so she asked Hampton to hold on and handed Ben the phone. Ben walked into the den, but Belinda could hear them talking about Hampton hiring Juan Marcos to be the maintenance man at an apartment complex he owned. His working there would also allow his family to live there. Belinda was glad that was worked out. Brittani and Brianna would be glad too. Now if they could get the new church building squared away, Hampton would be out of their lives forever. She would only have to deal with April to find their new house.

Hampton was shocked when Belinda answered Ben's phone. He knew he sounded like a smitten teenager when she answered. He had to learn how not to choke when she was around. She had an effect on him that he couldn't describe. He really wanted to know what Carlos was going to find through his investigation.

The twins and Ben went to Hattiesville. He had business to take care of and would be back in a couple of days. The girls were staying for two weeks. They were spending a week with Auntie and Grammy, and a week with Enoch, Kirby, and the boys.

It was rare for Belinda to be home alone, but she had to work. Two doctors requested her for their surgeries that week. It turned out that one surgery was postponed so she had the afternoon off. She knew there was plenty to do at home or at the church, but she decided to go to the park and read. She found a swing beside the water. She was there for about thirty minutes when she heard someone call her name.

Hampton was walking in the park and decided his last lap would be around the pond. He was totally surprised to see Belinda sitting on one of the swings beside the water. He had to think quickly as he was approaching her. He stopped walking and watched her for a few minutes. He didn't know what he was going to say. He just wanted to be close to her.

"Belinda, how are you?"

She looked around to see a man standing there in a long-sleeved T-shirt, gym shorts and shoes, a baseball cap turned backward, and sunglasses. She didn't immediately recognize him. When he removed his sunglasses, her defenses went up.

"Good afternoon, Hampton." She wanted to ask if he had followed her there but she didn't. It was an awkward moment.

"That's a good spot to read."

"Yes, it is."

He decided he better talk about business. "April told me you all are meeting this week to talk about your new house. I hope you will consider letting us build you a custom home."

"My husband and I will consider all our options." Hampton went on to tell her about a lot they may be interested in. He wanted to engage her in conversation, she wanted him to leave. He was looking directly into her eyes and smiling at her. She was very uncomfortable. After another minute he decided he needed to move on.

"Well, let me know if you want to see the lot. I guess I need to get going so I won't cool down too much." He said good-bye, put his earphones back in, and walked away quickly.

Belinda looked back down at her book but she couldn't concentrate. Kirby was wrong; Hampton was flirting with her. She was going to tell Ben as soon as he got back.

CHAPTER THIRTEEN

Jill and Raja were married in an elaborate ceremony about a year after they met, on a Sunday. It was one year to the day that Leah and Grant would have gotten married. Kathy and Tara had been her bridesmaids, but she did not have a maid of honor. Instead, she had a special candelabra designed to stand in the spot where Leah would have stood. Jill had convinced Raja to have a two-part wedding. She was so intrigued with the wedding of his cousin that they attended in London, she wanted to add some of those customs to their plans. They had a ceremony the night before the actual wedding that resembled a traditional Indian wedding and then a Christian wedding at Hattiesville Community Church the next day. The wedding party was the feast following the Indian ceremony. Jill followed the trend Leah set: not having a bachelor's party or a bachelorette party but having one big party for their family and friends.

For the first year of their marriage, they commuted between Chapel Hill and Hattiesville. After they seriously decided to start a family, Raja joined her father's practice and moved to Hattiesville. Being able to maintain his privileges in Chapel Hill was a bonus, and he would be called to consult and perform surgery there from time to time. They were still living in Jill's townhouse, a sign of how frugal Raja was. She knew the eleven-hundred-square-feet house would be too small once the baby came, but her mother told her to just wait. Raja would soon figure it out.

None of Raja's family from London or India came to the wedding though they were all invited. His parents didn't even acknowledge the invitation. He hadn't had any contact with his parents since they gave him the ultimatum to choose between them and Jill. His cousin Yash did call to say he and his wife could not come. Tara and Raja seemed unconcerned by it all, but Jill took offense considering Raja spent a considerable amount of money for them to go to London for Yash's wedding.

Today would be an interesting one. Grant was coming home for the weekend, and he had called Jill to ask if they could have brunch. He told her there was something he wanted to talk with her about. They talked fairly regularly, but they hadn't seen each other in months. Jill was curious about what Grant wanted to say.

Jill was really glad to see Grant, and he was glad to see her. They met at Lola's. Jill was craving maple syrup so she ordered pancakes. He teased her about her baby bump and laughed about her cravings. They both admitted they never imagined this season in her life without Leah. Grant had never imagined any season in his life without her.

Finally, Jill asked him what he needed to tell her. Grant reached into his jacket pocket, took out an envelope, and handed it to Jill. She looked inside, and there was a check for ten thousand dollars made payable to the Strauss Foundation.

"What is this for?" she asked Grant.

"I sold Leah's wedding rings, and I want to do something with the money that will last. Something that will honor Leah, leave a legacy for her."

Jill had tears in her eyes and a lump in her throat. "Thank you, G." He went on to tell her that he didn't know how he wanted to grant the money, and he trusted her to do the best thing. She assured him she would give it special attention. Then she told him she would personally match the gift.

"I need to tell you something else. I haven't told anybody else, not even Clay." Grant looked very serious. Whatever he was about to say was very important if he hadn't told Clay. They shared everything. He reached in his pocket again and handed Jill a picture of him and a lady. He was dressed in his formal uniform, and she was in an evening gown.

"The military ball?" Jill asked.

"Yes," he said quietly.

Jill thought of the year Leah went to the ball with Grant.

Grant continued. "Her name is Sunny. She works in human resources at the hospital. We have been seeing each other for about ten months. I never thought I would or could love anybody else, but I love her and I am going to ask her to marry me."

As he was talking, Jill was staring at the picture. Sunny was the exact opposite of Leah. Leah was five feet five inches and a size eight. Sunny looked to be five feet eight inches or five feet nine inches and about a size twelve. Leah's complexion was the color of milk chocolate. Sunny was the color of dark chocolate. Leah was beautiful. Sunny was gorgeous in a made up kind of way. Jill finally took her eyes off the picture. She swallowed hard, but she couldn't find her voice. Grant knew she was surprised, but he also knew she knew he would eventually move on with his life. The truth was he hadn't believed that, but he did. Sunny had been a good friend and now she was going to be his wife.

Jill knew Grant had the right to move on, but she wasn't sure how she really felt about all this. "Grant, I am feelin' some kinda way about this."

"I knew you would; that's why I wanted to tell you first."

"Even if you like Sunny, ten months is not long enough for you to know her well enough to marry her," Jill said.

Grant laughed. "Jill, you and Raja were engaged in a year. What's the difference?"

"The difference is Raja and I had not been in love with and planning to marry somebody else the year before we met. I just think it's too soon for you to be talking about getting married!"

When Kathy took the mail out of the box and saw the certified letter notice, she knew it was an answer about either her graduate school application or her application to teach in Paris. She didn't mention it to Sterling when she saw him that evening or to her mother when she talked with her. If it were an acceptance letter from either one, then she could get out of the situation with Sterling. He, her parents, and Michelle were too serious about this relationship.

Grant walked Jill to her car, gave her a big hug, and made sure she was buckled in. As he walked to his car, he thought about Jill saying it was too soon for him and Sunny to be getting married. He was on his way to meet Clay, Enoch, and Sterling at the church gym to play basketball, but he decided to call Sunny first to tell her about his time with Jill.

She answered quickly and was genuinely happy to hear his voice. He told her he gave Jill the check and showed her their picture from the ball. He didn't tell her that he told Jill he wanted to marry her. They talked as he drove, and she caught him up on her day. They hung up when he stopped to get gas. Just as he put the nozzle into his tank, he heard someone call his name. He turned around, and it was Janis.

"Hi Grant, how have you been?"

"I'm good, how are you?" Grant asked very formally.

"I am pretty good. Are you living here now?"

"No, just here for the weekend."

Janis and Grant hadn't seen each other in over two years. He went to see her in the hospital once after the incident, right before he moved to Washington. He heard from Clay that she had fully recovered. Her pump clicked, so Grant hoped she would just walk away.

"Grant, can we talk? Will you come by later?"

"No, Janis, for what?"

"I think we need to have some closure."

The gas pump clicked, so he turned his back to her to replace the nozzle and replace his gas cap.

Closure, he thought to himself.

"No, Janis. I won't come by, but you may be right. We do need some closure. I will call you."

That wasn't the answer she wanted, but talking on the phone was better than nothing, and she would have his number. She gave him her number, and he typed it into his phone. "What time are you going to call?" He didn't respond to her. He got in his truck and pulled away. She followed him out of the parking lot and stayed behind him until he made the turn onto the street where the church was. Janis kept going straight. She had no intention of going near that church. She knew that's where he was headed.

CHAPTER FOURTEEN

Kathy was right about her certified letter. It was an acceptance letter for graduate school at Columbia University in New York City. She was accepted into a program to earn a master's and PhD in four years. Four years. That was a long time to be away from her parents, the church family, and her friends . . . even Sterling. But being away from Sterling would keep her from having to get married and have children. Being away from home would keep her parents from hovering.

The telephone ringing interrupted her thoughts. It was Michelle. Kathy shared her news. Michelle congratulated her and then asked, "Where in the world did that come from?"

"You knew I was applying to grad school," Kathy said.

"Yes, I did, but I didn't know you planned to go that far or go into a four-year program."

"Chelle, this is a great program and a great opportunity for me. Can you please be more supportive?"

They debated for a few minutes, and Michelle finally asked the question Kathy didn't want to answer: "What about Sterling?"

"What about Sterling?" Kathy raised her voice. "What does he have to do with it? Why do I have to consider him? So I can get married and have kids and be who Leah was supposed to be?"

"Kathy, what are you talking about? You started seeing Sterling. You introduced him to the family. Nobody made you do anything!" Michelle raised her voice too. "What *is* your problem? One minute, you are inviting him to Sunday dinner. The next day, you askin' what does he have to with your future plans. I don't get it, Kat." Kathy was silent. "Hello. Hello!"

"I'm here. Chelle, you don't get it. I want my life to stay on its original tract. I never intended to do the wife-and-mother thing. When Sterling came back into my life, I thought a relationship was what I wanted, but now that I have the opportunity to go back to school and accomplish my goals, that's what I want to do."

"Don't you think you can have both: school leading to a career and a relationship?"

"I don't want both. I want a PhD. I want to teach at the university level and one day be a college president."

"Well, you know what, Kathy, you can put him back out there if you want to!" Michelle hung up.

Kathy didn't understand why Michelle was so over the top about this. All their growing-up years, she and Leah talked about husbands and children and all that, but Kathy always wanted to be the career girl. That hadn't changed. What had changed was Leah was gone, and "they" expected Kathy to rearrange her life and pick up where Leah left off.

"Sterling is a great guy, and we have a good friendship. He will understand and support my decision," Kathy said out loud.

She started to call Michelle back but decided against it. She called her mother. Interestingly, her dad answered.

"Hey, Daddy! I'm surprised you're there."

He laughed. "Yeah, your mom was surprised too! She was really surprised because she had to cook dinner."

Kathy could hear her mother saying something in the background. Her dad was laughing. "Put Ma on speaker so I can hear what she's saying."

They talked a few minutes, and then Kathy told them why she called. Her announcement was met with complete silence. After a few seconds, Kathy asked if they heard what she said.

He dad spoke up. "I guess congratulations are in order, but I admit I am caught off guard. I knew you wanted to go back to school, but four years and that far away was not what I expected."

Katherine was silent, keeping her eyes on her husband.

"Daddy, it's a great opportunity for me. I have applied for a fellowship that I expect to get. The timing is right. I feel good about this."

Her mother finally spoke. "You certainly deserve the best, sweetheart. When are you coming over so you can tell us all the details?"

"I'll be over tomorrow."

"Okay, let's talk then." Katherine tried to sound upbeat.

"Okay, talk to you guys later."

Katherine and Lee just stood there looking at each other.

One last call, one more person to tell—Sterling. Kathy looked at the clock. It was just after six o'clock, so practice would be going on at least another half hour. She decided to ride over and meet him when he was finished.

Sterling saw her before she saw him. He was surprised and approached her with a big smile on his face. "Hey there. What are you doing here?"

"Hey Coach, how was practice?"

He laughed. "It was pretty intense."

"Are you ready to leave?" she asked.

"I can be. What's up?" He noticed she seemed excited.

"I have some incredible news to share."

"Hold that thought. Let me get something out of my car and I'll ride with you. You can buy me dinner and tell me your incredible news." As he walked to his car, Kathy thought to herself that Sterling was always hungry.

They went right around the corner to a small Chinese restaurant that they both liked. "Okay, what is your incredible news?" Sterling asked as soon as they had ordered.

"I found out today that I have been accepted into the masters and PhD dual degree program at Columbia University!"

The expression on Sterling's face gave him away. He did not particularly like what Kathy just said. There was a thick silence between them for over a minute. "Wow! That certainly isn't what I expected you to say."

"Sterling, I told you I applied to grad school. Why are you surprised? Did you think I wouldn't get accepted?" Kathy was smiling, trying to defuse the tension.

"It never crossed my mind you wouldn't get accepted, but it also never crossed my mind you were going to New York. I thought you would be here at DavisTown or maybe at UNC Charlotte. Columbia was never in the mix." There was another huge silence.

CHAPTER FIFTEEN

As Jackson was driving home, he noticed how late he was. It was almost eleven o'clock. He couldn't lie and say the game ran over. Min was probably watching the game herself. He just wouldn't say anything. This was the second time in three weeks that he had been late. As he pulled into the garage, he heard the text message alert on his phone. He turned the ignition off and read the message: *Sorry for making you late again. Maybe you should send some flowers tomorrow! Good nite.* His reply was only *Good nite.*

When the flowers arrived the first time for no special occasion, Min laughed. Jackson was never one for flowers. He said they were a waste of money because they would die. He bought nice gifts, just not flowers. Then there was the bracelet and the perfume, all for no special occasion. So when the flowers arrived this time, Min was curious why he sent them.

Jackson usually called Min a couple of times during the day, but she seldom called him. When he looked at his phone and saw it was her, he was concerned. "Hey sugar, you okay?"

"Yes, I'm fine. Want to thank you for the flowers."

He laughed. "You are so welcome," he said in a sing-song voice.

"I am amused that you sent them for no special reason, and this is the second time."

"There is a special reason. I sent them because I love you." Min didn't want to sound like she was making an accusation, so she chose her words carefully.

"You have loved me for thirty years, and all of a sudden, you are sending flowers. Hmmm!"

He laughed. She went on. "What about your philosophy that they only die?" He felt uncomfortable and guilty. He had to say something to get out of this.

"Okay, Min, the truth is . . ." He sounded very serious. "Jacksa told me I should be more romantic. So that's what I'm trying to do." That was not the absolute truth, but he knew she would accept that and she would not question Jacksa about it. "I thought I had done a good thing."

"You did a good thing and I appreciate you and the flowers," Min said smiling. They talked a few more minutes, and she asked what he wanted for dinner.

"Well, since you obviously had Wheaties for breakfast and are feeling your oats, calling up here questioning my motives . . ." She was laughing. "I am going to take you out to dinner. So you get dressed, madam, and I will pick you up around six o'clock. And decide where you want to go."

After they hung up, he sat there for a few minutes in deep thought. His thoughts were interrupted by another call.

"Hello."

"How are you?"

"Good. Little busy." He didn't want to talk right then.

"Okay, just wanted to tell you I sent your wife some flowers."

"What! Why?"

"Because you were out late again last night."

"I already sent flowers."

"Oh, wow! I'm sorry. You never said yes or no, so I was trying to be helpful."

"You should have checked with me first. Umm, look I have some work to do, I'll call you later." He hung up. This situation was getting raggedy, and Jackson didn't like raggedy.

Jackson arrived home walked into the living room and saw two bouquets of flowers: the basket of tulips and lilies he sent and the dozen long stem red roses. He sighed loudly, and he knew he had to get on offense. "Where did the roses come from?" He asked as he leaned down and kissed Min. She looked at him and smiled.

"What? The card said they were from you."

"No, the basket is from me."

She just looked at him. He didn't meet her glance. "I think the florist made a mistake," Jackson said.

She was still looking at him. "They came from two different flower shops," she said very matter-of-factly. He felt a pang in the pit of his stomach. Raggedy. Min picked up her purse, reached for her walker, and walked out of the room. Raggedy.

CHAPTER SIXTEEN

Natalia reached the post office door before Chloe, both their arms were full. The man coming out of the door held it for them. When Chloe looked up to say thank you, she realized it was Enoch. She hadn't seen him in over a year. She stopped going to church while she was pregnant and hadn't gone regularly since she went away in college.

"Thank you, sir. Oh, um, Enoch, hi, um, how are you?"

"Hello, Chloe. How are you? It's nice to see you."

She was just standing there. Natalia walked back to the door and took the package out of her arms.

"I'm doing fine. Thank you for asking," Chloe finally answered Enoch. All in the same breath, she asked about Nicholas.

"He's good. He's growing up!"

"Do you have a picture of him?" Chloe asked.

Enoch hesitated. It was an awkward moment. Chloe started to say never mind, but Enoch interrupted her.

"It's okay." He took out his phone and showed her a couple of pictures: one of Nicholas and Blake and then one of Nicholas by himself. Chloe stared at the picture. She thought Nicholas looked like Campbell. Campbell was biracial and light-skinned, and Nicholas was a shade darker, but they had the same light brown eyes. Natalia was walking back toward the door. Chloe didn't want to explain to her who Enoch was so she gave him back the phone. When Natalia approached them, Chloe introduced the two of them. Enoch recognized Natalia. She politely shook hands with Enoch and asked if he attended Hattiesville Community Church.

"Yes, I do."

"You have the twin boys! I've had them in children's church."

Enoch laughed. "They aren't twins." He didn't offer any further explanation. They chatted for only another minute, and Enoch excused himself.

Chloe was very quiet on the ten-minute ride back to work. When they got back, she went straight to her mother's office. Sandra was on the phone but motioned for Chloe to sit down.

CHAPTER SEVENTEEN

Hampton Josephs was glad that Ben introduced him to Juan Marcos. He worked hard and took so much pride in his work. Hampton did something he didn't usually do. For the project to up fit the school for the church to use, Hampton decided to compile his own subcontractors. He chose Juan as the superintendent, and that was a good decision.

When Carlos first approached Juan at the job site, Juan thought he was looking for work. Then Juan became nervous, he was afraid the man was from Immigration. Carlos told Juan he was new to the area, and he and his family were looking for a church. He wanted to know about the pastor and if the congregation was diverse. Juan was glad to tell him about Landridge Community Church and about Ben being a great pastor. "Is he a family man?" Carlos asked.

"Si. He has a wife and daughters."

"Is Pastor Coffey from this area?"

"No, he came here from North Carolina."

"What about Belinda Coffey?"

At that moment, Juan knew what Pastor Coffey called the prompting of the Holy Spirit. He knew what discernment was. He didn't need to answer any more questions. That was one question too many. Juan had not told Carlos Belinda's name. There were many ways he could have known her name, but that was enough. He told Carlos he should call the church office to make an appointment to talk with Ben himself.

"And you should come to our worship service on Sunday." Carlos started to ask another question, but Juan interrupted him and said he needed to get back to work.

Carlos thanked him for the information, said he would accept his invitation and visit with his family on Sunday. "Gracias, amigo. Gracias."

"De nada," Juan said with a nod. As Carlos drove away, Juan got a good look at his car and wrote down his tag number.

Carlotta was studying with the Coffey girls, so Juan called Lili to say he would pick her up. He told Lili he needed to talk with Ben, but that's all he told her. For the rest of the day, Juan became more and more curious about Carlos and why he was asking about Ben and especially Belinda. He would protect them no matter what. They were his spiritual leaders but also his friends. They had been really good to his family. Juan prayed a prayer of protection for Ben, Belinda, and the girls. "El nombre de Jesus. Amen." Feeling peace in his spirit, Juan got back to work.

After talking to Juan, Carlos left the building, feeling good about his inquiry. He thought he made an inroad with Juan. He would definitely attend church on Sunday. If he befriended Juan, maybe he could get even more information. He knew Mr. Josephs would pay a bonus for extra information. He left a message for Hampton to say he was headed to North Carolina and would call him in a day or so. His original plans had changed due to a complication with another case. He did not want to disappoint Hampton Josephs. He was not the kind of man you wanted to cross. He wielded a lot of power and influence, and being in his good graces was important to Carlos personally and professionally. Hampton Josephs got what he wanted, and if he wanted Belinda Coffey, Carlos was going to do his part to see that he got her.

CHAPTER EIGHTEEN

Juan arrived at the Coffey home to find the girls still working on a project and Ben was not there. Belinda invited him in, but he said no because his boots were dirty. As Carlotta gathered her things, he asked Belinda to have Ben call him.

"I need to talk to him about something on the job site."

"Is everything okay, Juan?"

"*Si, señora.* Nothing is wrong, the work is going well. Just want to update him." Juan smiled confidently.

Belinda hugged Carlotta as she walked out the door and told Juan she would give Ben his message. She smiled to herself as she thought of how Brianna's good deed to help her friend ultimately helped the whole family. Juan had a good job, they had an apartment, Lili was able to work part time, the children were in school and doing well, and they had plenty to eat.

The next morning, after Ben dropped the girls off at school, he went to the job site to see Juan. He wanted to talk with him anyway about taking a leadership role in church.

They walked through the building, and Juan gave Ben a detailed assessment of what had been done and what was left to do. "Señor Josephs y Señorita Josephs will be here this afternoon to check everything, and they will give you the timeline."

Ben was pleasantly surprised. The project was moving more quickly than they anticipated, so he had to get the church family prepared to move, and he needed to give notice to their current landlord.

As they walked back to the front of the building, Juan asked Ben to take a seat. He told him he would accept the position and thanked Ben for his confidence in him.

"I don't want to alarm you, sir, but there was a man here yesterday asking a lot of questions. He said he wanted to know more about the church and to bring his family. I didn't believe him, but I did invite him to come, and he said he would be here on Sunday."

"Why does that disturb you Juan?" Ben asked.

"You know how you say we know in our spirit?"

"Yeah." Ben frowned as he answered.

"Well, that's why it disturbed me. He asked personal questions about you and a lot of questions about Señora Coffey."

"A lot of questions about my wife?"

"*Si, señor.* More about her than you."

"Okay, now I'm disturbed too. What sort of questions did he ask? What did this character look like?"

Juan told Ben about Carlos, describing him in detail and repeating their conversation almost word for word. Then he handed Ben the note where he wrote the tag number and description of Carlos's car. Ben chuckled. "You would make a good detective, Juan."

They sat for a few minutes. Ben was staring into space; Juan was looking at him. Ben was deciding how he should react, how he should approach this situation. Finally, Juan told Ben he needed to get back to work.

Juan stood to leave, deciding to leave Ben with his thoughts.

"Juan, before you go, let's keep this situation between us."

"Si, señor."

"I want you to do me a favor," Ben said, looking off in the distance.

"Si!"

"If this Carlos guy does show up on Sunday, make sure you point him out to me. When I see his face, I will know what to do."

"*Si, señor.* The Spirit will tell you."

CHAPTER NINETEEN

Clay had Jeremy's game schedule for a couple of weeks. Delia e-mailed it to him, just an attachment, no note in the e-mail. He intended to go before now, he just hadn't made time. Cicely was working, so tonight was a good time to go.

He arrived early enough to see the warm-ups. There was no sign of Delia. Jeremy started and scored the first four points. He looked good out there. About the end of the first quarter, Clay saw Delia, Crystal, and a man come in. He assumed he was Javier. They didn't see Clay. Jeremy's team won and Clay decided he would hang around to congratulate him. He stayed back and watched the interaction between Delia and Javier as he had throughout the game. They were affectionate toward each other, and Javier and Crystal appeared to have a good relationship. Seeing Crystal reminded Clay of how long it had been since he was in their lives. Crystal had really grown up.

As Clay stood in the lobby of the gym waiting for Jeremy to come out, suddenly, somebody grabbed him around the waist. It was Crystal. She and Clay hugged. He looked up to see Delia.

"Hello Clay" was all she said.

"How are you, Delia?"

She didn't answer.

Clay extended his hand and introduced himself to Javier. It was an awkward moment. Crystal told Javier that Clay had been Jeremy's big brother. Javier knew who Clay was. Delia had told him the whole story. Crystal and Clay kept their conversation going, and it wasn't long before Jeremy joined the group. He shook hands with Clay, and they hugged. He greeted his mom and Javier, and with some prodding from his mom, he hugged Crystal.

"I see you two still love each other," Clay said laughing.

They all laughed. Jeremy and Clay walked away from the group for a few minutes. They talked about his game, and Jeremy told him that he has some interest from a few college scouts. After a few minutes, Crystal came over to tell Jeremy they needed to go. Clay told him that he would try to come to another game soon. Clay looked toward the car and saw Javier open the door for Delia. Then he saw Jeremy open the car door for Crystal.

As Clay drove home, he thought about Delia. He pictured her in his mind. Her hair, her smile, and the jeans she was wearing. How she looked in the jeans. He had not seen her in years, but she hadn't aged and obviously she was taking good care of herself. He was puzzled why she wouldn't or didn't talk to him. He had put their past behind him, but based on her behavior, she had not. Clay chuckled to himself. "After all these years she still feelin' me."

Cicely was working and wouldn't be off for a couple of hours so Clay decided to get something to eat. He would get it, go to her place, and be there when she got in. They had keys to each other's homes, and Clay didn't think it was practical for them to be living separately, but he knew that was their situation until they were married. "Married," he said out loud. He had to go ahead and make the move. Her lease was up in three months, so he needed to go ahead and make it happen. He was already committed, and he loved her, so he didn't know why he wouldn't bite the bullet. He thought to himself that he was very unlike Grant. He was planning to marry Sunny, and they had only known each other about a year.

When Grant was home, he told Clay about Sunny and showed him the same picture he showed Jill. He confided in Clay that he and Sunny were "practically living together," which meant they were sleeping together, and that was out of character for Grant. He never moved this quickly. Clay thought this was a rebound relationship, and he told him that. Grant denied it and assured Clay he was in love with Sunny.

Grant told his twin sister, Gretchen, about Sunny, but he hadn't told his parents. That was another indication to Clay that he was acting differently. As Clay pulled up to the speaker in the drive-thru lane, he decided he needed to go to DC to meet Sunny for himself. As he pulled around the building to pay and pick up his food, he saw Delia and Jeremy walking though the parking lot. They didn't see him. He couldn't take his eyes off her. When she was inside the restaurant and out of his sight, he pulled away. He thought about Delia as he drove to Cicely's apartment. He wondered about her relationship with Javier, but he wanted to know why she wouldn't talk to him at the game. He decided he would call her and ask.

When Cicely walked in, Clay was on the sofa, half-asleep and half-watching Will Smith in *Ali*. He had left her a message that he brought her some food. He got up, gave her a hug, and went to the kitchen to get it. While she ate, they talked.

"I was thinking today that I want to go to DC to see Grant." Cicely laughed.

"You really want to meet Sunny, don't you?"

"Yep! She got my man actin' out!" They both laughed. "Can you take a couple of days off to go with me?"

"Sure, I have plenty of time. Just let me know when." They talked about the trip for a few more minutes, and then Clay changed the subject.

"When you get the notice to renew your lease, let them know you'll be moving out," he told her.

"And where do you plan for me to live?" she asked folding her arms and sitting back in her chair.

"Let's just say I have a plan," he said kissing her hand. "Do you work Saturday?"

"I get off at seven o'clock in the morning. Why?"

"I want to show you something." He wanted to show her his home. The house he grew up in. It would take some work, but he hoped she would agree they could live there to raise their family. It was a big house with a big yard, trees, flower beds, and a porch swing. Nobody had lived in it regularly for years. He kept the water and electricity on and would go out there occasionally in the winter. In the warmer months he would have cookouts and parties. From time to time, he would take his uncle Paul for a visit. The adjoining lots to Clay's house were where his father and uncle grew up. The old house had been torn down for decades, but Uncle Paul just liked to see the land. He had hoped that Gretchen and Grant would build on the land and raise their families there.

"Okay, I tell you what. Get a nap and we'll have a late lunch. That good?"

"That's great babe," she said smiling. "You know I like surprises!"

He kissed her forehead. As they did many nights, they stayed up late talking, and Clay fell asleep. Cicely looked at him. He looked like a little boy, so innocent. She wanted to get under the covers with him, but she was determined not to. Clayton Sturdivant had come a long way, and worked hard to earn her love, but they weren't married yet. She smiled at the thought of him telling her not to renew her lease.

CHAPTER TWENTY

Two Thursdays in a row, JJ had home games, so Jacksa and Jackson drove to Durham to see him play. The first week, Jackson skipped his hair cut. The second week, he got his hair cut on his lunch hour. Min watched both games on television with friends. The conference tournament was in Charlotte, and Jacksa was determined to take Min. With Anderson's help, they worked it out, and the four of them went to the game. Min was excited that Jacksa asked Anderson to go with them. She whispered in Jackson's ear for him to be nice. He was being the typical father who thought nobody was good enough for his daughter. He asked question after question about Anderson being a police officer. Min gave him the eye, and he finally backed off. Being out in the crowd seemed to give Min energy. She had a great time. She felt so good she attended all three games.

Jackson was away from his "other situation" for weeks. They spoke by phone, sent a few e-mails and texts, but hadn't seen each other. In a way, it was a relief to Jackson. Trying to live two lives was getting to be too much.

JJ was able to spend about thirty minutes with them after the last game. He was glad to meet Anderson but almost as bad as his dad about Jacksa. He was ecstatic to see Min and turned into a big baby. He asked his mother for money, whining about the food on campus, and he wanted his mother to see the bruise on his shin. Jacksa just looked at him.

Anderson went to get the car, while Jacksa and Min went to the ladies' room. Jackson was waiting for them and decided to check his phone. He had two text messages. He responded quickly, *At JJ's game. TTYL.*

Min was in the front seat with Anderson. He reached over, put his arm around her, and asked if she wanted a nightcap.

"What do you have in mind?" she asked.

"A banana split!" They all laughed. They stopped at an ice cream shop and Anderson doted on Min like she was his real date. They talked about his family and growing up on the reservation. He told her that his grandmother, mom, sisters, and aunt had been in town a few weeks before, and Min said she wanted to meet them the next time they came. He promised her he would make sure they met as he looked at Jacksa.

Jacksa and Anderson stayed at her parents' home briefly when they dropped them off. Min was exhausted, but she had a wonderful outing.

"How are you feeling, sweetie?" Jackson asked Min as they were getting ready for bed.

"I couldn't be better!"

She gave him a kiss as she walked into the bathroom. He decided to go into the other bathroom, so they would be done at the same time. He didn't want her to be asleep when he finished his shower. When they were both in bed, he pulled her into his arms like he often did. She snuggled close with her head on his chest. She could hear his heartbeat. He sang into her ear Luther Vandross's "If This World Was Mine." He played with her hair and rubbed her back. They came together that night in a way they had not in a very long time. Jackson was very careful with Min. He knew she could not bear his weight, but he needed his wife.

Jackson awakened first. It was just after six o'clock. Min was still in his arms. He eased out of bed and looked out the window; it was raining. They could stay in all day or maybe go to the mall, see a movie, and have lunch. He laughed to himself. He was making plans, and he hadn't asked if she already had plans for the day. He picked up his phone and walked out of the bedroom.

He purposely did not check his phone the evening before. He had turned it off. Min, Jacksa, and JJ were with him; he didn't need to hear from anybody else. He started some coffee and turned on his phone. There were eight messages—four text messages and four voice mail messages. They all basically said the same thing: asking Jackson to call, reminding him they had not seen each other in weeks. He deleted all except the last text so he could respond. He fixed his coffee while he thought about what to say. He knew he couldn't just walk away without an explanation. He could hear the wind and the rain and then a crack of thunder.

"A spring thunderstorm," he said out loud. He reached for his phone. He responded to the text. *I will see you Thursday.*

CHAPTER TWENTY-ONE

Sandra ended her call when she realized Chloe was crying. Chloe told her mom about seeing Enoch at the post office and about seeing the pictures of Nicholas. She cried uncontrollably for a few minutes.

"Ma, he is so cute," she said, smiling and crying at the same time. "I can't believe I gave him away."

Sandra had to get control of the situation. She sat beside Chloe, took her by the hands, and looked directly into her eyes. "Chloe, you made—you and Campbell made a good decision. It was the best decision you could have made at the time."

"I know, Ma, but you should see him. He has Campbell's eyes and my smile, including the dimple. Oh God, I can't believe I gave him away." She started to cry again.

Sandra wanted to tell Chloe that little boy, no matter how cute he is, would have ruined her life and he is better off with the Casebiers. But she couldn't. She knew the only way to deal with Chloe was to be firm with her.

"Chloe, when you and Campbell made the decision to have an open adoption without talking to anybody about it, you subjected yourself to this. You know Hattiesville is a small community."

Chloe covered her face with her hands. When she finally looked at her mom, she asked if they could call Kirby and ask to see Nicholas. Sandra did not think that was a good idea. They were both quiet for a moment. Finally, Sandra answered her. "I don't think that's a good idea. She probably won't agree to let us see him anyway."

"But we won't know unless we ask."

They talked back and forth for a while, and Chloe finally talked Sandra into making the call. They decided to call from home that evening. Chloe stayed in her mother's office for a while longer until she regained her composure and could go back to her office without answering questions. She washed her face and reapplied her makeup. But despite her efforts, Natalia still knew she had been crying and asked her about it. "I'll tell you later" was all she said.

Natalia was in the office, but she was actually doing her homework. She was working on her last project. Final exams would be the following week, and then she would be in the office thirty hours per week. She was considering getting another part-time job. She was saving to buy a car. The extra ten hours per week would allow her to save more, but if she could get a job at the mall that would be great.

Roderick Matthews, Chloe's dad, offered Natalia and her three friends a trip back to Haiti for a week. He was having difficulty finding them a place to live and a chaperone. Chloe volunteered to chaperone, but Rod didn't agree to that. He told her he needed her in the office. Natalia had no home or family who survived the earthquake, the State Department had confirmed that. One of the three others had an aunt and uncle who survived but were living in a tent camp with their children, and one had a grandfather who survived but urged him to stay in the United States "for a better life." Natalia and her roommate talked about home a lot, but they were both settled into a life in the United States. They were thriving in their new community. Natalia was particularly happy because she was spending so much time with Chloe. Sandra was concerned that Natalia was Chloe's project, something to keep her mind off Nicholas.

Belinda left Ben a message that she was headed home. She didn't feel well. She had assisted with a very early surgery and thought she was just tired. She hadn't felt well the last few days. She knew her family was perfectly capable of getting themselves dinner so she was going to bed. By the time she got home, she realized she hadn't eaten so that was probably part of the problem. She made a sandwich and had a glass of lemonade. She did feel better. After a shower, she got in the bed and went to sleep quickly. She didn't hear Ben and the girls come in, and when he finally awakened her, she had slept three hours. She apologized and started to get up. "Where are you going?" Ben asked.

"To check on the girls. I cannot believe I slept that long," Belinda said.

"They are fine. The kitchen is clean and homework checked. I told them to come in and say goodnight before they go to bed."

Belinda was sitting on the side of the bed. She really didn't feel well. Ben propped the pillows against the headboard and told her to sit back and relax. She sat back but didn't tell him how horrible she was feeling. He told her that he met with April and Hampton Josephs earlier in the day. That made her feel worse. He updated her on the church renovation project and then told her he and April discussed getting started looking for a house. She knew she had to tell him she didn't like Hampton, but she wasn't ready to tell him Hampton was flirting with her. She let out a big sigh.

"Sweetie, I'm good with getting started and meeting with April, but I don't want to work with Hampton."

Ben looked puzzled. "What's your beef with him?"

"I don't have a beef. I just think he's a little over the top, a little 'extra,' like the girls would say." Ben laughed. Belinda continued. "He will probably try to build us a mansion that we cannot afford, and I'm not going to clean up! He'll want us to have a four-car garage, and we don't even have four cars!" He was really laughing now.

"Woman, you are funny!"

She was laughing too. What she said was a mild exaggeration but not totally inaccurate. They continued to talk about what they needed in a new home and what they wanted. As was his way, Ben was writing everything down. With the money Grammy gave them, they could afford more house than they originally talked about. Belinda needed to get Ben to agree not to work with Hampton, so she had to steer the conversation back that way.

"Did April say she knew of any lots we could look at?"

"Yeah. As a matter of fact, she mentioned a fairly new development that backs up to the park. We could see the lake from the deck on the back!" He was smiling.

Belinda was thinking about seeing Hampton at the park. She was feeling sick on the stomach. Just as she excused herself, Brianna was at the door.

"Mommy, what's wrong with you?"

"Will you get me some ginger ale, please?"

A few minutes later, Belinda was back in bed. They prayed with the girls, who prayed for her, and Ben was rubbing her back.

"Babe, I want you to see a doctor tomorrow."

"I don't need to see a doctor. I'm sure it's just a virus." She wasn't sure.

CHAPTER TWENTY-TWO

Chloe was anxious for her mom to get home so they could call Enoch and Kirby. Sandra was hoping she had changed her mind. She knew in her heart that Chloe was going to be even more upset if Kirby said no, and there was a good chance that's exactly what she would say.

Chloe talked with Campbell shortly after she got in from work. He tried to cheer her up. He had to work until ten o'clock but told her he would see her as soon as he could. He also tried to talk her out of calling Kirby. Like Sandra, he knew nothing good would come out of a "no" from Kirby.

When Natalia called, Chloe wasn't surprised. She started the conversation asking Chloe if she would help her look for a car and gradually worked her way to why Chloe was crying at work. "The man we saw at the post office was someone from my past."

Exasperated Natalia said, "He was your boyfriend? He's too old for you!"

Chloe laughed. "No, girl, he was not my boyfriend! It's a very long story. I promise I'll tell you later. Campbell has to work Saturday, so we can hang out, look at some cars, and I'll tell you." Chloe wanted to get off the phone; she heard Sandra come in.

Chloe met Sandra in the hallway as she came upstairs. She didn't have to say anything; her mother knew what she wanted. A few minutes later, Sandra called the Casebier home. Enoch answered and didn't seem surprised that they were calling. It was not in Sandra's nature to beat around the bush, so she didn't. It wasn't in Enoch's nature either, so neither did he. Sandra asked, and he said no. Sandra asked him if he would at least talk to Kirby about it, and he said he didn't need to. The answer was no, and he was sure that was best for everybody involved. As if he were reading Sandra's mind, he asked her not to call back to ask Kirby.

"Sandra, please tell Chloe that Nicholas is fine. We are taking good care of him. He is loved. We want Chloe and Campbell for that matter, to get out of school, maybe get married, and move on."

"Enoch, do you think there will ever be a time when you will let Chloe see him?"

"Maybe. But not now. This is not that time." They ended the conversation.

Chloe burst into tears. Later that night, after they put the boys to bed, Enoch told Kirby about the day's events.

Carlos went to North Carolina and found out more than he expected. He paid for some of the information, but he was sure it was worth it. In order to tie up the loose ends, he decided he should go to church on Sunday. Then he would meet with Mr. Josephs on Monday, tell him what he knew, and collect his bonus. It was an interesting story to say the least.

Juan noticed Carlos a few minutes after he arrived. A woman and two young boys were with him. Juan assumed they were his wife and sons. He walked over and shook hands with Carlos making sure Ben saw him. After the service ended, Juan introduced Lili to Carlos and his wife. They chatted for a few minutes before Carlos excused himself; he had spotted Hampton. They acknowledged each other but did not talk. Carlos got a close look at Belinda. He felt bad for her, but he knew Mr. Josephs would fix it. He had a way of making things better. He felt bad for, Ben too. He seemed like a great man. No matter how great a guy he was though, if Hampton Josephs wanted his wife, he would have her.

After Enoch and Kirby talked about Chloe and a few other things, she went to the bedroom to call Belinda. Belinda told her about being sick.

"I didn't go to work today."

"Yeah, you really are sick. Are you going to the doctor?" Kirby asked.

"I guess I will try to see somebody tomorrow. My husband is insisting."

Finally, Kirby told Belinda about Chloe. "Well, I'm glad Enoch handled it," Belinda said.

"Me too, but I have a funny feeling it's not over." Kirby sighed.

"Why?" Belinda asked.

"Sandra called before, and she e-mailed me and asked to see pictures of Nick. I told her no when she called, and I just didn't respond to her e-mail. I hear from Campbell a couple of times a year and I have responded to him. He only inquires. He never asks for anything or asks to see him." Kirby explained.

"But, Kirby, you knew this was a possibility when you agreed to the open adoption."

"You're right. But I guess I thought almost four years later they would have moved on with their lives. They are in college. I just felt sure Nicholas would be a part of their past by now."

When Campbell arrived at Chloe's, they sat outside on the deck. She was clearly upset. Campbell knew he had to be firm with her but also not upset her further.

"Chloe, you and I both knew there would be consequences to our actions."

"But, Campbell, you don't understand."

"Yes, I do! I feel the same way you do. I think about him every day. But we made the decision to give him up so he could have a better life and we could go to college. And we also made the decision to have an open adoption, so we could have the option to be in his life."

"Well, I want my option now!"

"But the Casebiers have options too. They are his parents, and they get to make decisions for him."

"We are his parents!" Chloe was screaming by now.

Campbell got up and walked to the other side of the deck. He felt so defeated. He took this whole situation very personally. He hadn't ever told her how this whole thing weighed on him. He sat down directly in front of her and took both her hands in his. They sat quietly for a bit. He was looking at her. She was looking into space. Finally, he broke the silence.

"Sugar, I apologize." She slowly moved her eyes toward him. "I have never asked you to forgive me for all this. When you told me you were pregnant, I wasn't in a position to say 'its okay, we can take care of our baby.' I didn't have anything to offer you."

"Campbell, this is not your fault. We were seventeen years old."

"Let me finish, Chloe. Yep, we were seventeen, but I didn't have anything. I was living in a two-bedroom duplex with my mother and five brothers. Let's just say we hadn't put him up for adoption. I wouldn't be in college. We would be bouncing him back and forth from me to you, and he sure wouldn't be in that expensive private Montessori school."

"How do you know what school he goes to?" Chloe asked Campbell.

"Last year, I e-mailed Mrs. Casebier to ask about him, and she told me he was doing fine, and it happened to be his and his brothers first day at DavisTown Montessori."

"DavisTown Montessori," Chloe repeated.

"Chloe, the point is I was not, am not, in a position to give Nick the kind of life he deserves."

"But you would love him so much."

"Sure I would, but I wouldn't have much time with him. I would be working two jobs . . ."

"You know my parents would have helped us," Chloe said.

"But *our* child is not *your* parents' responsibility," Campbell responded.

"He's their grandson, Campbell."

"But he's my son, Chloe. My dad was in and out of my life, and I refuse to be that person. When I told my mom you were pregnant, the first thing she said was that I was following in my dad's footsteps! I wanted more for Nick than that, and I knew—I know the Casebier's can give him more."

Chloe was crying. Campbell put his arms around her and let her cry. He couldn't believe they were doing this again, almost four years later and all because she saw Enoch at the post office. What would she have done if Nicholas had been with him? She stopped crying, but she was really quiet.

"Sugar, I don't know if you will believe me, but I love you." She sat up and looked directly at him. "I love you and want us to be together for always. There are a lot of things to work out, but will you marry me?"

CHAPTER TWENTY-THREE

When Raja looked at the screen on his phone and saw his parents' names, he expected bad news. He hadn't heard from them since before he and Jill got married. When he talked to his cousin Yash, he would let Raja know they were doing well.

"Hello."

"Good evening, Manavendra. It is your father."

"Good evening, Father." Raja didn't really know what to say. It had been such a long time. "Is everything all right, Father?"

"Yes, we are fine. Calling to tell you we are in a hotel in New York City. We will be flying to Charlotte tomorrow."

Raja swallowed hard. There was a few seconds of silence. "It is quite unlike you to make an unannounced visit, Father."

"Perhaps, but I hope that you will accommodate us."

Raja's mind was racing. They didn't have room for his parents. But even if they did, there was no way he would bring them into their home, especially unannounced and uninvited.

"Who is traveling with you other than Mother?"

"Just the two of us," Mr. Rajagopal answered.

"What time do you arrive?" Raja asked.

"In the afternoon at two o'clock."

"All right, I will pick you up and have all the arrangements made for you."

Raja's father thanked him and they hung up. Raja shook his head to make sure he wasn't dreaming. "Where did all this come from?" he wondered out loud. He sat down in the patients' chair in his office. He had to call Jill. She was going to flip!

Jill and LaLa were spending the day with her mother. Jill left them for a while to run some errands, and she stopped by the office to check on some things. She was slowly working her way back to work full time. Ellen agreed to continue helping her at the foundation and to help with the baby. But Jill and Raja knew they would need a backup plan. Ellen and Dr. Strauss took several vacations per year.

Raja took a deep breath and called his wife. She answered cheerfully. When he told her why he was calling, she laughed. "Well, I'm glad you see the humor in this." She continued to laugh.

"Honey, I'm laughing because I don't know what else to do. Your parents are headed here with no warning," she said it loud enough for her mother to hear.

Ellen put her hand over her mouth as she saw Jill fighting to keep her composure. Raja explained he was surprised too, but he knew they were up to something. They talked a few more minutes, and he told her he would get them a hotel room.

"I am going to call Yash as soon as we finish talking."

"Go ahead and call him now. Let me get the baby's things together, and I'll see you at home."

Jill wanted to call Tara, and she needed to talk to her mother. When they hung up, she plopped down on the sofa like she used to when she was a teenager. She groaned loudly.

Her mother laughed. "Jillie, maybe they are coming around. Maybe they are extending the olive branch."

"Mom, they flew from London without saying they were coming. That's not an olive branch. That's a thorn bush!"

She called Tara while at her mother's. When she told Tara the news, Tara cursed. "I'm coming too!" she said matter-of-factly.

"Can you get off?" Jill asked relieved.

"Sure. Plus, Robert is playing in a golf tournament this weekend, so I would have been home alone anyway." Jill was so glad Tara offered to come.

"Tell Raja to book me in the same hotel. I will get to the bottom of this."

At the same time Jill was talking with Tara, Raja called Yash. He claimed he didn't know Raja's parents were even away from home.

"They cannot be here for any good reason if they didn't tell your parents they were coming," Raja said to Yash.

"Because I didn't know doesn't mean my parents didn't," Yash responded.

"That's true. I am just so puzzled about this. I'm actually worried."

"I don't think you should worry, cousin. Keep an open mind. Maybe they are coming to make amends." Yash sounded more confident than he really was.

"They could have done that over the phone. I don't like this at all. But I'll see what happens. They're here now, so there's not much I can do."

CHAPTER TWENTY-FOUR

Clay called Grant to tell him what he did and to let him know he and Cicely wanted to come for a visit. Grant was excited. He couldn't wait to tell Sunny. He was glad Clay was accepting his relationship with Sunny. He knew almost everybody else at home thought it was too soon. But it had been three years. If he had died, which he could have that same night; he would hope that by now Leah would be moving on.

Clay went to his safe deposit box and got his mother's ring. He took it to the jeweler's, had it cleaned and sized. This was the two-carat emerald-cut diamond set in platinum that his father gave his mother on their eighteenth anniversary months before he died.

Clay made a salad, prepped salmon for the grill, cut fresh strawberries, and chilled a bottle of Dom Perignon. All things were ready. He laughed. Bishop Robinson would often say "All things are ready."

On his way to get Cicely, he replayed in his mind the conversation with Delia. He called her a couple of days ago to ask why she wouldn't talk to him the night he saw her at the game.

"Clay, I spoke to you. What else was there to say? Jeremy told you what's going on with him and Crystal likewise."

"Oh, since you were with your man, no talk for me."

"Clay, I don't even understand why you called me. I haven't heard from you in three years. Now all of a sudden, you have so much to say," Delia said.

"Delia, we were friends. Why wouldn't I touch base from time to time?"

"I think because I was 'with my man' as you put it, you were jealous."

Clay laughed. "No, Dee, not jealous."

"Yes, you are, or just surprised that I am with a man who loves me, is good to me, and takes care of me and my kids. In your mind, all I'm good for is having sex."

"Well, Dee, you are living with him and not married to him, so that hasn't changed."

"If you must know, we're getting married, and we're building a house. We put both houses on the market. His sold quickly, so we are living in mine until our new house is ready."

"That's what's up. When are you getting married?" Clay asked.

"Why? Why do you care?" Delia raised her voice.

"I just asked, don't mean no harm." The conversation didn't last long after that. He would talk to her again, another time.

When he arrived at Cicely's house, she was ready and very curious about his "surprise." When they didn't go to his house, she got really curious. "Where are you taking me?"

"Just ride, ma'am!" When they approached the house, Cicely gasped.

"Is this your parents' house?"

"Yes, my childhood home." When they were out of the car, he showed her where his grandparents' home was and where Enoch and his family had lived down the road. They sat in the porch swing for a while. He broke a few roses off a bush and gave them to her. "Let's go around back and fire up the grill." He cooked; they ate and had strawberries and champagne for dessert.

"Dom Perignon, what's the occasion?" Cicely asked.

"How would you like to live in this house and raise a family?" He was looking directly in her eyes.

"I think I would like that." He stood, took her by the hands, and picked up their glasses. They walked through the house. He showed her all the rooms. They talked about a room for their son and a room for their daughter. They talked about what they would and could do to renovate and upgrade the house. Eventually, they made their way back through the kitchen and out on to the deck. It was getting dark. Clay lit a lantern and sat it on the table. He waited purposely for her to sit first. He fumbled with the lantern for a minute and then poured more champagne into their glasses. He took a sip of his and then handed Cicely her glass. She took a sip and then gasped loudly. The lantern light hit the glass just right, so she could see the diamond sparkling in the bottom.

Clay took the champagne flute from her, took a gulp, and got down on his knee. "Cicely, I love you so much." He put his fingers in the glass to fish out the ring. He took her hand in his. "It would be my honor to give you my name, be with you here to turn this house into a home again." Tears were streaming down her face. "Will you marry me?"

She looked at it for just a second and then looked into his eyes. "Clay, I love you very much, and it would be my honor to have your name and to live in this amazing house and make a home and have a family with you. Yes! I will marry you."

He slipped the ring on her finger.

"Neither DavisTown nor UNC Charlotte have the PhD program," Kathy responded.

The server brought the food, so for a couple of minutes, they were both distracted. Kathy said the grace, but when she finished, Sterling was still sitting there looking at her.

"Sterling, don't let your food get cold."

"Kathy, what about us?"

"What do you mean when you say *us*?"

Sterling looked at her with amazement on his face. He shrugged and asked, "Do you really need me to answer that?"

She put her chopsticks down and folded her hands in front of her. "Going back to school, earning my terminal degree, and becoming a college president one day are my ultimate career goals. Now that I have the opportunity to do it, that's what I want to do, intend to do. I hope you understand that."

"I do understand. I just don't necessarily agree with your method of accomplishing your goal."

"Can you say you wouldn't leave DavisTown if the right coaching offer came along?" Kathy asked him seriously.

"No, I can't say that, but what I can say is I wouldn't make that kind of decision, a life-altering decision without talking to you about it," Sterling answered just as seriously.

Kathy didn't really know what to say. They ate in silence for a few minutes.

"Kathy, what about us? I thought we were on the road to marriage."

"Marriage! Sterling, we never talked about marriage."

"That is the natural progression from courting," he said it very sarcastically.

"Even if I were not going back to school, we are a long way from getting married. You are still working on your career. It would be four years before we tried to do anything anyway . . . if we were going to."

They had both finished their food. Kathy was ready to go, but Sterling was ready to talk. He asked the waitress for more tea.

"Kat, when I met you five years ago, I told you I wanted to marry you. Why do you think that has changed?"

"But, Sterling, I didn't tell you that I wanted to marry anybody. I don't want to be anybody's wife or mother!"

"What a selfish thing to say."

"Why is that selfish, Sterling? This is not the 1960s, when women didn't have options. I can get an education, have a career, and take care of myself." Kathy's voice had gotten louder and gone up an octave as the conversation continued.

"You are your parents' only child now. Why would you deprive them of a son and grandchildren for your own selfish reasons? You can have a family and a career, Kathy. You don't have to make a choice."

She was fuming, and Sterling could tell by the look on her face.

"Why is it my responsibility to give them what they want? I didn't take it away from them, God did. They can't be angry with anybody but Him. How can you say you want to marry me when you can't even be happy for me? You didn't congratulate me. You can't or won't share my accomplishment. You're the one who's selfish!"

Sterling didn't respond. They sat in silence for a couple of minutes, and finally, Kathy was ready to go. They rode back to campus in silence. When she pulled in beside his car, Sterling looked at her and said, "Goodbye, Kathy."

He opened the car door, got out, and looked back in. "Congratulations."

CHAPTER
TWENTY-FIVE

Campbell awakened in the middle of the night and realized he had asked Chloe to marry him, and she said yes. What had he done? He asked her out of emotion, wanting her to feel better. Sure he loved her, such as it was. He looked around the room. He was a twenty-one-year-old college student. He lived in a residence hall with hundreds of other students. He worked two jobs, had less than three hundred dollars in the bank, a twelve-year-old car, and if not for his scholarship, he wouldn't be in school. He could barely take care of himself. How was he going to be a husband?

They would have to talk, as soon as the sun came up. How could he tell her he reacted to the situation and maybe getting married was not the answer? He couldn't hurt her. Campbell was afraid he had made a bad situation worse. He wanted to marry Chloe—in five or six years, after law school. He would have to tell her the truth. He had to once again take responsibility for creating a situation with Chloe. Campbell drifted back to sleep thinking maybe they could get married between undergrad and law school.

CHAPTER TWENTY-SIX

"Hey, honey".

"Daddy, its Bree. We're at the mall, and Mommy is sick!"

Ben got up from his desk, got his keys, and started toward the door. As he was getting into his SUV, Brianna was explaining that Belinda fainted. The mall security called the paramedics, and they were taking her blood pressure. She was conscious, and she said she was okay. Ben told Brianna to tell her to stay where she was until he got there. When Ben arrived, the medic told him that her blood pressure was low and suggested she see her doctor as soon as possible.

Belinda knew Ben was going to be angry. She cancelled her appointment earlier in the week because she was feeling better. They dropped the girls at home and, in spite of her protest, went to the emergency room. Through the course of the examination, the doctor asked her when she had her last period. She hesitated. At that moment, it occurred to her that she hadn't had one in maybe two months. The doctor did a pelvic exam and a urine test and confirmed what she suspected—Belinda was pregnant. When the doctor left the room Belinda was staring straight ahead, she was perfectly still and not saying anything. Ben was laughing. The doctor assured them everything was fine. Belinda needed to start taking prenatal vitamins and she should see her doctor right away. She congratulated them.

When Ben finally got a hold of himself, he put his arms around Belinda. She started to cry. "Babe, what is it?" She kept crying. "Why are you crying?"

"A baby! We didn't plan this. We didn't talk about being pregnant, and I haven't been taking extra care to watch what I eat." she went on and on.

"Belinda . . . honey, come on now."

"Ben, are we ready for a baby?"

"Ready or not, here he comes!" Ben was excited.

On the ride home from the emergency room, they decided not to tell the girls or anyone for that matter until after Monday when she could see her gynecologist. Before they left the hospital, they prayed and thanked God for a happy healthy baby.

"Do you think we will have twins?" Ben asked Belinda.

"One baby will be fine," she responded with a smile.

They walked in, and the twins were waiting. "Mommy, what did the doctor say?" Brianna asked.

"She said I am going to be fine, need to get some rest and take some vitamins."

"Oh, because Grammy said you might be pregnant!" Brittani said.

Belinda purposely didn't look at Ben. "Who called Grammy?"

"We did, and she asked where you were so we told her."

"Well, I'll call her later" was all Belinda said.

"What's for dinner?" Ben asked trying to change the subject.

He walked into the kitchen, and Brittani followed him. Brianna lingered in the den, but Belinda walked away, headed toward her bedroom. Brianna reached for the phone to call Grammy and report that Belinda was at home and what the doctor said. She thought there was more to this doctor's visit than her parents were telling.

"Well, good. Glad it wasn't anything serious. Let me speak to your daddy."

Brianna walked into the kitchen to give Ben the phone. "It's Gram," Brianna said.

"Hey, Gram. What's going on?" Ben knew the phone didn't ring, so Brianna made the call. They chatted briefly, and then Grammy asked, "What did the doctor really say?"

"Britt is cooking me dinner, so I'll have Belinda call you."

Grammy wasn't satisfied with that answer, but she knew the girls were standing there. She would give them time to call her back.

Belinda went to her room to call Kirby. "That's exciting, Belinda. Why are you upset?"

"I just don't know if we are ready for a baby. I'm working, and Ben is involved in the renovation of the building for the new church. The girls have a dozen things going on."

"Are you looking for some sympathy from me?" Kirby asked laughing.

"No, not really," Belinda laughed too.

"Look sis, you are working because you want to. You know you can stop at any time. The church stuff is not going to stop and the girls are always going to be busy. So if you have a baby now or a year from now, that won't be different." Belinda knew Kirby was right. She didn't know why she felt so strange about it. She went to the bathroom to wash her face. She needed to get herself together. The last thing she wanted was for the girls to think she was seriously ill, get upset, and get Grammy upset.

Ben walked in, and she looked at him and smiled. "You good?" he asked.

"Yep, I'm good. I am just so surprised!"

"Me too! But I like surprises! We need to call Gram. Bree called her to tell her you were back . . ."

"And she asked you if I'm pregnant," Belinda said, interrupting him.

"Yes, but I didn't answer her." Belinda took a deep breath and called Grammy. Ben went back to the other part of the house to keep the girls distracted.

"Hey, Auntie."

"Hey sugar, you feeling better?"

"Yes, I am. Is Grammy close by?"

"She is. Hold on," Aunt Avis said.

"Well, just put me on speaker," Belinda heard Grammy say hello and then ask her what happened at the mall. Belinda told them the whole story.

"So you were right, Gram. I am going to have a baby."

"I knew it" was Grammy's response. Grammy and Auntie laughed.

"I told Avis it was you."

"How did you know?"

"Avis said she dreamed about fish." They all laughed. "We are just glad it wasn't Kirby! Lord, that child has her hands full!" Grammy said. They laughed again.

"We aren't going to tell the girls until after I go to the doctor," Belinda said that to make sure they, especially Grammy, didn't say anything. They talked awhile longer, and Belinda felt good when they hung up.

CHAPTER TWENTY-SEVEN

Min and Jackson decided to stay in, at least until the storm passed. He cooked breakfast, and they were playing Scrabble. Later in the day, they went out. Min wanted to do a little shopping. They had dinner out and decided to see a movie. It wasn't anything she particularly wanted to see, but she wanted to accommodate her husband.

When they came out of the theater, it was raining again. Jackson went to get the car so Min sat and waited. She was really tired, but she wouldn't tell Jackson. They were finding their way back to each other, and she refused to let her body stand in the way. Min wanted her husband back. She wanted him to be 100 percent her husband. Whatever she had to do not to share him, she would.

Jackson helped her into the car, folded the walker, and put it in the backseat. When he got in Min leaned over to kiss him. Neither of them noticed they were being watched.

"I called in the reinforcement," Jill said to Raja as he took LaLa from her arms. He looked puzzled.

"Tara is on her way. She said to tell you to book her in the same hotel."

"You really do want to start a fight," Raja replied.

"Raja, I don't know what your parents are up to, but I don't feel good about it. Tara can say to them what I can't."

"You're right about that. I talked to Yash, and he said he didn't know they were coming. For some reason I don't believe him."

"Do you think he would lie to you?" Jill asked.

"I don't want to think he would, but I'm just not convinced he had no knowledge of them flying eight hours to another country."

Fortunately, the house was in good shape. The maid service had been there the day before. Mrs. Rajagopal didn't like Jill anyway. All she needed was to come to an untidy house. This whole situation was weird. LaLa was almost a year old. Raja and Jill had been married almost three years, and neither of those facts had been acknowledged. Now out of the clear blue sky, they show up.

"When we get to their home, we have to be very nice to Jillian. Otherwise, she will not leave the baby with us." Mrs. Rajagopal was speaking to her husband. "Manavendra has become so Americanized. He has forgotten about his roots. We mustn't let our granddaughter grow up in that environment, with those people."

"I still think we can talk them into letting us have the baby, rather than us taking her from them," Mr. Rajagopal responded.

"Well, if that doesn't work, we still just have to take her. I will buy a car seat once we get to Charlotte. I did bring Jillian and Manavendra a gift. That should soften them up."

Tara arrived at the hotel earlier than the Rajagopal's on purpose. She wanted to put them on defense immediately, and she was sure it wouldn't take her long to figure out what they were up to.

CHAPTER TWENTY-EIGHT

"Well, did she say she would marry you?" Grant asked Clay.

"Yeah, man. I wouldn't have put myself out there if I thought there was a chance she would say no!"

"That's hot, man. Congrats."

"Thanks. I'm pretty pumped about it."

"Clayton Sturdivant turning in his playa card. Wow!" Grant laughed. "Never thought I would see that day!"

"Dude, that whole pregnancy scare with Delia put a new perspective on the way I was livin'."

"You better be glad it was a false alarm, and you better be even gladder it wasn't HIV."

"Don't think I don't know that," Clay said shaking his head.

Grant and Clay confirmed Clay and Cicely's plans for coming to Washington, and after they hung up Clay decided he would call Delia. He called her work number. She was absolutely annoyed that he called, and she told him so. "Clay, I really want you to stop calling me!"

"Dee, I know you miss me."

"Clay, you are being disrespectful to me, to my fiancé, and to our relationship. Please don't continue to call me." Delia was serious.

"I need to share some news with you." Clay said.

"What is it?" Delia asked, rolling her eyes.

"No, I want to tell you in person."

"Is it that important?"

"Yes, Dee. It's pretty important." Clay sounded really serious.

Neither of them said anything for a few seconds. Finally, Clay asked if they could meet for lunch the next day.

"Maybe, I will call you in the morning."

Delia was concerned about what he needed to say that was so important. She hoped it wasn't bad news like he was sick or something. *Oh my god,* she thought. *What if he is HIV positive or something like that?* She took a deep breath and willed herself not to panic. She would call him in the morning, meet him for lunch, and get it over with. Whatever it was, she would be completely honest with Javier. They were committed to each other.

CHAPTER TWENTY-NINE

Carlos called Hampton and told him they needed to meet privately. He thought it would be better for Hampton to come to his office. Carlos was able to obtain Belinda's birth certificate. He handed it to Hampton. The baby's name: Belinda Denise Craig; mother's name: Shona Denise Craig; father's name left blank. Place of birth: University Medical Center, Augusta, Georgia. Hampton sighed loudly after he read the birth certificate. Before he could say anything, Carlos handed him two other papers. Both were death certificates: one for Shona Denise Craig and one for Andrea Renee Coffey. The dates of death were the same, the cause of death was the same: severe head trauma. Hampton looked from one to the other, over and over, like the information was going to change. Carlos began to speak. What he said was almost a monologue. He didn't wait for Hampton to respond or comment in any way. He started by telling Hampton that Benjamin Coffey had been raised by his grandparents, Victoria and John Coffey, because his mother had been killed in an automobile accident when he was three years old. He told him about Ben's college career and how he ended up in Landridge.

"Basically, he's just a regular guy," Carlos said. Hampton was listening intently. Carlos continued to talk. "Señor Josephs, this part is the part of the info that gets complicated." Hampton shifted in his chair. "Shona Craig moved from Augusta, Georgia, to DavisTown, North Carolina, to live with a cousin and go to school. One morning, she was driving too fast in the rain, ran a red light, and collided with Andrea's Coffey's car. Shona had a baby in the car with her. Andrea had a toddler in the car with her. Those children were Belinda and Ben." Carlos paused. But Hampton spoke.

"Belinda's mother caused the accident that killed Ben's mother."

"*Si, señor.* I'm afraid so."

"Oh my god," Hampton said as he leaned back in the chair and covered his face with his hands.

"Señor, I told you it was terrible news."

"Carlos, it's worse than you know." He sighed.

Grant kept his word and called Janis. She was lying in bed thinking about their conversation. He was very formal with her, like they just met. Her attempts to butter him up failed. He also refused to come see her or even to meet with her. He told her he was living in the Washington DC area, working at Walter Reed Hospital, and had been promoted. He was now the chief of Physical Therapy. He asked how she was doing from the shooting and if she had any lingering effects. She told him no, and he said he was glad. He told her how devastated he had been to lose Leah and how it took him a long time to recover. His voice cracked while he was talking. The last thing Grant told her rocked her.

"Grant, now that we have cleared the air, I have apologized for everything I've done, and you accepted my apology, can we move forward?"

"Yep, Janis, I want us to move on with our lives."

She remembered smiling and anticipating what he was going to say.

"I will be getting married later this year."

Her smile faded, and she couldn't believe what she had just heard.

"Married! To who?"

Grant went on to tell her about Sunny. She could hear the happiness and excitement in his voice. Janis was stunned. She asked him why he wouldn't give them a chance. She pled her case for why they should be together, including surviving the gunshot. He told her no and said that they both needed to move on separately. Grant said that he was looking forward to making a life in DC with Sunny, and this would be their final conversation.

As Janis lay there, she thought about Sunny. Obviously, she didn't understand. Nobody would have Grant if she couldn't have him.

On Saturday, Chloe and Natalia met for breakfast and then drove to Charlotte to look at cars. As she promised, Chloe told Natalia about Nicholas. Chloe cried a little and Natalia did her best to comfort her. Natalia hated seeing Chloe sad. Chloe told her about the open adoption and how she thought the Casebiers should and would be more reasonable about her being able to see Nicholas.

Through the course of the conversation, Chloe also told Natalia that she and Campbell were getting married.

"Well, when you all get married, I'm sure you will have more children," Natalia said to Chloe, hoping that would make her feel better.

"Yeah, I know we will!" Natalia continued talking about what kind of wedding Chloe could have trying to change the subject and lighten the mood.

Natalia couldn't really afford any of the cars they looked at. She was discouraged, but Chloe had a plan. She was going to ask her parents to buy her a new car, and she would sell Natalia her car really cheap. Chloe kept her plan to herself. She would talk to her dad about it first.

"Chloe, you don't need a car," Roderick said, knowing that wasn't the end of the discussion.

"Daddy, my car is five years old. It's time for a new one!"

Rod looked at her over his reading glasses. "I'll buy you a car if you pay your tuition!"

"Daddy!" Chloe wasn't making much headway with Roderick, but she was determined to help Natalia get a car. Plan B, talk to her mother.

CHAPTER THIRTY

Ben and Belinda dropped the girls off at school, went to breakfast, and on to her doctor's appointment. When everything was said and done, they determined she was ten weeks pregnant. Her hemoglobin was low, and she was slightly dehydrated. Nothing was going on that couldn't be managed. Belinda was at peace; Ben was absolutely ecstatic. She reminded him they agreed not to tell anybody for a while. "Can I tell Bishop?" he asked.

"Of course," she answered smiling.

While they were driving home, they decided to find a creative way to tell Brianna and Brittani. "Are we going to tell the church or just let them figure it out?" Belinda asked Ben.

"Good question. What would you prefer?"

"I would prefer we wait until I start to show and then confirm their suspicions."

"You're funny," Ben said laughing.

They talked a few more minutes, and then Ben said he hoped she would seriously consider not going back to work after the baby came.

Okay, there it is, she thought. She wasn't surprised. She knew Ben hadn't ever wanted her to work anyway. Even knowing how hard she had worked to prepare herself to be a great nurse, all the extra training and certifications to be a surgical nurse. The best surgeons in the area would request her to be in their operating rooms. And he wanted her to give all that up to be a stay-at-home mom. They had the conversation more than once about the advantages of her being at home, including they could manage nicely without her salary. And while she agreed with Ben and totally understood why he wanted her at home, she wanted to work. She loved being a nurse.

"Babe, can we make that decision later?"

"Sure, but I want to state my position up front. It's not necessary for you to work with three or four children . . ."

"Where did you get four from?" Belinda interrupted. "May I please get through this pregnancy before you start talking about another one?"

Ben was laughing. "You are so cute when you fuss!"

She rolled her eyes at him.

"Well, you know this pregnancy may produce twins."

"Ben, please. Let's pray for one, healthy happy baby. When the girls were born, I was ten years younger. I'm not sure I can handle two babies now."

"You will have plenty of help, and maybe then we can get Grammy to move down here."

"I think we missed our opportunity to get her here. I just don't think she'll come now."

"I think if she was going to move down here, she would have when we first moved."

"I don't know, babe. A little baby may get her to change her mind." Ben wanted Grammy in Landridge with them. Belinda was thinking as he was talking.

"Note to self, add a room and bath for Grammy in the plans for the new house."

"I don't know why she won't move down here, and give Kirby and Enoch that big house with all that yard and upkeep."

"Have you suggested that to her?" Belinda asked.

"No, I just thought of it." Ben said frowning.

"What about Auntie?"

"I don't think she wants to be any further from her kids."

"True, and somebody needs to be there with Blake and Nicholas!" They both laughed.

"I am going to tell Grammy she should move here, give them her house, and Auntie can move in their house. Yep, that's the plan." Belinda looked at her husband. He had a plan, had everything worked out. The only problem was that he hadn't discussed his plan with any of the people involved. The diagnosis: OCS—only child syndrome!

CHAPTER THIRTY-ONE

Clay was surprised when he and Cicely arrived at the airport and Sunny was there to meet them, without Grant. She explained that he had a meeting, but by the time they were settled at the house, he would be done.

Clay liked Sunny immediately and felt a little guilty that he did. She had a slight accent, and Cicely asked her about it. "I was born in the Bahamas, on the island of Eleuthera, but we moved here when I was thirteen. So I've lost most of the accent. It only shows up in certain words." Cicely knew Clay was sizing her up so she kept the conversation going with Sunny. She made them laugh about how she got her name. "I was born in October, which is the rainy season in the Caribbean. It had been raining for five days. My father told my mother he was going to name the baby, Rain. The morning I was born, the sun was shining, so he named me Sunny. My mother told me she was glad there wasn't a tornado or a hurricane!"

Sunny and Cicely had a lot in common, starting with being the older sister of younger brothers. They talked a lot, and Clay was glad because he knew when they got home, Cicely would give him the scoop on Sunny.

When Grant got there, the energy level increased by 100 percent. He and Sunny were very affectionate with each other. He and Clay were playful as usual, and he decided Cicely was his new best friend.

Grant and Cicely cooked while Clay and Sunny entertained them. They were eating when Grant noticed Cicely's engagement ring. He held her hand for a moment, kissed the ring, and looked at Clay. They were all very quiet. Finally, Grant broke the silence. He looked Cicely directly in the eyes and said, "He loves you." She nodded in agreement.

"I was with him when he put this ring away, and he said he wouldn't take it out until he found 'the one.'" Grant moved his fingers in the quotation sign.

Cicely looked at the ring and then looked at Clay. She smiled at him. He winked at her. The moment was really intense. Cicely and Sunny had tears in their eyes. Clay had to break the tension.

"The other part of the story is my mom and Grant adored each other. As far as my mother was concerned, Grant could do no wrong. I got my butt beat many days because Grant said I did it, and he was the one."

Grant jumped in to defend himself, and he and Clay started telling stories about growing up together. They told the ladies about their grandparents' house and all the hiding places. Cicely told them about the plans she and Clay had for renovating his parents' home.

"I would love to help you!" Sunny said to them. "I sew. I made the window treatments in here, and the comforter and window treatments in our room." Cicely walked over to the window and felt the valance, and looked under it.

"Why do women feel stuff?" Clay said to no one in particular. They all laughed.

"Sunny, these are great. I would love for you to help me."

"Okay. We can talk about it more tomorrow, and we'll drive over to a fabric store I like."

"Tell them who painted," Grant was saying to Sunny.

"We painted!" Sunny said.

"Well, I helped," Grant said pouting. The conversation shifted to renovating the house. Clay was watching Grant and Sunny. He knew Grant had loved Leah, and Clay never thought he would see that look in Grant's eyes again. But he did. Grant loved Sunny. It was all over his face.

It was Thursday. Jackson left work and went to the barbershop. After his hair cut, he went to visit his friend. It had been weeks. They were glad to see each other, but Jackson intended to end things that night.

After a couple of beers and talking about their lives over the past few weeks, Jackson admitted he couldn't live this double life anymore. "This just isn't working anymore." Jackson said.

"Why? What's the problem? I haven't broken any of your 'rules' and I apologized about the flowers."

"Look, I don't want to do this anymore. We're getting careless. I don't like it."

"I think it's more than that. Are you seeing somebody else?"

"No, I am a married man. I told you when we got into this. You have to understand that."

"I do understand. I know she's your wife. I know she's not well. I know stress exacerbates her condition. And I know you need me." Jackson dropped his head, took a deep breath, and blew it out slowly. He leaned back against the sofa. The shoulder massage felt good. He started to relax. He closed his eyes and gave in to the attention. Against his better judgment, he stayed too long.

After dinner with Anderson, Jacksa went to see her mother. Min was trying to carry a basket of laundry and maneuver her walker at the same time. It wasn't working very well. "Mom, what are you doing?"

"I need to fold these clothes." Jacksa picked up the basket and the clothes that had fallen out and proceeded to the den. Min was hoping Jacksa wouldn't come over tonight. She adored her daughter and loved spending time with her, but she hated that Jacksa felt compelled to be there with her because Jackson wanted to be out, away from home and away from her. As much as she knew he loved her, she also knew she was a burden to him. He would never admit it. He was a kind man, but the truth was the truth.

"Jacksa, I thought you had a dinner date with Anderson."

"I had dinner with him. He had to go back to work." That was only partly true. He didn't go back to work. She sent him to do some investigating: to find out where Jackson was spending his Thursday nights.

Since Min confided in Jacksa that Jackson was having an extramarital affair, Jacksa had been incensed. She always held her father in high esteem and wanted a marriage like her parents. The news shattered her. What added fuel to her fire was how loving and attentive he was to her mother when they were together.

Anderson wasn't excited about what Jacksa asked him to do. He was shocked that she shared that information, and even more shocked that her dad was having an affair. If Anderson had to pick a person to be in that situation, he wouldn't have chosen Jackson Baye.

He also knew that he may not tell Jacksa everything he found out, if he found out anything. He had no intention of adding to the ruin of a marriage or making Jacksa anymore unhappy.

Anderson's first thought was to show up at the barbershop and ask Jackson to have a drink with him. So if he and his barber really were going out, they would ask Anderson to join them. When he got to the barbershop he decided not to go in. He waited in the back of the parking lot. He only waited about ten minutes when Jackson came out to get in his truck. They traveled about fifteen minutes toward Charlotte. Jackson turned into a subdivision and drove past the pool and clubhouse. When he turned into a cul-de-sac, Anderson stopped on the cross street. As he slowly drove to where he could see Jackson, he saw a garage door go up. Jackson drove in and the door went down. After a few minutes Anderson drove by the house, wrote down the address, and left. Anderson drove to the shopping center and parked. He accessed the computer in his cruiser and typed in the address to see who lived there, still not sure what he intended to do with the information.

CHAPTER THIRTY-TWO

Clay decided to check his e-mail before he went to sleep. There was an e-mail from Jeremy with his new AAU basketball schedule. Seeing the e-mail made Clay think about Delia and their conversation at lunch.

They met at a sandwich shop in the building where she worked. She had plenty of attitude, but Clay thought it was funny. She looked good, more stylish. She was obviously making more money or handling what she was making better. But then Clay remembered Javier was probably paying her mortgage—their mortgage.

They talked about Jeremy. He was doing well in school, and for the first time really talking about going to college. She talked about how much better he was about everything since Javier had come into their lives. She wasn't giving Clay credit for anything.

"Dee, you know he made a turn around long before Javier, and you know I had a lot to do with that."

"Yes, Clay. I guess you did your part," she said very sarcastically.

"Does Javier have children?"

"He has a son who's in Texas with his mother. He's nineteen, in college. Why are you asking so many questions? I thought you had something to say." Clay looked at her. Delia had changed, and he wasn't sure he liked this Delia.

Delia seemed a little nervous about what he was going to say and obviously wanted him to get it over with. She had her hands folded in front of her. Clay reached over and put his hands on top of hers. "Dee, I think you should reconsider getting married."

"Why would you . . ."

"Let me finish. Based on your reactions to me, seeing me, hearing from me, you aren't ready. You obviously still have feelings for me." She looked at him but didn't say anything for a few seconds. She sighed deeply.

"Clay Sturdivant, I love Javier and I am going to marry him. You are the last person to tell me what I should do in a relationship. Because remember, you told me we didn't have a relationship."

Clay looked at her and smiled. He gently drew his finger across her chin. Delia jerked her head away from him. She reached for her bag and stood to leave the table.

"Wait, Dee. Don't go. I didn't tell you what I came to tell you." She sat but her bag stayed on her shoulder. She folded her arms again.

"Delia, I am getting married too." She shrugged. He continued. "Cicely and I . . ."

"Good, Clay. Good for you. Now she can deal with you, and you can leave me alone." She stood and walked out of the restaurant.

When Raja arrived at the airport to pick up his parents, he couldn't believe how much luggage they had. How long did they intend to stay? This was getting worse by the minute. Raja and his father shook hands, but when he leaned down to embrace his mother, she was very stiff. He took part of the luggage. He drove back around to the curb pick up area. While his parents were getting in, he texted Jill to tell her they were on their way to the hotel.

"Manavendra, please take us to your home. I need to rest a bit."

"Mother, I have arranged for you and Father to have a suite at a hotel close to our home. You will be more comfortable there."

"I guess your wife made that decision."

"Mother, my wife's name is Jill, and I made these arrangements. I know you will need more space than you will have at our place."

"I'm sure your wife . . ."

"Mother, stop it right now! Let's settle this once and for all. I haven't had any contact with you in years. Then you show up unannounced. I don't know why you're here, but you are not going to disrespect Jill or upset our routine." His father remained silent.

"We came for a visit with our only son, and he doesn't appreciate us being here," Mrs. Rajagopal said to her husband. He didn't comment.

"Mother, what I would have appreciated is you acknowledging my decisions—my marriage to Jill, my daughter Leah's birth. No, I don't appreciate you showing up three years later like nothing happened." Raja raised his voice, and he promised himself he wouldn't. His mother brought out the worse in him. The remainder of the ride was in silence.

When they arrived at the hotel, Raja stopped at the front door, helped his father unload the luggage, then moved the car. His first thought was to keep driving. When he walked into the hotel lobby, his parents were standing there looking like a deer caught in headlights. Tara was in the lobby waiting for them. Raja stood back and watched. His mother's arms were flailing. Tara had fury in her eyes and her arms folded. She looked up and saw Raja. She motioned for him to join them. As he approached the group, he heard his mother tell Tara that she should mind her own business. Tara laughed. "Raja, Jill, and LaLa are my business."

Raja checked his parents in, and he and Tara escorted them to their suite. Tara told her aunt, "Don't bother to unpack all that. You won't be here long enough to use it all."

"Son, we would like to see the baby," his father said.

"I will talk with Jill about it."

"Hmph," his mother said and walked into the other room.

As Tara and Raja walked down the hall toward her room she told him, "I know in my heart they're up to something."

"I agree with you, but I don't know how we can find out."

"I don't either, and I can only stay 'til Sunday."

"My mother is impatient. She'll show her hand before then," Raja said with a sigh.

CHAPTER THIRTY-THREE

Hampton Josephs had been out of sorts since his conversation with Carlos. He missed a meeting, missed a deadline, and was being short with his staff. April finally confronted him about it. His explanation to her was that he just had a lot on his mind.

"Is there something I can do to help? 'Cause this is getting crazy," April said.

"I know and I apologize. No, you can't help me with this. I have to figure it out." April looked at her father, not satisfied with his answer.

"Are you in some kind of trouble?" she asked him.

"April, no, I am not in any kind of trouble." His voice was firm. "I have some personal things on my mind that I need to work through. I will tell you when the time is right."

"Okay, Daddy. Then I need you to focus. We have a lot to do, starting with a status report for LCC." As soon as she said that, Hampton's heart sank.

"When is our meeting with them?"

"Thursday of next week. Pastor and Mrs. Coffey and their team are coming here. I am having dinner catered."

"Will Bishop Robinson be coming?" Hampton asked.

"I haven't confirmed that. Why don't you go out there and ask somebody to find out and apologize while you're at it." April wasn't smiling. She didn't know what was eating her father, but she knew it was serious. She hadn't ever seen him so off his game.

"A dance with boys?" Ben was asking the twins as they were going over their calendar for the next few weeks. The girls looked at him and laughed.

"Yes, Daddy!" Brianna answered.

"I'm not sure how I feel about that." They laughed even more. The school year was coming to an end, and there was a lot to do: a concert, a dance recital, a play, the school dance, and finally, graduation.

"Daddy, we're getting ready to go to middle school, and in middle school there are a lot of dances with boys." Brianna was explaining things to Ben. He groaned and acted like that was the worst thing she could have told him. Belinda and Brittani were laughing at him.

At the conclusion of calendar time, the plan was that Brittani and Ben were going to Hattiesville to get Grammy so she would be there for all the activities. Brianna couldn't go; she had rehearsal for the play. Auntie was coming with Enoch and Kirby for graduation. They couldn't get away for the other activities.

Belinda hoped both girls were going. She just wanted to be home alone so she could sleep. And of the two of them, having Brianna at home would require more of her attention. She made a decision at that moment to ask for some help. She knew Thelma would help, and when Grammy got there, she would take over. Belinda and Ben also decided not to tell the girls about the baby until after graduation. They wanted this time to be special for them and not be about the new baby.

Belinda was just praying she could hold it together until then. She was so sick. What she ate wouldn't stay down. Smells made her sick, and she was so very tired, so very tired. She called the doctor back, who prescribed an additional iron supplement. Belinda agreed with what Kirby said when she was expecting Blake. The baby had to be a boy; a little girl just wouldn't act like that.

As excited as Belinda was about everybody being there, she was tired just thinking about having six more people in the house. Their four bedrooms would seem really cluttered, but Brianna and Brittani wanted Nicholas and Blake to be there with them. The four of them under one roof for three days, all Belinda could do was laugh.

When Brittani and Ben got to Hattiesville, Grammy had a list of things for him to do, including going to the bank with her. She was making the final arrangements to move the money to his account and getting the girls checks for their graduation to go into their savings accounts. They were also getting some cash to spend on anything they wanted. In the midst of all that, Ben wanted to see Bishop Robinson. He was excited to tell him about the baby, and he needed to discuss some church business as well.

Ben was like a kid going to tell his parents he made straight As. He went to Katherine Robinson's office first, and asked her to go with him to the bishop's office. When they were both seated, he broke the news. "How would you two like to be 'grand-godparents' or 'god-grandparents'?" Katherine gasped. Lee leaned back in the chair and laughed a hearty loud laugh.

"A baby? Oh my!" she said smiling. She got up and hugged Ben and held him for a long moment. She had tears in her eyes. Lee stood and shook Ben's hand.

"Wow" was all he said at first and then finally, "Congratulations, son, and we are honored to be grand-godparents or however you say it."

Ben told them about Belinda getting sick at the mall but assured them she was fine now. Katherine reached on Lee's desk, got his phone, and called Belinda.

They had a good conversation with her for a few minutes, and then Katherine excused herself. Ben and Bishop Robinson talked only a few more minutes about the baby, and then Ben told him about Carlos and how he was asking questions about Belinda. Lee shifted in his seat, leaned forward, and looked at Ben seriously. "What do you want to do?"

"I'm not sure, sir. He hasn't been back to the job site or the church."

"Did you contact anybody to run his license tag number?"

"No, sir. I didn't know if I should. I didn't want to overreact."

"Let me have it," Lee said to Ben, who handed the note to him.

Lee went to his desk, made a phone call, but didn't reach his party. He left a message and then went back to his conversation about Landridge Community Church.

About ten minutes later, his call was returned. Lee told the caller what he needed, gave the information he had, and asked the caller to get back to him as soon as possible. Another ten minutes passed, and Lee's private line rang again. He talked about five minutes. "Let me know. Thanks, man. Later."

"The character's name is Carlos Reyes. He lives in Atlanta, and . . . he's a private investigator."

"What the hell?" Ben said.

"Don't worry about it. My people will get to the bottom of it," Lee assured Ben.

CHAPTER THIRTY-FOUR

Jackson and Min had a great day. She was hoping he would want to be intimate with her when they got home. She was tired, but she didn't care. They talked about the movie and made plans for Sunday.

"Maybe we can have brunch with Anderson and Jacksa," Min said casually.

"Yeah, that's a good idea. I need to talk to that boy some more."

"Jackson, he's not a boy. He's a grown man, and you might as well get used to him. I don't think he's going anywhere."

"Honey, the man carries a gun for a living. I don't want him seeing my daughter."

"You wouldn't want him to see your daughter if he worked in a pie factory!" They both laughed.

"That's okay. JJ will be here next week. He'll shut it down."

"Let it go, Jack. You don't want her to be mad at you." He mumbled something. It was barely audible. Min didn't bother to ask him to repeat it.

Min came out of the bathroom barefoot and without her walker. She stumbled a little before she reached the bed. Jackson was already in bed, and he was dozing. She eased in beside him. He pulled her close, kissed her forehead, and went to sleep.

Jacksa asked Anderson what he found out when he followed her father. He couldn't lie to her but he was careful with his reply.

111

"I followed him to a subdivision on the outskirts of Charlotte. He went into a garage. I didn't see anybody."

"Why didn't you get the tag number on the car?"

"Jacksa, it was a cul-de-sac. If I had followed him to the house, he would have seen me."

"I see. Thank you, Anderson. Just let me know what you find out."

"I will, don't worry." Anderson needed a little more information but if what he suspected was true, Jacksa was going to be really angry.

Anderson had a more pressing issue right then. He had gotten a call from Bishop Robinson. He needed to give that request his immediate attention.

Chloe told Natalia she had some errands to run at lunch and she was going a little early. She told her that because she wanted to go out by herself, and they usually went together. The truth was she was going to DavisTown Montessori School to see if she could see Nicholas. She couldn't tell anybody. She looked at their website to try to determine when they may have recess. She was guessing, but if she was right, they should be outside shortly.

Chloe guessed correctly. The children were outside. She parked in the church parking lot next door, where she had a pretty good view of the playground. It was funny—all the kids looked alike in their uniforms. "I should have brought my binoculars," she thought. She couldn't spot Nicholas. For that matter she didn't see Blake either. After almost an hour, she gave up and left.

She was headed back to the office and decided to get something to eat. Surprisingly, Campbell was there too. He was with a couple of guys from work. He introduced Chloe to everybody and left his friends to sit with her. "What are you doing all the way over here?" Campbell asked Chloe.

"I had to run an errand, and I'm headed back to the office now." She couldn't tell him the truth.

"Can we get together later?" he asked her.

"Sure. What do you have in mind Mr. Rice?" She was smiling and winking at him. He intended to tell her they couldn't get married until at least after they graduated.

"Just wait and see, Miss Matthews."

As she drove back to Hattiesville to the office, she thought of how happy she, Campbell and Nicholas would be as family. "The Casebiers have another son. They will be fine without mine."

When Chloe got back to the office, she took a notepad and went into the library. She wanted to research the North Carolina case law on adoption. She knew there was other work to do, but as far as she was concerned this was more important. The decision had been made—she would file for custody of Nicholas. It would work well because she and Campbell would be married.

CHAPTER THIRTY-FIVE

Kathy's visit with her parents hadn't gone any better than her visit with Sterling. They asked some of the same questions and made basically the same comments. She left their home feeling very alone. She had no support, so she would have to do this on her own.

Kathy always thought her parents were open-minded and fair. They always supported her and Leah's dreams. But since Leah passed, they changed. They wanted her under their thumb or in her dad's words, "at arm's length." Her parents refused to accept what she wanted, what she thought was best for her. They raised her to be strong and independent and taught her the value of education. But no matter what she said, they would not support her plan to move to New York.

She stopped to get some sushi, and to add salt to her wound, there was Sterling and a date. Kathy was going to turn around and leave, but he saw her. She took a deep breath.

"Hey, Kathy. How are you?"

"I'm fine, Sterling. How are you?"

"I'm good."

His date looked familiar, but Kathy didn't know her name. When Sterling introduced her, Kathy realized she was the volleyball coach from DavisTown College. From what Kathy could remember, she was "famous." She had played on a winning Olympics team. She had a to-go container in her hand, so Kathy excused herself to get her sushi. When she had her food, she walked in a different direction so she wouldn't have to pass them again.

As soon as she got in the car, she called her cousin Michelle.

"Well, I told you not to put him back out there like that," Michelle was saying to Kathy.

"Is 'I told you so' the best you can do, Michelle?"

"What did you expect? That he was going to sit at home and wait for you to come home from school?" "No, but he was talking about us being in a relationship. Obviously, he got over that quickly."

"Kat, if you're looking for some sympathy from me, you aren't getting any. I hate it, but you made this bed."

Kathy's conversation with Michelle didn't last much longer. She went home, ate the sushi, and sat quietly for a few minutes. She thought through the situation she found herself in. The bottom line: what she had always wanted was within her reach.

"I'm going to New York. I'm going to earn my degrees," she said out loud. *Sterling can do Sterling*, she thought. "But I have to make peace with my parents." Kathy knew her parents loved her, but since Leah died, they were different. "If Leah and Grant were married and starting their family, Mom and Dad would have a totally different attitude. God, why am I dealing with the consequences of Your will?" Kathy said out loud.

"Lee, we can't keep her from going," Katherine said to her husband with tears in her eyes.

"What do you want me to say, Katherine? I don't want my only child over six hundred miles away. Don't tell me how great an opportunity it is for her. I know that. I just can't let her go."

"Lee, honey, we can't stop her. She wants to do this, and for all our best efforts, our power in this instance is limited."

Katherine started to cry. Lee put his arm around her and tried to comfort her, but he wanted to cry too. Life as he knew it, as he planned it, had changed. And though change was constant in life, this was simply more change than he wanted to face.

"Life comes at you fast, darling, and I guess all we can do is adjust."

"I miss Leah so much. What am I going to do without Kathy?" Katherine said in the midst of her tears.

They continued to talk late into the night.

CHAPTER THIRTY-SIX

Anderson went over his notes with the information Bishop Robinson gave him. He needed to track Carlos Reyes, and he needed to find out what Carlos knew, why he needed the information, and who he was working for.

"This is Detective Thorn, Hattiesville North Carolina Police Department, Badge 8408. I need some data on Private Investigator Carlos Reyes." He was talking to an officer at the Georgia Bureau of Investigation. The officer told him Carlos was "duly licensed and in good standing with the Bureau." He also told Anderson that Carlos applied to take his weapon with him to North Carolina for a few days. "That's interesting," Anderson thought. He thanked the officer for his help and hung up. "So he tracked them here. I need to pick up his trail and see where that leads me."

It didn't take Anderson long to find out that Carlos had been to the County Office of Vital Statistics, and that he ended his search at the State Office of Vital Statics with a copy of a birth certificate and a death certificate. He had learned in his reasonably short tenure as a detective not to burn bridges, pay his informants well, and ladies like flowers. A dozen roses went a long way with an acquaintance at the North Carolina Bureau of Investigation. She told Anderson whose birth certificate and death certificate Carlos obtained. The death certificate puzzled Anderson. Maybe Bishop Robinson could shed some light on that. But what he still didn't know was who Carlos was working for.

"Good evening, sir. AT here." Bishop Robinson laughed. He and Katherine were in the car headed to Sheldon's. They called Kathy and asked her to have dinner with them. They had also called Sterling, but he declined without much explanation. Katherine fully intended to ask Kathy about that.

Anderson told him what he knew, but assured him he had another avenue to follow for what he didn't know. "I am puzzled though about this death certificate. The name is Shona Denise Craig. She was nineteen at the time she passed. Hmmmm . . . My wife and I are headed to dinner. Can you come by my office tomorrow, and let's see what we can get done?"

"Yes, sir. I'll call you before I come." Anderson knew that was Lee's way of saying we need some privacy to discuss this.

Kathy was surprised when her mother called, but she agreed to meet them. She declined their offer to pick her up. If this was their way of trying to change her mind about school, she wanted to be able to leave.

When the Robinsons arrived at Sheldon's, Kathy was already there, seated and engaged in a conversation with Campbell. They were still very close, and she was telling him about going back to school. He was excited for her. The first person she told who was. He caught her up on things at school and then told her he needed to talk to her about Chloe. Kathy really hoped that ship had sailed, but obviously not. They made a dinner date for later just as Lee and Katherine approached the table. After Campbell took their beverage and appetizer orders, Katherine asked Kathy about Sterling.

"Hi, Mommy!"

Belinda awakened to Brianna standing in the bedroom door. She sat up in bed, but Brianna told her to lie back down. She just wanted her to know she was back. Belinda looked at the clock and realized she was asleep for over two hours. She came home to a clean house, dinner cooked, and a note from Thelma saying she would pick up Brianna from rehearsal.

"Come in, Bree. Is Thelma still here?"

"No, she left, but she said for us to call her if we need anything."

Belinda asked Brianna to get her some water, and she propped herself up in bed. Bree came back and sat on the foot of the bed, and they talked awhile. Rarely did Belinda get to spend any alone time with either of her daughters. With a new baby, that time was going to be even less. Belinda's cell phone rang, and it was Brittani calling to check on her but also to talk with Brianna. Brianna left the room, and Belinda went to the kitchen. She wasn't very hungry, but she needed to eat. All she wanted to do was sleep.

Belinda confided in Thelma that she was pregnant and didn't have a taste for anything. So Thelma cooked several different things, hoping she would eat something. Ben said he would hire Thelma full time if he needed to. He just wanted things to be as easy on her as possible. But if they convinced Grammy to move, they would still only need Thelma part time to keep Grammy from doing so much.

Belinda wanted to go back to work after the baby came, and whatever she had to do to make that happen was what she wanted. She could have a career and a family and be the first lady. She wouldn't, she couldn't defy Ben, but she had to make him understand how important it was to her to continue working as a nurse. That's what she always wanted to do. She prayed her career wouldn't get cut short. Before long, she went back to bed.

The twins talked about everything that was going on in Landridge and everything going on in Hattiesville—everything they cared about. Brittani reminded Brianna to make the appointments to get their hair done and reminded her to get fresh flowers for Grammy's room.

"We'll be there around two o'clock, but I'll call you when we get close."

"Okay," Brianna said, writing herself a note.

"Bree, is Mommy still sick?"

"Yep, she has been sleepy all the time. But I don't think it's real sick. I think Gram is right. I think Mommy is going to have a baby!"

"Brianna!"

"Well, that's what I think!" They giggled and giggled.

Raja and Jill were meeting his parents for dinner. It was Tara's idea for them to meet on neutral ground. When Raja, Jill, and LaLa came in, Tara took LaLa from Raja and she squealed with excitement. "Mr. and Mrs. Rajagopal, it's nice to see you again," Jill extended her hand but neither of them responded. *Strike one*, Tara thought. Mrs. Rajagopal only nodded. Mr. Rajagopal said hello. Mrs. Rajagopal reached for LaLa, but she laid her head on Tara's shoulder and wouldn't go to her grandmother. The waiter brought a high chair, and Tara sat the baby between her and Jill, across from her grandparents.

The conversation at dinner was formal and awkward until LaLa decided to eat her mashed potatoes with her hand and offered some to her mother. When Jill declined, she insisted by putting her hand full of potatoes on Jill's mouth! The laughter at the table amused her, so she continued to entertain them.

"Father, I still don't understand why you and Mother came all this way without telling anybody."

"Son, your mother and I wanted to come here to determine why your life here has taken you away from your real family."

"My *real* family? Father, Jill and LaLa are my real family. What are you talking about?"

"In other words, cousin, they want to know why you are so happy and prosperous without them," Tara said to Raja.

"Tara Rajagopal, you are so disrespectful. Why are you here? You were not invited," Mrs. Rajagopal said curtly. Tara laughed.

"I was invited; you were not!" she continued to laugh. Jill sat quietly, cheering for Tara on the inside. The conversation continued for a couple of moments, but the Rajagopals were not giving any real answers. Tara had enough of them sidestepping. "Look, why don't you two just state your business!"

Mr. Rajagopal looked at his wife. He spoke. "Son, we want to spend some time with Leah, your daughter."

"Our granddaughter," Mrs. Rajagopal added.

"That's really interesting, Mother, since she is almost two years old, and you haven't ever acknowledged her."

"Manavendra, it was the circumstances. But now we think she should come to London to live with us." Tara slapped her hand on the table. "So that's it. You are crazy!"

All of a sudden, Jill's face turned beet red. She looked her mother-in-law directly in the eye. "Live with you! Really! Seriously! My child is not going across the street with you, so you can forget it!" LaLa was looking from one of them to the other.

"She is my flesh and blood and should not be reared in your culture," Mrs. Rajagopal continued. "Mother, you are completely out of line. And, Father, you obviously support her in this fantasy." Raja was trying to maintain his composure.

Tara, on the other hand, was talking loud and had added a few curse words to her rant. As Jill was cleaning LaLa's hands, she told Raja she was ready to go. He stood to gather the baby's things.

"Manavendra, take your seat. I am still talking to you."

"Aunt, this conversation is over, and so is your stupid plan to take the baby back to London with you. I can't believe you!"

Jill didn't breathe until she was in the car in the backseat with LaLa. Tara was in the front with Raja. Jill literally had her hand over her mouth. She was afraid if that she moved it she would scream and scare the baby. When they got home, Tara took LaLa in the house so Jill and Raja could have some privacy. He put his arms around her and held her tight. She was trembling.

"Sweetheart, nobody is going to take our daughter anywhere. My parents can go back to London just like they came here: under the cover of darkness and without a relationship with us." After a few minutes she calmed down, and they went inside. Tara had LaLa in the bathtub.

"Cousin, why don't you finish up here?" She wanted to talk to Jill.

Mrs. Rajagopal was furious; her husband was passive. Tara's presence had complicated her plans, and she was angry with her husband for not demanding that Raja be more respectful. He knew that it was not uncommon for grandparents to keep the children while the parents worked. If she could get her hands on the baby, she knew she could get Raja to come back home. And maybe she could save face with the family of the young lady who they originally arranged for him to marry.

They took a taxi back to the hotel. Mr. Rajagopal prepared a cup of tea for both of them. Mrs. Rajagopal wasn't interested. She wanted to talk about how they were going to execute another plan to "take the baby."

CHAPTER THIRTY-SEVEN

Janis looked online to read up on Walter Reed Hospital, to see if she could find Grant's office number and if she could find a number for Sunny. At the moment, she wasn't sure what she intended to do with the information, but Grant couldn't marry Sunny.

God has moved Leah out of the way, she thought. *There's no way I am going to miss my opportunity again to be his wife.*

The website was helpful but not fully. She found a number for the Physical Therapy Department and a general number. She realized that she didn't know Sunny's last name or the department she worked in. Grant only told her that she worked at the hospital.

Janis went to an Internet directory and put in Grant's name and Washington DC. There wasn't a listing for him. With so many suburbs in Maryland and Virginia, she knew it would be hard to find it this way. Her best bet was his work information. She looked at the clock. It was after 6:00 p.m., so chances were they wouldn't be at work. She called the main hospital number, listened to the recording, and dialed the extension for Physical Therapy. It was a general voice mail and did not mention any names specifically. She hung up. As soon as she had, she realized that she should have dialed zero for the operator. Janis called back and this time dialed the operator. "Grant Sturdivant, please." Several rings and then voice mail. It wasn't his voice, but the message stated it was his office. A big smile came across her face. She had a way to access him. She was going to call back and ask for Sunny, but before she could do that, her daughter came in, and she stopped her research to attend to her. Janis prided herself on being a good mother.

Grant would be impressed, she thought. *And when we are married, we will have lots of children.*

After getting Carmen settled, Janis went back to her research. She called the hospital again.

"Good evening, I hope you can help me. I shared a cab with a lady who works there, and she left her camera in the cab. All I know is she said her name is Sunny. I would really like to get it back to her."

"So you don't have a last name?" the operator asked.

"No, I'm sorry I don't."

"Without a last name, I won't be able to help you, but I will transfer you to our Human Resources Department. Maybe they can help. They are closed for the day, but you can leave a message."

"Thank you," Janis replied.

After the operator transferred the call, and it rang once, Janis hung up. She wasn't about to leave a bogus message with her name and number. For now, she needed to keep a low profile.

Feeling really good about what she found out, Janis was shutting down the laptop when she decided to check one more thing: flight schedules and fares to Washington.

CHAPTER THIRTY-EIGHT

Belinda got some rest. She had been taking her vitamins for over a week, and she was feeling much better. She needed to. There were six extra people in her house. Two of them were four-year-old boys with more energy and curiosity than all the rest of them combined. Interestingly though, Brianna and Brittani seemed to have them under control. They were really good with their younger cousins. Belinda was glad, but she knew that by the time their new brother or sister was four, they would be teenagers who probably wouldn't want to be bothered with a kid sibling.

The play and concert went well, and everybody was in town for the graduation and the party. Thelma cooked, and Grammy organized everything. They invited Carlotta and her family to the party. With Grammy, Auntie, and Thelma at the helm, there wasn't anything for Belinda to do.

Just as they were getting ready to leave home to go to the ceremony, the doorbell rang. Auntie went to the door, and to everyone's surprise, there stood Bishop and Mrs. Robinson. "Can we get in on the celebration?"

"Yes, sir!" Brittani screamed. Of course, they were invited, but nobody expected they would come.

Both girls graduated with academic awards, perfect attendance awards, and awards in their "majors." Her girls were going to middle school. For the first time in a long time, Belinda thought about Canady, the twins biological father. He was killed in Iraq almost eight years before. That seemed like a lifetime ago. He would be so proud of his girls.

As the evening progressed, Ben, Enoch, Juan, and Lee ended up in the den, the ladies in the kitchen, and the kids in Brianna's room that the girls were sharing while their company was there. The ladies whispered about the new baby coming, but the men were having a very serious conversation about Carlos Reyes.

Juan assured Enoch and Lee that he would keep an eye on Ben and his family.

"I know you will," the bishop said to Juan. "And I appreciate that."

Enoch made sure he and Juan exchanged phone numbers. He wasn't quite as kind and understanding as the rest of them. He said he thought they should just find "this Carlos dude and confront him."

"No, let Thorn have a chance to see what he's up to," Lee responded to Enoch, but was really talking to all of them.

"Well, sometimes the law can take too long," Enoch said.

"We don't want to overreact if it turns out to be something good, like she's being vetted for a government job or something." They all looked at Lee with puzzled looks on their faces. Ben spoke up. "I've already told Belinda I don't want her to go back to work after the baby comes.

"You TOLD Belinda? My sister-in-law Belinda?" They all laughed. Enoch continued. "Maybe this clean country air has cleared her head, but the Belinda I know, loves being a nurse and she probably didn't take that real kindly."

"*Si*, Señor. I think Señora Coffey would not like that." They were laughing.

"My beautiful wife and I will reach a compromise I'm sure. I admit she was not immediately on board." "If you make that work, I want you to run for Congress. You will be the best negotiator ever!" Enoch was still laughing.

After all the guests left and the girls were in bed, Ben asked everybody—Grammy, Auntie, Enoch, Kirby, and Belinda—to come into the den. Belinda knew what was on his mind, but she didn't know how the rest of them were going to feel about it.

"Belinda and I are starting the process of building a house." He looked at Grammy and winked. She smiled. "So as we were talking about that and the new baby, I was thinking Grammy should move down here with us." She sat back in the chair and folded her arms.

Kirby started to protest. "Wait a minute, Sis! I got you. Auntie would stay in Hattiesville with you guys so she wouldn't be any further from her family, and you, Enoch and the boys could move into Grammy's house. That big house and all that yard would be perfect for Nick and Blake." Ben and Kirby were looking at each other. Everybody else was looking from one to the other.

"You know, bro, with all the insane ideas you've had, that one might just work," Enoch said looking at Kirby. They started talking back and forth, except Auntie and Grammy hadn't said anything. After a few minutes, Grammy spoke up.

"Benji, I am too old to move. And what am I gone do with all my stuff that's in that house? Kirby and Enoch have their own things, and what are they gone do with their house?"

"Grammy, we have to work all that out. I just wanted to mention it while we are all together. But now I may need you here before the actual move. Thelma will help us with the house and the girls, but I need you here to help us with the baby, especially if we have twins!" He looked at Belinda just in time to see her roll her eyes at him.

Auntie looked at Belinda. "Sweetie, are you expecting twins?"

"No, ma'am, not that I know of." They all talked for a while, and it was settled. They would implement Ben's plan. It was a good plan for everybody involved, and they all knew it. There just seemed to be so many adjustments. The other thing they needed to talk about was that Grammy's eightieth birthday was coming, and the twins wanted to have a party.

CHAPTER THIRTY-NINE

Katherine wanted to know what was going on with Sterling. She told Kathy about their conversation.

"He's seeing somebody else."

"What? Sterling is cutting out on you?"

"No, Ma. It's not like that." Kathy explained what happened with Sterling and was completely truthful with her parents. "But obviously, he has moved on, so he didn't really care anyway," Kathy said ending her explanation.

Lee defended Sterling, and that made Kathy angry. But she decided not to fight with him. The bottom line was she was going back to school regardless of what her dad, Sterling or anybody else thought.

Obviously, Katherine was making peace with the situation. She had a totally different approach. "Kathy, tell us your plan. You can't continue to work and be in school full time." Kathy told her about the fellowship, her budget, and even that she was considering having a roommate. They debated the situation for almost an hour. At the end of their time together, Lee and Katherine still didn't like that she was going so far away, but they agreed not to try to stop her.

Lee was not "all in," but Katherine convinced him that he was pushing his daughter away. She planned to suggest he give her an allowance too.

Jackson was back to being out on Thursday nights. He was coming in at a reasonable time. Things were back to "normal." Anderson had followed him and confirmed his suspicions. The other person in Jackson's life was a coworker of Min's, another professor at the college. Anderson had to decide how much information he was going to give Jacksa. The problem was he didn't know if he could trust her not to tell her mother. He wanted to confront Jackson. He hated to lie to Jacksa, but for now he just wouldn't say anything.

Jackson's other life was back on track. He didn't feel as guilty because JJ was home and Min didn't seem to notice he was out of the house. Jacksa was there almost every day too. Min seemed to have more energy, and she was laughing a lot. Her children brought out the best in her.

Hampton didn't have a good night's sleep for weeks after he talked to Carlos almost a month before. He held on to the information, told Carlos not to do anything further, and thought long and hard about what to do. The one person he trusted more than anybody was his daughter, but he didn't even know if April was ready to hear this story. Ben and Belinda deserved to know, but did they need to know?

Hampton was totally smitten with Belinda, and giving her this type of news and being there to support her may endear her to him. Or it could make her hate him forever. And it may ruin her marriage. Her mother was responsible for his mother's death. That had the potential to drive a permanent wedge between them.

Anderson backtracked and caught Carlos Reyes's trail. What he found out didn't make sense to him, but he figured Bishop Robinson would know. They were meeting for breakfast in the bishop's suite. That was cool with Anderson because Bishop

Robinson had a female chef that could cook better than any chef at any five-star restaurant. He hoped she made some biscuits and pear preserves. She did, and Anderson ate two before he even took out his notebook.

"Sir, I don't know if this means anything to you, but Reyes is working for some big-baller real-estate guy in Landridge, Georgia, whose name is Hampton Josephs."

"Hampton Josephs! What the hell! Why would he have a private investigator getting intel on Ben and Belinda?"

"So you know him?" Anderson asked.

"Yeah, that's the guy LCC is buying the new building from. He and his daughter are the architects too, and she is helping them look for a new house. This is crazy!" Bishop said, throwing his napkin on the table.

"What do you want me to do?" Anderson asked between bites.

"Nothing, I will deal with Hampton Josephs myself."

"You need me to ride down with you? You know, your people, my people. Your enemies, my enemies."

"I don't know. I need to decide how I want to handle this. How did you find out?"

"Long story short: I bought a lady some flowers, she accessed his bank account for me, and I put two and two together. It's confirmed, don't worry. And Josephs paid Reyes well for the information."

"I bet he did," the bishop said frowning.

"From what I gathered, Boss, this Josephs dude has plenty of paper."

"Yeah, I'm sure. But Ben and Belinda are like my children, and I don't like this one bit. Mr. Josephs doesn't know me." Anderson looked at Bishop Robinson thinking to himself, *No, he really doesn't.*

CHAPTER FORTY

Clay almost tripped over the box at the front door. Sunny sent it to Cicely. It was the second one this week. He laughed. They were sending fabric samples and pillows and flooring samples—just "stuff," like Clay called it. Cicely was in overdrive; Clay had to laugh. He knew his mom would be pleased with her choices and how she was pulling it all together. She was definitely turning the house into a home.

They decided to go to Hawaii for the wedding and honeymoon, and have a reception when they got back. The staff from Lola's was going to cater the reception under Gretchen's supervision. Most of their family was not coming to Honolulu. Sunny and Grant were going. Gretchen was going, and Cicely's brothers were going.

They had so much to do: deciding about what furniture and other "stuff" they would keep and what they were giving away. There was no hurry to move; they hadn't done anything with the house he was living in. The good thing was Cicely knew how to stretch a dollar. She was well within the budget he gave her. She was spending a reasonable amount of money. She was amazing. He loved her so much.

He had called Delia a few days after she walked out on him at lunch. She didn't answer or return his call. He called her at work because she blocked his number from her mobile phone. Clay made a couple of Jeremy's AAU games and saw her there with Javier. There was something he didn't like about that guy. *I don't think she should be with him*, Clay said to himself. *I need to tell her that.*

Clay showed up at her office one day, but the receptionist told him Delia was in a meeting. He decided to go back after work. Delia saw him before he saw her. "What the heck does he want?" she said out loud. There wasn't a way to get around him seeing her. She walked by casually, like she hadn't noticed him.

"Dee, can I talk to you a minute?"

"Clay, what are you doing here?"

"I want to tell you something."

"Again, Clay? Really!"

"Give me two minutes." She stepped to the side, and he walked over to her.

"Dee, I don't think you should marry Javier. He isn't . . ."

"Clay Sturdivant, you don't have the right to tell me anything. I wasn't the one for you, so don't concern yourself with who I marry. Clay, this is the last time I'm going to tell you to leave me alone." She walked away.

Clay was home when Cicely came in. He came straight there after trying to talk to Delia. Her smile melted his heart. He really did love her, and he knew she loved him. This whole thing with Delia was crazy. He didn't want Delia. He just didn't want Javier to have her.

"Hey, you!" he greeted her with a hug.

"Hey, yourself," she said. "I didn't expect you to be here."

"Got off a little early. What's all this?" He took a stack of mail and her bag out of her hands. He put the bag down and started to flip through the mail. There was a letter from the management company of her apartment complex and a big packet from the travel agent. He had a huge grin on his face. "You can send this back unsigned. Tell them you have a new home with your new husband!" He took her by the hands and spun her around. They danced around for a minute.

"I've already informed them I am not renewing my lease!" she said placing a light kiss on his lips. "I haven't been through the packet yet. I wanted to wait until we were together." They sat and went through the information. Clay told her that he was taking her downtown to the courthouse to get married, and their honeymoon was going to be at Myrtle Beach.

"Girl, you costing me too much money. I gave you a ring, gave you a house, you fixin' it up, now you want me to take you to Hawaii. When does it stop?" She had her hands on her hips, as she stood there watching him pretend to be serious.

"It's not going to ever end. Because there will be baby furniture and ballet lessons and sports equipment and . . ."

"Okay, that's enough. I can't take it." He was laughing. She tried not to laugh, but she couldn't help it.

As was his way, Clay looked at the numbers. Money wasn't a big issue for him, and he had pretty much given Cicely a blank check on the house and the wedding plans. He wasn't concerned about it, she was very practical. Gretchen was handling the wedding plans and reception, and she was pretty practical too. At the moment, they were both still in his good graces. He offered to fly both of Cicely's brothers to Honolulu, but only one accepted—the younger one who was still in college. The other one said he could handle his ticket. Clay was paying for all the hotel rooms.

"Are you okay with the cost?" Cicely asked Clay.

"Yep, this looks good. All I care about anyway is the bed. You have made me wait so long; we may not get out of bed all week!" Cicely was blushing. He slapped her on the bottom as she walked by.

Clay called Grant to see if they received their info from the travel agent. "Yeah, man. It looks good. Sunny showed it to me earlier. But let me tell you this while she's not in here: I am thinking we should go ahead and have a double wedding."

Clay laughed. "For real man? You there?"

"Yep, I'm there." Grant answered. "But I haven't given her a ring yet. She may want her own wedding."

"Well, dude, why don't you ask her and see what she says. Have you bought a ring?"

"Yeah, had it a few weeks."

Clay was frowning. "A few weeks. Are you having second thoughts or got cold feet? Realize you haven't known her long enough?" Clay was serious.

"None of the above," Grant answered. "I just had a bit of reflection about Leah—proposing to her, planning the wedding, her getting sick, and well . . . the way it ended." Grant was serious. His voice cracked.

"Are you still in love with Leah?"

"I will probably always love Leah, but I put those feelings in perspective."

"Have you talked to Sunny about this?"

"Yep, she brought it up first."

"But I mean, since you got serious, have you discussed it?"

"When we first started talking about getting married, she brought it up. She helped me work though it for the army, so she knows the whole story. She was the one who sent me to counseling. We don't have any secrets. She knows I gave Jill's foundation the money from Leah's ring."

"So what's up then?" Clay asked.

"I just can't imagine going through that again. Man, sometimes when I can't get a hold of Sunny, I panic, scared she's not coming back," Grant said.

"Do you need to go back to counseling?"

"I still go periodically at her insistence."

"G, all I can say is, be sure. You can't take Leah into this marriage. Three's a crowd."

"I get it," Grant said.

They talked awhile longer, but Clay decided he needed to talk to Sunny. He would talk it over with Cicely first. He also needed to tell her the proposal of a double wedding may be coming. He wasn't sure how she would feel about that.

CHAPTER FORTY-ONE

Ben and Belinda had the plan in place to tell the twins about the baby. They had T-shirts made that said "I'm the big sister" and a letter to them from the baby. Ben was the grill master for the evening, and he prepared their favorites: grilled barbeque chicken with pineapple slices and grilled corn on the cob. The girls made the salad, and when Belinda came in from work, everything was ready.

They ate and talked about their plans for the rest of the summer. They voted on their family vacation destination. Brianna said she had Grammy's proxy, so the girls won. Vacation would be in the Bahamas at Atlantis so they could be at the beach and have an adventure with the dolphins. Ben and Belinda wanted to do something they hadn't done before and stay closer to home. "We'll go with that for now." Belinda said looking at Ben with a "let it go" look. Ben was excited, and when they finished eating he promised they would go to get ice cream sundaes.

"We have something for you before we go get the ice cream." He handed each of them an envelope.

They looked a little uneasy but took the envelopes and opened them slowly. Brittani was reading faster than Brianna and started jumping up and down. "Grammy was right! We are having a baby!"

The celebration went on with hugs and kisses for a few minutes. Finally, they settled down, and their mom gave them the T-shirts. They started firing questions. The baby would be here in November, they didn't know if it would be a boy or girl. The girls agreed they would like a brother but another sister would be okay.

"Oh, so that's why you don't want to go to Atlantis!" Brianna was talking to her mom. "You don't feel like going that far."

"That's partly true, plus we need to get ready to move into the new house," Belinda responded to her. "Bree, let's do something else," Brittani said to her sister.

"Sure, Britt. No problem." Brianna was on the phone. "Gram, you were right! We are having a baby!" Ben and Belinda just sat and watched what was going on around them. They all talked with Grammy and Auntie, and when the girls were satisfied that they had all the information available to them, they told their dad that they were ready for their sundaes.

Delia was furious with Clay. "How dare he tell me I shouldn't marry Javier," she said out loud when she was in her car. Delia hadn't told Javier about the phone calls or having lunch with Clay, but this was the last straw. She would tell him everything when she got home.

Clay couldn't believe Delia walked away from him. He was telling her for her own good. She simply did not need to marry Javier. The truth was Clay didn't know the guy and had no real reason to tell Delia not to marry him. After all these years, why did he care what she did?

Delia told Javier she needed to talk to him away from the kids, so after dinner they went for a walk. She told him the whole story. "Sorry, I didn't tell you when he first called." Javier looked at her.

"It's okay, Delia, really. I just wonder what he's up to and why now. Do you want me to say something to him?"

"I'm not sure if we should draw any attention to it," Delia said.

"Well, it's up to you. I'll handle it if you want me to," Javier said with a serious look on his face.

"Let's hope my telling him to get lost today will do it. If not, then yeah, I do want you to say something to him." Javier nodded, not saying anything. But as they walked in silence for a few minutes he was thinking he would beat the hell out of Clay if he didn't back up.

On Sunday, when Kirby dropped the boys off at children's church, Natalia was the one who greeted them. She immediately recognized them, and she knew which one was Nicholas. Throughout the morning, she watched them interact with each other, the other children, and the teachers. They were really active, not bad, but very curious and very mischievous. Natalia paid special attention to Nicholas.

When Kirby came back to get them, Natalia wrote her cell phone number on the back of her business card from the Matthews Law Firm. She gave it to Kirby. "Mrs. Casebier, if you ever need a sitter I would be glad to keep your sons. I know CPR and I have good references!" Kirby smiled at Natalia. "You have a good job at the law firm. Why are you sitting with children?"

"I am saving to buy a car and pay the insurance, so I need to make as much money as I can!" They both laughed.

"I will hold on to your number, Natalia. Thank you." Natalia hugged Kirby and handed her the boys backpacks and gave them a hug. She did need the money, but she wanted to get to know Nicholas and Blake better. If she could earn their parents' confidence, then maybe she could make a way to let Chloe spend some time with Nicholas.

CHAPTER FORTY-TWO

Mrs. Rajagopal called the concierge and asked him to get them a car to go to Raja and Jill's house. She didn't want to call first because she didn't want Tara to know they were going. She decided that after a good night's sleep, Raja would be more reasonable.

Jill saw the black town car first and was not surprised to see her in-laws get out. She had regrouped from the night before, and she was ready for them. Raja and Tara went to play tennis, but she was expecting them at any moment. She opened the door before they rang the bell.

"Yes, may I help you?"

"We would like to see Manavendra," Mrs. Rajagopal was speaking.

"He's not here. May I give him a message?" Jill asked very politely.

"I will come in and wait," Mrs. Rajagopal replied.

Jill's first thought was to tell her she wasn't welcome. But she thought better of it and invited them in.

"Please have a seat." Jill waved her hand toward the sofa. They sat, but nobody said anything. The silence was huge.

"You have a lovely home, Jillian," Mr. Rajagopal said.

"Thank you, sir. May I offer you some tea?" Jill replied, looking at her father-in-law. Her back was turned to Mrs. Rajagopal.

"No, thank you," he said. "I would like to see my granddaughter if I may."

"She should be up from her nap shortly," Jill responded.

At that moment, Jill decided that was enough small talk. She walked over to the chair directly in front of Mrs. Rajagopal and sat down.

"Mrs. Rajagopal, why are you here? Why have you come to my home uninvited? I made it—Raja and I made it very clear to you last night that we are not amenable to your idea, your plan to take LaLa back to London with you! You have treated me like dirt since I met you, and you think you can just show up and make a decision for my family."

"Jillian, in your culture, things are done differently . . .," Mrs. Rajagopal said before Jill interrupted her.

"Don't talk to me about the differences in our culture. My husband, your son, has the right to love who he wants to love, and he loves me. He tried to stay in touch with you, but you forced his hand. Now three years later, you show up to take my daughter . . ."

Before she could finish her sentence, the door opened. Tara and Raja walked in.

"What the hell?" Tara asked, looking around the room.

"Father, Mother," Raja said as he walked in, "what are you doing here?"

"Nothing good," Tara said.

"Being disrespected by your wife mostly" was Mrs. Rajagopal's answer.

"Disrespected by me?" Jill looked directly at her mother-in-law. "You come here to kidnap my daughter and you call me disrespectful!" Jill was screaming.

Raja put his arm around Jill, but before he could address his mother's comments, Tara was literally in her face.

"My dear aunt, your scheme didn't work. You need to pack your things and get out of town, as a matter of fact, out of the country. I am checking you out of the hotel tomorrow morning. Go back to London, mind your own business, and leave Raja, Jill, and LaLa alone. And if you don't, I will deal with you myself."

Mrs. Rajagopal was looking at Tara with real fear in her eyes, but Mr. Rajagopal spoke up. "Tara, you have no right to speak to an elder like that. Who do you think you are?"

She spun around on one heel and faced her uncle. "The better question, Uncle, is who do you think you are, marching in here behind your wife and her foolishness? As I said, check out of the hotel first thing in the morning and go home. I am not kidding. Leave now." Tara pointed to the door. Mr. Rajagopal stood and looked at Raja.

Raja lifted his hand, indicating to his father not to say anything. He took Tara by the hand and nodded to Jill for the two of them to leave the room. "Father, Mother, this situation is completely out of hand. I absolutely do not appreciate any of this. You say my wife and my cousin disrespected you. You disrespected all of us first. My daughter is not going to London with you, now or ever. And you have ruined any opportunity you may have had to spend any time with your only granddaughter. Jill will never allow it now."

Before Raja could continue, his mother interrupted him. "You are her husband. She must do what you say."

Raja laughed. "Mother, I will not fight her on this. Now I agree with Tara. You two should leave now and make arrangements to check out of the hotel in the morning."

"May we see Leah before we go?" Mr. Rajagopal was asking. Raja went into the other room, and brought the baby back with him. Her grandfather reached for her, but she clung to her dad. When her grandmother reached for her, she buried her face in her dad's chest.

The Rajagopals checked out of the hotel the next morning and checked into the one across the street.

CHAPTER FORTY-THREE

Janis was a little nervous, but she had planned her trip well. She found a hotel room close to the hospital, and she made arrangements for a rental car. She had her story straight in her head. Ms. Sunny needed to know there was no chance for her with Grant. And Grant needed to know she would do what she had to do to be with him. Carmen was settled for the weekend, so she could go to the airport early. In the midst of her nervousness, she was excited. She could hardly wait to see Grant.

The flight seemed to be over quickly. Before she knew it, Janis was getting her rental car. She engaged the GPS and drove to the hospital and from there to the hotel. Now that she had her bearings, she would check into her room and put her plan in motion.

She showered and changed into an outfit she knew Grant would like. She applied his favorite perfume and made sure her hair was beautiful. Grant always told her how beautiful she was. He liked to play with her hair. She never cut it because he liked it long.

Janis arrived at the hospital just before lunch. She went to the second floor of the administration building, where the Human Resources Department was located. She told the receptionist she was there to see Sunny. "I don't see an appointment for you, Ms. Mitchell." Janis was prepared for her to say that.

"Oh no! Grant must have forgotten to tell her I would be here today."

"Grant?" The receptionist questioned Janis, looking at her sideways.

"Yes, Grant Sturdivant referred me to Sunny."

"Yes, apparently, he did," the receptionist replied. "What is this in reference to?" Janis smiled before she answered. She was expecting that question too.

"I am relocating to the area in preparation of us getting married, and he said Sunny would help me get settled." The receptionist looked amused.

"Please have a seat, Ms. Mitchell." She left her desk and went through a door behind her. She walked down the hall to Sunny's office. She sat in a chair in front of Sunny's desk and burst into a hysterical laughter.

"What is your problem?" Sunny asked laughing too, but not knowing why she was laughing. The receptionist told Sunny about Janis being in the lobby and what she said. Sunny could not believe her ears.

"You cannot be telling the truth! You cannot be! There is no way that crazy girl is here asking for me!" Sunny said.

"What do you want me to do?" Sunny's coworker asked still laughing.

"Tell her I will see her in ten minutes."

Sunny sat at her desk for a minute, totally flabbergasted. She had to make Janis understand once and for all she was not going to play with her. She picked up the phone and called Grant's office. No answer. She looked at the clock. He had probably already left for lunch. She called his cell hoping he wasn't too far away. He answered. "Hi, Grant. Are you alone?"

"Don't try to seduce me over the phone, woman."

Sunny laughed. "No, not this time. There is a situation over here I need you to help me handle."

"Are you okay, Sunny? Is it my dad?"

"No, no, nothing like that. Just come over here, but don't come through the main lobby, come through the employee's entrance."

"Sunny, what is going on?" Grant sounded annoyed.

"Please Grant, just come."

"Okay, I'll be there in a few."

She didn't tell him because she didn't want him to be prepared. She wanted and needed to see their natural reaction toward each other. Sunny touched up her make-up, put some perfumed lotion on her hands, called the receptionist, and asked her to show Janis to her office.

"Ms. Mitchell, I'm Sunny Dorsette, please have a seat. How may I help you?"

Janis was a little taken aback. The picture she had of Sunny in her mind was totally different from the woman in front of her. She pictured someone more like Leah. Sunny couldn't be more different. On the credenza behind her desk were two pictures: one of Grant and one of them together. Janis moved her eyes away from the pictures.

"Sunny, we can cut the formalities and get to the point of my visit."

"Yes, Janis, I agree. Why are you here?"

Before she could answer, the office door opened. Grant walked in.

"Janis! What the hell are you doing here?"

CHAPTER FORTY-FOUR

Anderson decided it was time for him to talk to Jackson. He didn't tell Jacksa what he was going to do. As a matter of fact, he hadn't told her anything. All Anderson intended to tell Jackson was that he knew and that Jacksa knew. He couldn't make him do anything different. He hadn't broken any laws. Whatever decision Jackson made was on him.

When Anderson walked into the barbershop, Jackson was in the chair. "What's up, Detective?" One of the other patrons was speaking to Anderson. Jackson looked up.

"You on official business?" Jackson's barber asked.

"Naw, trying to catch up with my future father-in-law!"

Jackson frowned. "If that's what you want to talk to me about, the answer is no." A few of the guys laughed, but Jackson nor Anderson laughed.

"Jack, man, AT is good people," the barber said.

"I can't keep my daughter from marrying him, but a man who carries a gun for a living is not who I want for her."

"Good. You know, it's her decision," Anderson said looking at Jackson seriously.

They were off to a tense start, so Anderson knew the rest of their time together was going to be even worse. Somebody commented on what the sportscaster was saying on Sports Center and the conversation shifted. When Jackson was done, Anderson was on the phone, but he motioned for Jackson to give him a minute. What he noticed too was the barber wasn't preparing to leave. Jackson's consistent story was he and his barber have a drink on Thursday after his haircut. Anderson knew he couldn't hold him to that, he just hated a liar. And he hated a man who would have an affair, especially with a wife who had no control over her situation.

Anderson walked outside behind Jackson and finished his call. "Mr. Baye, let me buy you a drink."

Jackson looked at his watch. "What's on your mind, Anderson?"

"Sir, I need to have a private talk with you." The tone of Anderson's voice was firm. He was a little surprised at how Jackson was responding to him. It was almost like he knew he was busted.

They went to a sports bar about half a mile away. Anderson ordered a burger and an iced tea. Jackson ordered a beer. "I thought you said 'a drink,'" Jackson said to Anderson as they took a seat in a booth.

"I'm actually on duty."

"What's up, Detective Thorn? You really want to talk to me about my daughter?"

"Yep, but not for the reason you think. We'll have that conversation another day," Anderson chuckled.

"Jacksa asked me to investigate where you really spend your Thursday nights. She knows the story about you having a drink with the barber is not 100 percent true. I told her no, that I wouldn't do it, but I did. I know where you go and who you're spending your time with." Jackson started to interrupt, but Anderson continued. "Jacksa knows because her mom told her."

Jackson took a long swallow of his beer. He really didn't know what to say.

"How do you know what you think you know?" Jackson asked Anderson.

"Mr. Baye, I'm a detective. I investigate people for a living. It wasn't hard."

"So what do you intend to do with what you think you know?"

"I don't intend to do anything. Not now. But one thing's for sure, I won't keep lying to Jacksa and putting her off, trying to talk her out of what she asked me to do. What do you intend to do?" Anderson leaned over his plate and took a big bite of his burger.

"Anderson, I do appreciate you coming to me privately with this, and I appreciate you protecting my daughter. I don't know if I can give you the answer you want, and I don't know that I can make you understand."

"Start by telling me why you havin' an affair with your wife's coworker, who's supposed to be her friend?"

Jackson proceeded to try and explain the situation to Anderson. He told him how discreet he tried to be, how he took great care to make sure his outside life didn't enter his home. Jackson got personal and told Anderson how he and Min hadn't had a physical relationship in years.

"I love my wife. She's my world. But I am a man with a wife who has a debilitating illness and cannot make love to me. This other situation is purely physical."

Jackson couldn't believe he was having this conversation with somebody he didn't know any better than he knew Anderson Thorn. And if he really was working to establish a permanent relationship with Jacksa, how would this play out? How would Anderson respect him?

"But your wife's friend? Come on, man! You know that ain't right!"

Jackson ordered another beer; the waitress refilled Anderson's tea. Nobody said anything for a minute. They both knew Anderson had the upper hand. Not that he was trying to use it. Jackson didn't really know what Anderson wanted.

"Anderson, what do you want"?

"I don't want anything. Well, maybe I do but not for me. I happen to think your daughter is the most incredible woman I've ever met, so I want her happy, and that means not stressed out about how her mother is being treated by her father. And I also think Mrs. Baye is an amazing woman and deserves better than what you doin'. So I guess I want you to correct some stuff . . . whatever that means."

"I'm not sure what that means. I've tried to end it. I've tried to get out. I have gone weeks at the time, but I always—for whatever reason—go back."

"Yeah, when I was in college, we had a name for that!" They both laughed.

"I hate that you got dragged into the middle of this . . ."

"Don't be. Better we deal with it than you have to go around with Jacksa."

"You're probably right," Jackson replied. "But back up. You said Min told Jacksa."

"She told Jacksa. She knows you are having an affair. I don't think she knows who it is."

Anderson's comment was interrupted by Jackson's phone ringing. He looked at it and sighed. Anderson shrugged.

"Hello. How are you?" He was silent for a few seconds and then looked at his watch. "I don't see that I'm going to make it, but I will call you back." He hung up.

"Maybe you need to go and deal with that now."

"Naw, I need time to think."

That ticked Anderson off. "Think about it! What the freak?" Jackson started to respond but Anderson cut him off. "Tell you what Mr. Baye, you handle your business the way you do, but know that I am on Jacksa's side."

CHAPTER FORTY-FIVE

Campbell finally had an opportunity to have a heart-to-heart talk with Chloe. He was very honest with her. He told her he does love her, he does want to marry her, but his proposal was out of emotion. She agreed that neither of them are ready, but she told Campbell she didn't appreciate his patronizing her, especially not about something so serious. He apologized. They kissed and made up, and he told her the next time he proposes to her, things would be in order, and they would be headed down the aisle.

Chloe was fine after her conversation with Campbell. What she didn't tell him was she intended for Nicholas to be with them when they got married. She did some research and hoped she found a way to file for custody of Nicholas. She knew it was a long shot; but as far as she was concerned, having her son with her was worth it. She knew that if she did the preliminary work, her parents would help her, and Campbell would too.

She pulled into the parking lot next door to the school. She was spending many lunch hours there, watching the kids on the playground. Most days she would see Nicholas. But even when she didn't, she would sit and watch the children play.

Today there were only five or six children on the playground, on the opposite end from where Nicholas's class usually played. That was strange. She sat for a few minutes, ate her sandwich, and read an article in a magazine. No sign of the children. She decided to leave. As she was leaving the church parking lot, she saw a small bus pull into the school lot. She backed up so she could see the children get off the bus. Three cars pulled in behind the bus. As Chloe watched, children and parents slowly got off the bus. She saw Blake first, then a little girl, and then Enoch. Several other children got off before she spotted Nicholas. Mrs. Avis Johnson was with him. Chloe recognized her from church. She knew Mrs. Johnson was part of their extended family. Just then, she saw Kirby get out of one of the cars. Chloe's heart sank. A family outing, obviously a field trip. That should have been her and Campbell and their son.

Cicely was working her twelve-hour shift and left Clay a list of things to do. He needed to move some things she packed from her apartment to his house and some to the new house. The plan: she was moving into his house, and he was supposed to move into the new house. As far as he was concerned, that was a formality. He just didn't see the point when they were going to be married in about six weeks. But he was letting her call the shots. If Cicely was happy, Clay was happy. It wasn't rocket science.

Clay laughed when he got to the apartment. Cicely left the same list there. "She acts like I might forget something!" he said out loud. He moved some boxes to the front door and then started to take stuff to the truck.

As he walked down the stairs, he saw some ladies standing on the sidewalk. He thought he recognized one of them. When he got to the truck he realized who she was. It was Delia's sister-in-law. He met her only once, but he was sure that was her. As he turned to go back upstairs, he looked again, and there was Delia. She saw him at the same time. He walked over to where they were standing.

"Good evening, ladies," Clay said with a smile. They all spoke.

"Hi, Clay," Delia said last. He turned his attention to her sister-in-law.

"Good to see you again."

"Thanks, nice to see you too. Clay, right?"

"Yep. What are you ladies up to?"

"It's my cousin's birthday, so we're headed to dinner."

"Happy Birthday!" he said with a wink. He didn't know for sure, but he guessed it was the one smiling. He was right. "Thank you," she said blushing.

"How are Jeremy and Crystal?" Clay asked Delia.

"Fine," she laughed. "Crystal is planning to try out for the track team, so she has been working out." The sister-in-law chimed in. "Can you believe that? As prissy as she is, I am surprised she wants to break a sweat!"

"That's my girl!" Clay said.

Delia rolled her eyes. They talked as a group for a minute, and then one of the other ladies said something that moved the rest of them away from Clay and Delia. She was talking about Jeremy.

"When are you all getting back from dinner?" he asked her.

"Why, Clay?" Delia asked with a smirk on her face.

"I thought maybe you could meet me back here, and we can talk."

"No, Clay. Absolutely not," she was adamant.

"I'm not driving anyway," she said a little softer. "What are you doing over here anyway?" Delia was asking.

"Helping a friend move."

"Oh, I see," she said.

The conversation didn't last long after that.

"Since you walked out on me at lunch, you need to reschedule with me."

"Clay, take care. I'll tell Jeremy I saw you." That's what Delia said out loud, but she thought to herself she was going to tell Javier too.

He went back upstairs, brought down the rest of Cicely's boxes, and put them in the back of the truck. He decided he would stay awhile. He lay on the sofa and turned on the television. *I guess I should disconnect this TV*, he thought. As he dozed off his thought was where they were going to put the sofa. *Man cave in the new house*, he thought.

He was awakened by the doorbell. It was Delia. "What's up, Dee?" Clay stretched. "Glad you came back."

"Clay, I came back to set the record straight."

"Come in." She stepped right inside the door.

"Have a seat," he said motioning toward the sofa.

"No, thank you," Delia said. "I just want to clear the air. Clay, I am in love with and going to marry Javier. You are planning to marry Cicely, and I guess you're in love with her."

"I am," he interjected.

"There is absolutely nothing between us anymore. Please stop calling me, asking me to meet you . . ."

Before she could finish what she was saying, Clay pulled her into his arms and kissed her. She didn't stop him.

CHAPTER FORTY-SIX

Hampton Josephs had Lee Robinson's cell phone number, but he hadn't ever used it. He didn't need to. Their conversations were strictly business-related, and Ben Coffey was involved. But this time, Hampton and Lee needed to talk privately. Hampton just hoped Lee would be his ally, not his adversary. Hampton wanted to call from home. He couldn't take a chance on being overheard or interrupted in the office. It was nine o'clock on Monday morning. He hoped Lee would be at home too.

Lee looked at his phone and saw Hampton Josephs's name on the screen. He sat down at the kitchen table and wondered what the call could be about. Hampton quickly put Lee's mind at ease about the Landridge project. "Things are going really well on the job site. I'm calling about something personal, very personal. Can we talk privately?"

Lee was thinking how strategic it was that Hampton called that morning. He was at home alone and he agreed they needed to talk. He moved from the table to a more comfortable chair in the family room. Hampton took a deep breath. "Lee, I need to give you some news that will probably astound you, but I need your advice on how to handle this." Lee was listening, but at the same time trying to decide if he should interrupt Hampton to ask if what he is talking about has to do with why he was having Belinda followed by a private investigator. He decided to wait, to hear Hampton out.

"When I met Ben and Belinda Coffey, I was immediately attracted to Belinda. I couldn't take my eyes off her and I couldn't get her off my mind," Lee shifted in the chair. He didn't think he liked where this was going. Hampton continued. "There was something familiar about her to me. It was like I had met her before. I thought about her day and night, to the point that I had to know more about her, so I hired a private investigator."

Now we're getting somewhere, Lee thought to himself.

"What I found out blew my mind," Hampton proceeded to tell Lee what Carlos found. He told him about Belinda's birth certificate, and Shona Craig and Andrea Coffey's death certificates and the circumstances surrounding their deaths.

"Lord, have mercy! Are you saying the woman who caused the accident that killed Andrea Coffey, Ben's mother, was—" Lee said.

"Shona Craig, Belinda's mother," they said it at the same time.

"Jesus, Jesus, Jesus." Lee said.

They were both quiet for a minute. Hampton broke the silence. "There's another caveat here, Lee."

"It can't be worse than what you just told me."

"For me it is," Hampton said. "Belinda is probably my daughter."

"Hampton, are you serious?"

"Yep, I'm afraid I am."

Lee sat back in his chair, closed his eyes, put his hand on his forehead and exhaled.

Once again, Chloe got what she wanted—a new car. The only thing she didn't plan on was that she had to buy it herself. She couldn't believe her dad didn't give in. But her mom explained that he wanted to help Natalia with her tuition, and they decided that that was more important than Chloe having a new car. She agreed and moved on to Plan B.

When it was all said and done, Chloe sold her four-year-old car to Campbell, and he gave his twelve-year old car to Natalia. Natalia planned to drive that car until she could save more money, and she was ecstatic to have a car of her own. She washed and waxed it and parked it away from other cars in parking lots. But what she really couldn't believe was that Campbell gave it to her. She knew Chloe worked it out. They were so good to her. They were her family, and she loved them so much. When she came to America for five days to visit colleges, she never imagined how much her life was going to change. And when she had no home in Haiti to go back to, she never imagined she would be this happy. Now if she could get accepted into college, all would be well. But first she was going to do something special for Campbell and Chloe.

CHAPTER FORTY-SEVEN

Belinda knew she was quickly gaining weight, but her scrubs made her really look pregnant. She was feeling better—her energy was back, and her appetite was better. She was still dealing with some morning sickness, but a few saltine crackers and peppermint tea as soon as she got up was keeping the sickness to a minimum. The trouble with all this was it was familiar, too familiar. The last time she was pregnant was over ten years ago; she was in nursing school and gaining weight fast. She had to face the music. This baby may be babies. She wouldn't make an appointment for the ultrasound because Ben would want to go. She needed to find out first, and if there was only one baby, she wouldn't even mention it. If it were twins, she would need to get used to the idea before she told him, and they would both have to get used to it before they told the girls, Grammy, and Auntie.

Belinda called a friend on the ob-gyn floor and asked if she would do an unofficial ultrasound. Her friend happily agreed. At the end of her shift, Belinda went to have the ultrasound. As she walked out of the elevator, she made up her mind to be okay with the results. Her wonderful husband was going to be ecstatic no matter what. Her wonderful daughters were in overdrive planning to be big sisters. And as much as Grammy loved Brittani and Brianna, Belinda knew she wanted Ben to have a child of his own, and twins would be icing on the cake.

As Belinda walked down the back hall, she got really nervous. She decided to call Kirby. "I'll stay on the phone with you if you want me to," Kirby told her sister.

"Yeah, I want you to."

"Belinda, don't be nervous, it will be fine either way."

"Yeah, you just want me to go through what you're going through!" They both laughed.

"K, do you remember how you reacted when I told you I was having twins before?"

"Yeah, it freaked me out!"

"Okay, here goes," Belinda told Kirby.

The ultrasound technician ran a probe across Belinda's baby bump. It looked pretty small with her lying down. The tech slowed and detected two heart beats. "Look right there Belinda, one heartbeat, second heartbeat," the tech said.

"Two heartbeats, Kirby."

"I'm excited!" Kirby replied. She was determined to be upbeat. She wasn't sure how Belinda was really feeling. "Can you tell anything else?" Kirby asked. The technician was showing Belinda both babies were in one sack, which meant they were identical twins."

"We can see they are identical, but not if they are boys or girls."

"Aw, man!" Kirby said. The sisters laughed.

"Let me get cleaned up, K. I'll call you back."

"Ok, and Belinda, and I'm not freaked out!"

Belinda didn't change out of her scrubs. She went home, intending to cook for her family, spend some time with her girls, and have some quiet time with her husband. She was in a daze. She was grateful for her life, for her loving husband, and the church family who showered them with love. She and Ben often remarked that they not only loved their church family, they liked them too. Belinda did everything Ben asked her to do, and she loved her responsibilities in the ministry. But she also loved her job, and she knew this second baby would give Ben more ammunition to ask her to stop working. *Maybe this is God's way of saying I need to go home and care for my family.* Belinda said to herself with a sigh. She wanted to be happy about all of this, but at the moment, she wasn't. Then to top it all off, she had a message from April Josephs.

"Hello, April. This is Belinda Coffey returning your call."

"Hi, Mrs. Coffey. How are you? Thank you for calling me back! I want to schedule an appointment for us to meet and go over the plans for your new home."

"Yes, I guess we need to get started," Belinda said without much enthusiasm.

"You tell me what day and time are good for you, and I'll adjust my schedule. We need about ninety minutes."

"April, who's meeting with us? Do I need to check Ben's schedule?" What Belinda really wanted to know was if Hampton would be there.

"No, I think for this session the two of us can handle it."

"Great!" She hoped she didn't sound too excited. "Do you mind coming to my house? I'll fix us breakfast. I have one day off this week, and I need to multi-task," Belinda said.

"That's fine with me. What time?" They worked out the details. Belinda was relieved she wouldn't have to see Hampton.

Hampton started to tell Lee the story he hadn't told anybody. "Shona Craig was my high school girlfriend. When we started seeing each other, I was a senior and she was a junior. I left to go to college, left her in Augusta. She got pregnant while I was home for spring break the next year. Shortly before the baby was born, Shona told me the baby wasn't mine. I was pissed off, but I was more hurt. I never saw her again, and I never saw the baby," Hampton's voice cracked. He cleared his throat and continued. "When my mom let me know she had been killed in the accident, I was stunned. I went home for the funeral. While I was there, I talked to her cousin who told me the baby was put up for adoption at birth and that she believed the baby was mine, in spite of what Shona told me."

"What did you do to follow up?" Lee asked.

Hampton sighed. "I talked to a couple of people, but nothing really. My folks didn't have money and the coach told me to come back to school, get my education, play ball, and not concern myself with all that. They convinced me that even if the baby was mine, I couldn't do anything about it because my name wasn't on the birth certificate. So I went back to my life, and here I am thirty years later."

"I'm still puzzled about what drew you to the conclusion that baby was Belinda—well before you got a hold of the birth certificate which, as you said, doesn't list your name?" Lee asked. He was sitting up in his chair. His emotions were up and down. He would absolutely protect Belinda, but he had to think how this news would affect both Belinda and Ben. And he had some compassion for Hampton too.

"Belinda looks exactly like Shona—same height, same coloring, same size. Her mannerisms are exactly like Shona. They are both left handed, and both have a mole on their ear. And if you do the math, Belinda was born nine months after that spring break in Augusta, Georgia. All that cannot be a coincidence," Hampton said with a sigh.

"No, Hamp. I don't believe so."

"Lee, I need your help. I just don't know what to do next."

"Can I ask you to do nothing for a few days? Give me a chance to process all this?"

"Yep, no problem and thanks for listening," Hampton said seriously.

"I'm glad you trust me with something so sensitive," Lee was serious also.

"You are the only person I could trust."

CHAPTER FORTY-EIGHT

Janis was totally shocked when she saw Grant standing there. She planned to deal with Sunny; she never considered Sunny would call him. She decided she better play offense.

"Grant! Hi!" She stood and tried to hug him. He pushed her away.

"Answer me! What the hell are you doing here?" Grant was yelling.

Janis smiled. "Grant, it's okay. Just tell Sunny the truth. I wanted to tell her so she wouldn't be embarrassed in front of you, but since you're here, you go ahead and tell her we're back together."

Grant was astounded. He couldn't believe he was living the Janis nightmare again. A full minute passed, and he hadn't said anything. Janis spoke up.

"Sunny, I am in DC looking for a job so I can be here with Grant."

"You crazy . . ." Grant said before Sunny interrupted him.

"I got this," Sunny said. She walked around her desk, stood directly in front of Janis, and got right in her face. "Janis, hear me and hear me clearly. You can play the nut role if you want to. You can make up all the stories and live in all the fantasies you want to. But today ain't the day, and I ain't the one! I know you, and I know your kind. You have one chance to save yoself 'cause you don't want none-a-me."

Sunny's accent had kicked in. Grant was standing there in awe. Sunny had turned into somebody he hadn't ever seen before. By now, she had a finger in Janis's face.

"That is *my* man!" She pointed to Grant. "He is going to be *my* husband *for-ev-er*! Cross me and you will be sorry! Yo best bet is to take your ass back to Hattiesville and get on with yo life!" She took her index finger and pushed Janis's forehead.

Janis stood there and did not say one word while Sunny was talking. She was out of her element. Not in her wildest dreams did she expect Sunny to come for her like that. She was a worthy opponent. Janis turned her attention to Grant. Trying to recoup from what Sunny had just said and done to her.

"You ordered it, Janis. You eat it," was all Grant said.

"I told you—one chance to save yoself. I suggest you leave my office, leave this campus . . ."

Janis interrupted Sunny, "Ms. Dorsette, this is not over. I will have Grant . . ."

Grant knew he heard Janis talking, but all of a sudden, he heard a loud noise and saw Janis's head move from side to side. Sunny slapped Janis.

CHAPTER FORTY-NINE

Mr. and Mrs. Rajagopal rented a car. They were determined to see LaLa, even if they pretended to apologize to Jill and Raja. Tara went back home, and Mrs. Rajagopal was glad. She threw a kink in the plan.

"We have to try to see them today. We can't stay here much longer. We have spent more money than we planned," Mr. Rajagopal was saying to his wife.

"I know, and I'm sorry," she replied. "This just didn't go according to plan. Manavendra has just become so much like the people here. It's hard for me to accept."

"I know, dear. You're right, but I can understand them not wanting the baby to be so far away. Maybe if we lived here in the States, they would be more amenable," Mr. Rajagopal said.

"Then we shall tell them we are moving to North Carolina! That's it! Then we can take the baby and tell them she will come back with us."

"Dear, they are not going to go along with that. This is pointless. We should just try to visit one last time and then go back to London."

Mrs. Rajagopal knew her husband was right, but she couldn't stand the thought of Jill's mother having so much time with LaLa and so much influence on her.

The Rajagopals stopped at a toy store and bought a teddy with a red bow around its neck. They brought two sterling silver bangles from London and almost forgot about them in the midst of everything that happened. When they arrived at Raja and Jill's home, there wasn't a close parking space. Mr. Rajagopal let his wife out in front of the condo, and she stood there several minutes. When they finally rang the bell, a young man answered the door with LaLa in his arms. He knew who they were, but they didn't know he was Jill's brother, Trey.

"Raja, you might want to come in here," Trey yelled over his shoulder. LaLa was holding on to Trey. He kissed her cheek, and she giggled. Trey invited them into the foyer but no further. The Rajagopals knew they came at a bad time. Jill's parents, her brother, and some other people were there. Raja walked into the foyer. Trey took LaLa and walked away.

"Father, Mother, I thought you had returned to London."

"We are leaving tomorrow for New York City and then on to London the next day," his father responded.

His mother spoke up. "We have some gifts for Leah. May we see her please?"

Before Raja could answer, Jill came around the corner, drying her hands on a dish towel. She did not smile when she saw her in-laws standing there.

"My parents have a gift for the baby," Raja was talking to Jill.

She didn't say anything. Raja backed away from them, not taking his eyes off his parents. He said something they couldn't hear and then walked back to where Jill was standing. In a few seconds, Trey appeared again with LaLa. Raja took her into his arms. Her grandfather reached into the bag and gave her the bear. It was almost as big as she was. She took it but was focused on her uncle who was still standing behind her.

"Manavendra, your father and I—Manavendra and Jillian, your father and I have decided to move to North Carolina. We want to be close to you and be able to help you with Leah."

Jill folded her arms. Trey put his hand on her shoulder.

"You and Father need to make the decision that works for you, but don't make it based on me or my family." Raja was very serious.

His mother sighed. She handed Jill a white box. Jill opened the box to see the two bracelets. They were smaller but otherwise an identical set to the ones Tara wore and gave Jill as a gift years before.

"Thank you," Jill said.

"May I put them on her arm?" Mr. Rajagopal was asking.

"You do one and I'll do one," Raja answered.

LaLa was quite fascinated with the bracelets. She looked at her arm, turned it over and over. She showed it to Uncle Trey. "Pretty," was his response. She smiled.

CHAPTER FIFTY

Enoch, Kirby, Auntie, and Grammy talked at dinner on Sunday about how they would handle all the moving. They made one adjustment to Ben's plan. Auntie was going to stay with Kirby and Enoch and the boys, and they would sell their house. Auntie and Grammy knew they needed to go through the house first and decide what to keep and what to discard. Grammy was going to Landridge in a couple of months to be there when school reopened. So that was the priority—to get her settled. But she would move again when Ben and Belinda's new home was built.

Kirby and Auntie went through the house and made a list of updates and renovations like paint colors and changing counter tops in the kitchen. Grammy opted out of the walkthrough. Auntie was concerned about that. She knew her sister loved Ben more than anything or anybody on this earth, and she would do what he wanted her to, even if she didn't want to. Avis decided they needed to talk.

After Kirby and the boys left, Avis went in the kitchen and sat at the table. Grammy was standing in the pantry making a grocery list.

"Are you sure you want to move to Landridge?" Avis asked Victoria. Victoria waited a bit before she answered.

"No, Avis, I'm not sure. But what I am sure of is God has answered my prayers, and given me the desires of my heart: for my baby's baby to be happy. He has the family he's always wanted and the opportunity to lead a great church with great people. If all he wants from me is to be there, I'll do it. Neither of them has a mother, so you and I are it."

"You're right about that," Avis said.

"So be it. I'm moving to Georgia. The hard part is not being down there, it's leaving this house. Do you know I've lived in this house almost sixty years, through all the renovations and additions that my husband did with his own hands? Lord, I hope this house can stand up to Blake and Nicholas!" Grammy said. She and Avis laughed.

CHAPTER FIFTY-ONE

Neither Clay nor Delia said anything for a bit after the kiss. He took her hand and walked her to the sofa. He sat down, and she stood in front of him. He unzipped her jeans. Just as he was pulling them down, she noticed the picture of Clay and Cicely on top of the stack of books.

"Is this Cicely's apartment?"

"What difference does that make? Look at me."

She met his eyes, but she stopped him from pulling her pants down any further.

"Dee, this is not about Cicely. It's about you."

"No, Clay. I don't want to. I'm not going to do this to Javier. And you're pathetic. You want to get with me in your fiancé's apartment! You are just pathetic!" Delia pulled her jeans up, zipped them, and walked out of the apartment.

Delia got in the car and drove away as quickly as she could. She didn't want to leave, and she knew if Clay came after her, she would go back in. She was angry with herself for going back over there anyway. At least she wasn't so late; she would have to lie to Javier. *Why, after all this time, does Clay still drive me crazy?* she was thinking. The phone startled her. She knew it was Clay before she looked at the screen. She was wrong, it was Crystal. When they hung up, she was actually a little disappointed. "I can't believe he let me leave like that.

He didn't try to stop me, and he hasn't called. He makes me sick!" she said out loud.

Clay was still sitting on the sofa. He came so close that it frightened him. After all this time, he was still physically attracted to Delia. But he knew for sure it was only physical. He was glad she walked away. He would never forgive himself for going back to his old life and cutting out on Cicely. The phone rang. He knew it would be Delia. He was wrong; it was Cicely. "Hey, sweetie" was how he answered as he got up and started to get the last couple of things he needed to get ready to leave.

"Where are you?" she asked.

"Just leaving the apartment. You home?"

"No, but I will be leaving here in about thirty minutes."

"Meet me at the Pancake House."

"Okay, I will!" she said.

"I love you Cicely," he said and sounded very serious.

"I love you, Clay."

Clay was in the truck headed to the Pancake House when his phone rang again. It was Grant. "What's up, GP?"

"Man, I had one hell of an afternoon."

Clay laughed.

"Not funny man. I'm serious." Grant said.

"What happened?" Clay turned the music off. Grant told him about Janis and Sunny. Clay was in total disbelief. "Dude, you are lying!" Clay said.

"It was like television man. I'm tellin' you. Sunny has another personality. She turned into this other person. Straight girl gangsta!" Grant said.

Clay was laughing hard. He had reached the parking lot at the Pancake House. He sat in the truck waiting for Cicely. Grant went on to tell Clay that security had eventually escorted Janis out of the building. "Sunny slapped her, and I jumped between them, and Janis actually hit me. Man, she was going to fight Sunny! I had to make Sunny back up, and sit down at her desk. Then Janis wouldn't leave so we called security."

"But you know what? I'm disappointed in Sunny."

"I'm not," Clay said matter-of-factly. "Why are you disappointed in her? You know Janis is crazy."

"I know that, Clay, and Sunny knows that too. She should have just called security and had her thrown out."

"Naw, you wrong. It's about time she met her match. Sunny should have kicked her ass and told you about it later. You can't reason with people like her," Clay cursed.

"Janis pulled a gun on me and intended to use it. How did Sunny know she didn't have a gun? Why would she take that chance?" Grant asked seriously.

"You're right, and I'm glad she didn't. But I'm also glad she knows she can't run over Sunny. My girl Sunny!" They both laughed. "The girl gangsta!"

Clay saw Cicely turn onto the parking lot and blinked his headlights at her. He got out of the truck and went to her car, got in on the passenger side, and gave her a peck on the lips. He mouthed to her, "Grant." She waved.

"Cicely said 'hello,'" Clay said to Grant.

"Tell my darling I said 'hello' and 'I love her.'" Clay delivered Grant's message.

They talked a few more minutes, and Clay encouraged Grant to be okay with what Sunny did and to go ahead and give her the ring.

Clay and Cicely went in talking about Grant and Sunny and the Janis fiasco.

"OMG! I am so proud of Sunny for handling that lunatic!" Cicely said as they were seated.

"I agree with you. She should have kicked her butt. I hope 'Crazy' knows she can't mess with Sunny!" Cicely was laughing out loud. Clay loved the way she laughed.

"Let me change the subject slightly," he said.

"What's up?"

"Grant bought Sunny a ring. He hasn't given it to her yet, but mentioned us having a double wedding." Cicely was listening intently. Clay continued. "I told him it is totally up to you, and if you don't want to, it's absolutely perfectly fine. This is all about you." He leaned across the table and kissed her.

"Wow! Let me think about it," she said. "I'm just not sure."

"No pressure, I just want to get to the honeymoon."

"Clay!"

"Well, I'm just sayin'!"

CHAPTER FIFTY-TWO

Kathy's things were in order for her move to New York City, and this evening, she was having dinner with Campbell. She wanted to make sure he was situated for the upcoming semester. This would be his senior year at DavisTown College. Kathy wanted to be sure he was set to graduate on time and applied to go directly to law school. Maybe she could get him to come to New York. She liked Chloe, but she wanted to make sure there was some distance between them. She felt sure Chloe was coming back to North Carolina for law school because her parents went to North Carolina Central.

Campbell looked good, and Kathy noticed he was driving a different car. "It was Chloe's, I bought it from her. She has a new one, and I gave mine to Natalia."

"Of course, Chloe engineered all that," Kathy said.

"She put the plan in motion, but it was my decision not to sell my car to Natalia and to just give it to her." They took their seats and Campbell talked more about Natalia and how she was doing in the wake of all she had been through. "Mr. Matthews was going to pay for her and the other students to go back home to Haiti for a visit, but Natalia didn't want to go. She said it would make her too sad."

They ordered, and then Kathy asked about Chloe. As always, he was very honest with Kathy about Chloe, about their relationship, and their future. He told her about Chloe's depression and how she disappeared for a while but went to counseling and "is doing great now." He told Kathy about her seeing Enoch, asking to see their son, the Casebier's saying no, and how he acted out of emotion and asked her to marry him.

"You did what?" Kathy put down her fork and folded her arms in front of her.

"She was crying, and I didn't know what to say." Campbell went on to tell Kathy he went back to Chloe, told her the truth and told her he wants to marry her after law school. Kathy felt better, but she was more determined to get Campbell as far away from Chloe as possible.

They talked about law school, and Kathy was clear with Campbell what her expectations were for him. She knew his mother didn't even expect him to go to college, so she wouldn't encourage him to go to law school. She was glad to hear him say he was open to coming to New York.

What Kathy didn't know was Sterling was in the restaurant too. He was sitting at a table on the other side of the bar. He saw her come in. He was going to sit there until he saw her get ready to leave and then tell her he wanted to talk to her.

Sterling finally stopped avoiding Mrs. Robinson's calls. They talked a few days before, and she told Sterling he and Kathy need to clear the air.

"My daughter is much like her father—headstrong," she said. "She cares more for you than she will admit."

He told Mrs. Robinson that he was transparent with Kathy about his feelings but that hadn't "affected her."

"Well, Sterling, you want to know in your heart that you did all you could." He decided to give it one more try. His intention was to call her, but there she was across the room.

As Campbell and Kathy were about to leave the restaurant, she reinforced to him that because she wouldn't be living in Hattiesville full time didn't mean their relationship had to change. He agreed.

As they walked toward the door, Kathy was getting her keys when she heard Campbell talking to someone. "What's up, Coach?"

"Rice, what are you doing out with my girl?" Kathy looked at Sterling and half smiled.

"No harm, Coach. I am just protecting your interest!"

"Well, good. I appreciate that. I can take it from here." Kathy still hadn't said anything. Campbell and Sterling shook hands, and then Campbell and Kathy shared a long hug.

"Kat, we need to talk," Sterling's voice was firm. They walked outside, but Kathy didn't really react. "My place or yours?" he was asking.

"Mine," she answered.

He followed her home, thinking this may be their last time here. Once inside, he could tell she was almost ready to leave.

"What are you going to do with the place?"

"Nothing for the time being. This was Leah's condo and like everything else about her, my parents won't let it go." She handed him a bottle of water and the television remote. He took the water but laid the remote on the coffee table.

"Kat, I want to clear the air before you leave. I know I'm being selfish, not wanting you to go. But I just don't, the timing of all this stinks. After all these years, we reconnect, things are moving at a good pace, and then you decide to break camp."

"Sterling, you act like it's the end of the world. It's 'do or die' for you. You never gave us the option of having a long distance relationship. You gave me an ultimatum. You didn't consider that we can continue to communicate and visit," Kathy said. "You didn't consider anything but your own feelings."

"Do you love me Kathy?" She couldn't believe he was asking her that. She really didn't know what to say. He had taken her hand in his. He was looking directly into her eyes. He was waiting for her answer.

"Do you love me, Sterling?"

"Don't answer a question with a question. Do you love me Kathy?"

"I don't love you enough to change my plans."

CHAPTER FIFTY-THREE

"I have something to show you!" Natalia walked into Chloe's office and sat down in front of her desk.

"How was your weekend?" Chloe asked her.

"Great." Natalia handed Chloe her phone. On the screen was a picture of Nicholas. Chloe gasped.

"Where did you get this?" she was almost whispering.

"I babysat for them on Saturday evening." Natalia went on to tell Chloe about her time with Nicholas and Blake.

"Chloe, he is so cute and so smart. He likes to sing, and he runs everywhere he goes."

"What do you mean he likes to sing?"

Natalia laughed. "He sings all the time! I asked him what he wanted to drink, and he sang, 'May I have some juice please!' It was so funny! And when he was coloring, he was singing."

Chloe looked at the pictures on Natalia's phone over and over. Two of them were of Nicholas's, and two of them were both boys.

"Why don't you forward them to your phone?"

Chloe looked at Natalia and smiled. She sent the pictures to her phone and then to her personal e-mail.

"I can't wait to show Campbell! Thank you so much. You are an incredible little sister."

Natalia accomplished her goal. She wanted to make Chloe happy. But that was just the beginning. Next step, to earn Mrs.

Casebier's trust so she could take the boys on an outing and Chloe could spend time with Nicholas in person.

Chloe called Campbell to see if he could meet for lunch. "I can't leave, but if you want to pick up something and come over here, I can still get to see you."

"It's a date!" She was excited and anxious to show him the pictures. She hadn't told him about the research she was doing and her intention to undo Nicholas's adoption. Maybe she would tell him today.

Chloe picked up a pizza and went to Campbell's office in the DavisTown College Athletic Center. It was really small, just barely enough space for the desk and an extra chair. They sat in a common area, ate, and talked. When they finished eating, Chloe told Campbell she needed to show him something in private. They went back into his office where she closed the door and took out her phone.

"Check this out!" She handed her phone to him. Campbell looked at all four pictures before he said anything. "Isn't he adorable?" Chloe was smiling from ear to ear.

"Chloe, where did you get these pictures?" Campbell was very serious.

"Natalia took them. She was at their house on Saturday helping Kirby Casebier with the boys." Chloe told Campbell the story of how she came to have the pictures.

"Natalia shouldn't have taken these."

"Campbell! That's our son!"

"Yes, sweetie, that's our son, and he's amazing and cute like you, but he has other parents who would be very unhappy if they knew Natalia was with their boys under false pretenses."

"Campbell, they called her!"

"Chloe, I don't care what the circumstances were. She shouldn't have taken these pictures, at least not without telling their parents."

Chloe stood up and looked Campbell directly in his eyes; she didn't smile at all. He started to say something, but she put her hand up to stop him. She turned and walked out of his office. She didn't realize until she was halfway back to her office that she left her telephone on his desk. She would send Natalia to get it; she didn't want to see Campbell again.

CHAPTER FIFTY-FOUR

Min and Jackson had dinner and then went to a concert at the Blumenthal Arts Center in Charlotte. Going to the symphony was one of her favorite things to do. Tonight was extra special because the orchestra was featuring Motown hits, Jackson's favorite.

He felt like such a fool. He let his weakness cross a line that could potentially cost him everything, and now Anderson Thorn knew what was going on and with whom. If he told Jacksa, it was going to get really ugly. Dealing with Min would be easier than dealing with Jacksa. But Min knows, and she hadn't let on, and she wasn't acting any differently. The danger was this may be the quiet before the storm. And his beautiful daughter could and would be the eye of that storm. If Jacksa told JJ, both his children would hate him, and he would lose their respect.

Jackson was having all these thoughts as they were waiting for the concert to start. Min was chatting with the lady sitting beside her. When the lights dimmed, she turned her attention to Jackson. The concert was incredible—way better than Jackson expected. He had only been with her a few times, usually Jacksa would accompany her. He decided he would like to come again.

When they were driving home, Min was looking over the brochure for the next concert season. She was telling Jackson about the features—the Four Tops, the Duke Ellington

Orchestra, and Natalie Cole. "I tell you what, I'll get you season tickets for next year," Jackson told her.

"Thank you, dear!" Min said looking at him and genuinely smiling.

"As much as you like to go, I don't know why I hadn't already thought to do it."

"No problem. Next season is going to be good."

"I agree," he said "and maybe I'll go with you."

"It's a date," she said.

Jackson was thinking to himself, *do you think season tickets to the symphony will make up for what you've done?*

His phone was on vibrate, and he could feel the one quick pulse. It was his "good night" text. He wouldn't respond. They were both quiet for a few minutes, and then she broke the silence.

"Do you love me, Jackson?"

"Woman, didn't I just tell you I was going to spend money on you? Of course, I love you. If I didn't, I would let you listen to the radio!" She didn't laugh, and his heart dropped. "Yes, I love you. I love you very much." He didn't know what was coming next.

"You very seldom tell me anymore." He reached over and took her hand.

"I try to show you."

"You do, but I often think how things were when we were younger. We said it every day. I just don't want us to take each other for granted." Jackson kissed his wife's hand. They held hands the rest of the ride home. When they were home, he fixed her tea, rubbed her feet, and massaged her shoulders and back.

"I love you, Min."

"I love you, Jackson." He felt sick. He held her in his arms until she went to sleep.

CHAPTER FIFTY-FIVE

"I had a great meeting with Belinda Coffey this morning! Guess what she told me?" April was sitting at her dad's desk. Hampton stopped what he was doing to listen to her. "She's pregnant!" April said it very excitedly. "Pregnant!" she said it again. Hampton felt a pain in his chest.

"So what does that mean for the project?"

"Daddy, you are so funny, always about business. But to answer your question, the project has an addition. We were already doing five bedrooms, but we're adding a 'mother-in-law' suite, except we're calling it the grandma suite. Pastor Coffey's grandmother is moving in with them."

"She's coming here to stay?"

"Yep. She's coming in a couple of months. She'll be here before the baby comes."

April went on to tell him about the house plans and how she was going to show them a different lot that would better accommodate the new floor plan. She was talking, but he was half listening. He needed to talk to Lee Robinson. They needed a plan. Ben and Belinda would be excited about the baby, so maybe that would take the sting out of his news. He could only hope.

When April left his office, Hampton called Lee. "Just anxious about all this," Hampton was telling Lee.

"I know, but the situation is what it is. You can't change it. We just have to deal with it," Lee said. "What I do know is we need to tell Ben and let him advise us about Belinda and Ms. Victoria."

"Yeah, 'cause April just told me Belinda is pregnant."

"They told me," Lee said laughing.

"I know Ben isn't going to want to upset her," Hampton said with a sigh.

"Yeah, there are so many people to consider, including your daughter and the Coffey twins." Hampton had thought about the twins, but he wasn't even thinking this means April would have a sister. Hampton leaned back in his chair, closed his eyes, and rubbed his hand across his forehead.

"Lee, can you come down, so we can meet with Ben?"

"We are scheduled to do the walkthrough at the church two weeks from yesterday, so I'll be down then. I know two weeks seems like a long time, but the situation isn't going to change in that time. Let's see what we can work out."

"Unfortunately, you're right."

Lili Marcos took Brittani, Brianna, and Carlotta to see a movie. Juan, Ben, and Jorge went to a Braves game. Belinda was home alone and thankful for the peace and quiet. She talked to Kirby, and now she was in bed. She rubbed her baby bump. It was amazing that she was carrying twins again. She made an appointment to see the doctor the following week so they could do the official ultrasound and Ben could be there. The only downside to all this was she knew Ben was now going to insist that she stop working. They would have to compromise. She went to sleep thinking about how they could work it out.

CHAPTER FIFTY-SIX

"This is Sunny Dorsette."

"Oh, I have the wrong office. I was trying to reach Laila Ali."
Sunny laughed. She recognized Clay's voice.

"Oh, you got jokes."

"Ain't nobody joking. I heard about you!"

"I bet you did hear, and I can only imagine what you heard.
Do you know Grant Sturdivant is angry with me?"

"I don't think he's really angry. I think he's just protective,
and he doesn't want you taking chances with a crazy person."

"I'm not afraid of Janis, and she needs to know that. I'll kick
her butt and then go back to work. No biggie."

Grant was right, Sunny did have a gangster side, Clay was
thinking to himself. He laughed as Sunny gave him her version
of the story. It didn't differ from Grant's version, except he was
nervous and Sunny wasn't.

"I'm a city girl, Clay, and I've dealt with her kind before. I
love Grant, and I will fight for what I want. Anybody who doubts
that will see."

"I'm going to say this, Sunny, and I hope you won't take
offense, but you seem so refined, so lady-like."

"I am always a lady. But sometimes I'm a lady tiger!" She
laughed.

Clay went on to tell Sunny the other reason for his call.
He repeated portions of his conversation with Grant to her,

highlighting the part about Grant going into a panic when he can't get a hold of her and being afraid she won't come back. Sunny blew out a long breath. "Yeah, I know, and I try to always let him know where I am and to never miss his calls. I asked his therapist if he's suffering from post-traumatic stress disorder."

"What did he say?"

"He said Grant has some of the symptoms, but he wouldn't diagnose PTSD."

"So what did he suggest, medication?" Clay asked.

"No, he suggested we go ahead and get married. The rationale—if he can see it happen . . ."

"He won't worry about it not happening," Clay finished the statement.

"Right," Sunny responded.

They talked awhile, but Clay stopped short of telling Sunny about the ring. He didn't want to spoil the surprise. And he didn't want to get her hopes up if Grant didn't come through right now.

"I'll be honest, Sunny, I'm concerned about him."

"I know you are, but I'm taking good care of him. I love Grant. If he was in trouble, I would be the first to get him some help." Clay could tell she was sincere, and he was satisfied.

When Sunny got home, Grant wasn't there. His bicycle was gone, so she knew he would be gone at least an hour. She texted that she was home and decided at the same time that they would walk to a neighborhood bistro they liked for dinner. She lay across the bed for a few minutes thinking about her conversation with Clay. She hadn't ever loved anybody like this. Grant Sturdivant was an incredible man, and she would love him through this pain. She hurt for him when he first told her about Leah, but nobody had been on the front lines with him through the healing process the way she had. Grant was her man, and she was his lady. They loved each other, and that was all that mattered.

There was no crowd at the bistro, so it didn't take long for them to be served. After dinner, they shared some raspberry sorbet—her favorite. They walked back the long way, down the parkway and through the park. They were holding hands, and Grant led her to a bench by the water.

"We need to coordinate our schedules so we can go to Hattiesville in a couple of weeks," Grant told her.

"That's fine. Just let me know when. I have plenty of time I can take off."

"I want you to meet my parents, Gretchen and . . ." He paused.

"And beat Janis down!" she said, and they both laughed.

"Ugh, don't talk about her. One thing's for sure, Gretchen and Clay think you should have a fan club."

"What do you think, Grant?"

"I don't want to talk about that now. I also want you to meet Leah's parents and sister, and Jill, her best friend." Sunny didn't really know what to say. Meeting his family was fine, great in fact, but why Leah's family?

"I know you're wondering why I want you to meet Leah's family."

"Yes, I am."

"For one thing, Bishop Robinson is my pastor, so it's a matter of order and respect. But also, Leah and I were together for years. As much as I love you, I feel it's my place to tell them we're getting married, not let them hear it 'in the street' like my mom would say. Plus, Mrs. Robinson and my mom are still good friends."

"I understand, sweetheart. I really do, and it's fine. I would love to meet your family and your extended family," Sunny said with a genuine smile.

Grant stood up, and Sunny thought he was ready to go, but he got down on his knee in front of her. She wasn't breathing. He took the box out of his pocket, opened it, and took out a beautiful one-and-a-half carat round diamond set in yellow gold. He took her hand in his and, without a lot of fanfare, simply said, "Will you marry me?"

"Yes" she answered, just as tears spilled over her eyelids as he slipped the ringer on her finger.

He stood and pulled her into his arms. They held each other for a while. She looked at her ring; it was exactly what she wanted. When they broke their embrace there were two ladies standing and watching. They had witnessed the whole thing, and one of them had recorded it on her phone! They approached Sunny and Grant to congratulate them, and an impromptu celebration happened. They took a couple more pictures, forwarded the video and pictures to Sunny's phone and were on their way. As they walked away from the park hand in hand, Grant had a funny feeling. He knew in his heart those ladies were not there by accident. Leah sent them to tell him "it's okay."

CHAPTER FIFTY-SEVEN

Janis had once again been escorted away by law enforcement. The same thing happened when she went to Leah's hospital room all those years ago. Again, she was embarrassed. But this time, Grant was there. She had no chance of making him believe it wasn't her fault.

She circled back and waited in the parking lot to see if she could see Grant when he left. She didn't see him or Sunny. One thing was for sure, this was a military installation, and she knew she couldn't just be there. She didn't want to be arrested. She did not have a number for Grant so she decided to call his office. She tried twice, and both times the person who answered said he wasn't available.

It hit Janis suddenly that she knew Sunny's last name. She would look her up to see if she could find her address. There were two listings for S. Dorsette on the directory website. No Sunny, and the others had complete names. Janis mapped both addresses from the hotel. Now that she had that information, what was she going to do? Janis knew she couldn't go to Sunny's door. To her surprise, Sunny was a force to be reckoned with. She never expected that. She had totally underestimated this whole situation.

Janis drove to the first address, but she wasn't able to determine anything. She wasn't even sure what she was looking for, short of seeing Grant or Sunny. She got lost driving to the second address, and it got dark, so she didn't find it. She was totally frustrated. She was going home the next day empty handed, but determined to come up with another plan.

On the flight back to Charlotte, Janis replayed in her mind the encounter with Sunny. She refused to think about it before. Sunny had actually slapped her, and Grant did not defend her. Sunny humiliated her in front of her beloved Grant. She would have to pay.

Sterling was actually shocked by Kathy's response. He didn't expect her to declare her undying love for him, but neither did he expect her to be so matter of fact. Kathy knew she sounded harsh. That wasn't her intention, but she needed to make her point.

"Kat, I intend for us to continue to communicate, but being just friends isn't what I want."

"Sterling, that's all I can promise you. My studies will be my priority. I am investing a lot of money into this, so I have to invest the time too. I won't be able to come home regularly, won't have the time or money."

"Can I come see you?" Sterling asked very softly.

"Call first," she said, and they both laughed.

"Sterling, as soon as the season starts, your time is going to be limited too. Let's just play this by ear. You know events are going to come up that you will need a date for, and I don't expect you to go alone." Kathy started to ask him about the volleyball coach, but she changed her mind.

"Kathy, what do you expect?"

"I expect you to respect my choices and be my friend."

"So you are going to give me away when you know I want you." Sterling was serious.

"You do you, and I'll do me. At some point, if we can do each other, then so be it." Sterling was staring at her. She felt the need to say more. "Sterling, I wish we were in the same place. You just got here—to the relationship status quickly. I was concentrating on preparing to go back to school."

"Quickly? Kat, it's been years, and you know it. When we met originally, I told you how I felt about you and what I wanted."

"Yeah, and if you remember, you did the same thing then; tried to tell me what to do."

They went back and forth until the whole conversation was pointless. He tried, and he needed to make peace with that. "Kathy, can I see you again before you leave?"

"Sure, I'll let you know exactly when I'm leaving."

When Sterling was in his car headed home, he decided he was done. If Kathy really did let him know when she was leaving, he would take her to dinner and say goodbye. But he was moving on. Mrs. Robinson was right—he was sure he did all he could.

CHAPTER FIFTY-EIGHT

The third time Campbell called Chloe and got her voice mail, he left a message. He told her she needed to stop pouting and call him. Campbell was tired of Chloe's selfish antics. He knew how much she was hurting. He was hurting too, but they had to live with the decision they made, and Campbell knew he had to make her see that. If she couldn't or wouldn't respect his leadership on this, how was she going to respect him as her husband? If God was going to hold him responsible, then he had to make the hard decisions. He loved Chloe, but she needed tough love.

Chloe listened to Campbell's message, and she knew she needed to call him, but she was angry with him. She just could not digest him being so passive about Nicholas. He was their son! He was Nicholas's father, and he had a right to know. But she knew she was going to have to tackle this on her own.

Chloe took a deep breath and called Campbell. They made arrangements to meet later. She gathered her file and her thoughts. Chloe was done trying to reason with Campbell. He was going to have to hear her out today. She had to get this processed before it is time for her to go back to school.

Campbell brought a peace offering: a peach milk shake. Chloe smiled. He knew that was her favorite. "Sugar, I need you to hear me out, and understand I am very serious about this. I know you're angry because I didn't jump for joy at those pictures. My heart hurts for our son too, but you are being selfish."

"Selfish! Are you serious?" Chloe raised her voice.

"Yes, selfish. You are thinking about what you want, how you feel, what's best for you. Have you even thought about Nick or his brother or his parents?" Campbell's voice was firm.

"We're his parents!" Chloe was still screaming.

"Do you remember when you were pregnant, and we were talking, and we said and agreed God gave us Nicholas to bless another family? Do you remember how proud and happy we were that God chose us?" Campbell had her attention. Her body language had softened.

"Of course I remember that Campbell, but I feel differently now."

"Chloe, how can you feel differently? Don't you still believe we were God's instruments to get Nicholas into the earth?" She dropped her head. Campbell prayed he was getting through to her. "Maybe it would've been better if we had done the closed adoption like your parents said. But we wanted to choose our baby's parents remember?"

"Yes, I remember," she whispered.

"And we said we were going to college, get it together, get married, and have other children. We need to stick to our plan, not get sidetracked by emotion."

Her back stiffened. "I am not sidetracked by emotion. I want my, our, son back. I changed my mind."

"You can't change your mind. Answer this. Do you want to graduate from Spelman and go to law school?" Campbell asked her seriously.

"Of course I do."

"Can you raise Nick in an apartment in Atlanta with no job? Who's going to keep him while you're in class or in the library at night studying? Have you considered any of that?" The truth was she had not. She hadn't thought past her own wants. Campbell was right—she was being selfish.

Chloe started to cry, but Campbell wasn't shaken. He expected her to cry. This time he wasn't going to be moved by her tears. He was going for broke. "You say you love me . . ."

"I do love you," she interrupted him.

"And you accepted my marriage proposal . . ."

"For the future," she added. They both smiled. He winked at her.

"If I am your husband, the head of our family, then you have to trust me on this. And Chloe if you can't, I don't think we can get married." Her heart skipped a beat. She looked in his eyes, and he was serious.

"I realize you will be the head of our family, and I do respect that. But will you hear me out at least?" she asked.

"Sure," he replied. She reached in her bag, pulled out a file folder, and proceeded to explain to Campbell all the case laws she found to support wanting to file for custody of Nicholas.

"So you want to take the Casebiers to court and fight them over Nicholas?"

"Campbell, you make it sound so awful."

"It is awful. Why do you want to put yourself and them through that, especially when you have a one percent chance to win?"

"Why are you being the voice of doom?"

"Not doom, reality. Have you talked to your parents about this?"

"No," Chloe said.

"Why?" Chloe didn't answer. "You haven't talked to them because you know they won't support you." She still didn't say anything. "And who's going to pay for all this, you?"

"My parents are attorneys."

"Chloe, you expect them to represent you when you haven't even told them what you want to do?" Campbell raised his voice. "You keep saying me, represent me. It's us; it's our fight."

"No, Chloe. It's not us; it's you. I absolutely do not go along with this, and I will not help you try to take Nicholas from the only parents he knows." Chloe threw the file back into her bag. She stood up and started to walk away. "Chloe, if you walk out of here you are walking out of my life," Campbell sounded more confident than he felt. He got up and walked toward her just as she fell into his arms. She cried, and he let her. He held her until she got it all out.

CHAPTER FIFTY-NINE

Kirby and the twins worked out the family vacation schedule. The whole family was going to the North Carolina Outer Banks. They rented a five-bedroom, three-bathroom house on the beach for a week. Grammy's birthday party would be Saturday in Hattiesville, and then they would go to the beach on Sunday. The twins, Grammy, Auntie, and the boys were staying until Friday. Ben and Belinda and Enoch and Kirby were staying until Sunday. Enoch was concerned about them driving the five hours back. Kirby was concerned about them keeping up with the boys. Enoch hired one of the guys who worked for him to fly up on Friday morning and drive them back that afternoon. Kirby called Natalia and asked her to be available to help with Blake and Nicholas. She said she would be "delighted." All things were ready.

Belinda and Ben's appointment with the obstetrician was Friday before they left for Hattiesville. When the nurse weighed Belinda, she frowned. "Mrs. Coffey you have gained eleven pounds in three weeks." When they were in the exam room she measured Belinda's stomach and had a similar reaction. Belinda played along. Ben's eyes were wide. "You have a set of twins, right?" the nurse asked.

"Yes," Belinda said hesitantly.

"Let's do the ultrasound before we draw any conclusions," the nurse said. Ben reached for Belinda's hand. His heart was pounding.

The doctor came in to talk to them while the nurse set up the ultrasound machine. In about forty-five seconds they saw one heartbeat, and about ten seconds later she saw the second one. "There are two heartbeats," the doctor said.

"Twins!" Ben responded. He looked at his wife with a huge grin on his face. She looked at him very seriously. Even though she already knew, hearing Ben say it took it to another level. Belinda started to cry. "Babe, its fine. I love you and both our babies," Ben said. But the tears kept coming. The doctor and the nurse were still performing the ultrasound, trying to determine the gender of the babies.

"Well, they're identical. Both in one sack, but they are stomach to stomach so we can't see if they are boys or girls.

"It doesn't matter," Ben said.

When the doctor and nurse left the room and Belinda was dressed, she sat down beside him, totally overwhelmed by the reality of it all. He asked her to stand. Her stomach was close to his face. They held hands, and he prayed. When she looked down at him, he was crying, and that made her cry. After a few minutes, they gathered their composure and went to talk with the doctor. She assured them everything was fine. Belinda needed to take two vitamins a day and increase her calorie intake. Her only concern was the twins may come a little early. "Twins usually do," the doctor said.

"My girls were only three weeks early," Belinda replied.

"Yes, Mrs. Coffey. But you were ten years younger. I want you to also consider you may need to stop working several weeks before your due date."

"I'll work as long as I can. I have scheduling options, so I'll exercise those," Belinda's voice was firm. She didn't need to give Ben any ammunition. On the ride home, they decided to tell everybody about the twins while they were at the beach.

CHAPTER SIXTY

It had been a few weeks since the Rajagopals came to the United States unannounced. They talked with Raja once in the weeks that followed. He made it clear that he still didn't appreciate how they approached his family. And he let them know gifts to LaLa didn't make it okay.

What Raja was really concerned about was their announcement that they were moving to North Carolina. He didn't believe them, but he wanted to be sure. He spoke with Yash, who assured him he knew of no plans for them to move. He also told Raja that his parents had "scolded" Raja's parents for what they did while they were there. Raja and Tara talked. She was still angry at his parents' nerve and she cautioned Raja not to let his guard down.

Jill and Tara talked too. They agreed this may be the quiet before the storm. And they agreed to proceed with caution. Tara promised Jill she would gather more information. Jill felt confident in what Tara said, and she was sure she didn't want to know how Tara intended to accomplish that.

Mrs. Rajagopal finally admitted to her husband that she made a mistake in trying to force Raja's hand. She knew she needed to fix it, but she wasn't sure how without looking totally foolish.

"This is Detective Thorn."
"This is Jacksa Baye!"

"Hey baby, how are you?" Anderson asked her smiling.

"I'm great. How are you? I am returning your call."

"Have some news to share. Wanted to see if you want to come over for dinner."

"Wow. Are you cooking?"

"I am!"

"Yes, I will be there, and thank you for the invitation," Jacksa was smiling too.

Anderson had been successful in diverting her attention away from her parents, but he didn't know what Jackson did, if anything. He didn't intend to follow up unless Jacksa pressed him, and he hoped she wouldn't. At the moment, there were bigger fish to fry than a jerk like Jackson Baye. Anderson thought so much of Jackson until now. But he was falling for Jacksa hard and fast and if she supported him now, he would know she was the one. The next step was to introduce her to his sisters then to his mom, aunt, and grandmother. Once he "takes her home," there would be no turning back. He hoped his sisters would be nice. When he told them that Jacksa was half-African American and half-Korean, they told him that he and Jacksa would have strange-looking children. There were alluding to her genes added to his Catawba Indian genes. He didn't care. He was totally smitten with her. And he felt good that she felt the same way about him.

He cooked, but he wasn't quite ready when she arrived. She helped him finish, and when they sat down to eat he got right to the point. "I was notified today that my application to the FBI was accepted. Things are being processed, and I should be going to Quantico in about forty-five days!" He was obviously excited and grinning from ear to ear.

"Wow, Anderson. That's incredible. Good for you! I guess congratulations are in order." She lifted her glass for a toast. "What's left to be done in the process?" she asked. He told her the basics, including she would most likely be interviewed. "Why me?"

"Because they are talking to my family, closest friends, coworkers, former coworkers, church members, and everybody else I know." She laughed. They talked more about the training, and then he told her the hard part.

"I will probably have to relocate."

"Exactly what does that mean?" Jacksa asked.

"No doubt I requested Charlotte. But without any seniority, I probably won't be assigned here."

"So where do you think you'll be?" she asked very carefully.

"I have no idea. Maybe somewhere like Bangor, Maine."

"Where?"

"Bangor, Maine—somewhere in the middle of the state, which is at the top of the country," Anderson said seriously. "What do you think about that?" he asked her. She dropped her eyes.

"It doesn't really matter what I think, Anderson. This is an awesome opportunity for you."

"What you think about everything matters to me, sweetie. Look at me, and tell me how you feel." "Anderson, in a perfect world, you would be assigned to Charlotte, and we could continue to work on our relationship." That was exactly what he wanted her to say.

"Can we work on it even if I'm in Bangor, Maine?"

"Yes. We will just have to work hard and make it work." He fell in love with her at that moment.

For two Thursdays, Jackson stayed home. The second week, JJ was home, so the whole family was together including Anderson. Jackson felt uncomfortable with him around, but he was sure Anderson wasn't going anywhere. He told them about the FBI process. JJ was impressed. Min said the whole thing made her nervous. Jackson congratulated him, but he wasn't sure how he really felt, and the absolute truth was he didn't know if he wanted his daughter involved with an FBI agent. Being a police officer was bad enough. Federal agent was worse. And if they were married, he would be terrified for her. And Jackson knew they would probably move away. He wouldn't like that, but Min would be devastated.

During the time he was home, and especially while the whole family was together, he thought about his other life. He weighed the few pros against all the cons. The conclusion: he was going to end it once and for all. He wouldn't change his mind this time.

Thursday came. He got a haircut and went straight to her house. He wouldn't be late getting home tonight. As usual, when they hadn't seen each other in a while, there was food and ambiance. Jackson hated that she went to so much preparation considering why he was there. He ate, and they chatted, but he got right to the point. "What's on your mind, Jackson?" she asked. He was sitting across from her at the kitchen table. He moved his chair back from the table and leaned forward with this forearms on his thighs. He looked up at her and spoke slowly.

"We can't continue to see each other. I'm not willing to keep doing this to Min and my kids."

"What's wrong?" she asked.

"Nothing. I just don't want to live this double life anymore."

"Are you afraid the detective is going to tell Min who I am?"

"No, but not for me, because he won't hurt Jacksa," Jackson said with a sigh.

They both sat quietly for a minute. Jackson sat up straight, stretched his legs out in front of him, and reached for his hat.

"Don't go yet."

"Please don't do this," Jackson said standing.

"You have to give me a chance to say something." He remained standing, hat in hand.

"You know my birthday is coming." Jackson laughed.

"Your birthday is three months away." She laughed too.

"That's coming!" He knew what she was going to say.

"You promised me a long weekend away for my birthday."

"You're right. I did."

"Jackson, please don't disappoint me on this. I have been looking forward to it."

He sighed again deeply. "Let me think about it."

He left, glad things had not gotten teary or dramatic. He had no intention of spending a weekend away. It was over. He was done.

CHAPTER SIXTY-ONE

Cicely's and Clay's phones rang at the same time. It was Grant and Sunny. Sunny told Cicely that Grant had proposed. Grant was talking to Clay.

"So you asked the girl gangsta to marry you?" They were laughing. "Congratulations, man. That's what's up!"

Cicely was listening as Sunny told her about how he proposed and about the two ladies who were watching. "I'll forward you the video," Sunny told her.

"Well, are you going to have a wedding?" Cicely wanted to see what Sunny said, but she had decided against the double wedding.

Grant was telling Clay about the two ladies, but his explanation was different. He told Grant he knew they were "angels," and Leah had sent them. "Are you okay with that?" Clay asked Grant.

"Yeah, I'm great. I am at peace with the whole situation now."

"That's good stuff, man!" Clay said shrugging.

"Sunny and I are coming to Hattiesville the first weekend next month so I can introduce her to everybody."

"All right. You can stay here with us," Clay told him.

"Ya'll stayin' together now?" Grant asked.

"She's out of her apartment, so we're both here."

"In separate rooms?" Grant asked laughing.

"Yeah, man," Clay answered matter-of-factly.

"Dude, you and Cicely are practically married," Grant said. Clay changed the subject.

"Let me know what time you gettin' in. I'll leave work early."

"Okay, I will. And I'm gonna let the Robinsons know I'm comin' too."

"Leah's parents? Why?"

"I want them and Jill to meet Sunny."

Grant went on to tell Clay what he told Sunny. Clay wasn't sure he agreed with Grant, but he respected his right to make that decision. They talked about what had been done to Clay's house and what was left to be done. Then Grant brought up the double wedding. Cicely hadn't given Clay an answer on the double wedding. "Man, let the ladies work that out. Do what I'm doing: sign the check and show up where she tells you—on time!"

Cicely and Sunny were still talking too. Sunny told her she wanted a big wedding "back home in Eleuthera," and they would wait until after she and Clay were married. Cicely was curious why she wanted to go back there; she hadn't been there in so many years.

"It's a beautiful island, and that's where my parents are."

"But you know that means Grant's dad won't be able to be there. Have you mentioned that to Grant?" "Oh my god, Cicely, I didn't think of that. No, I haven't said anything to Grant. Wow, I need to rethink this."

Cicely was glad she didn't have to tell her no double wedding. She wanted her wedding day to be her day. As much as she liked Sunny and they had become friends, she wasn't going to share her day.

Cicely only let Gretchen see her dress, and only Gretchen knew any of the details. She waited her whole life for her wedding day. This was going to be a little different from her little girl vision of walking down the long church aisle on her father's arm. Since he was gone, she wanted to do something different.

Clay was an amazing man, and Cicely loved him completely. He honored her, taken good care of her and been true to her, even truthful about his past, and they had moved on. He was giving her a beautiful home and what she always wanted—security. And after they were married, they wanted to have four children, and she remembered promising Clay she would be a great mother. She told him, "I will never walk away from you and our children the way my mother walked away from us."

Chloe spent the night with Campbell. She finally went to sleep. She cried so hard, and as he lay across the room on the futon watching her hug the pillow, he could hear her whimper every once in a while. He sent her mother a text message telling her Chloe was with him, and he would explain later. One decision he absolutely made—she was going back to counseling. If she wanted him to go with her, he would, as long as she went.

Campbell was angry with himself. He ruined Chloe's life. He wasn't sure that even with counseling, she would ever get over this. He had made so many mistakes: first, getting her pregnant, agreeing to put the baby up for adoption, and then agreeing to the open adoption. If they didn't know where Nicholas was, that would be better, and if they knew but he wasn't in the same town, that would be ideal. How could he fix this? He had to do something to make this up to her. But short of getting married and having another baby, he didn't know what would fix it.

CHAPTER SIXTY-TWO

Katherine couldn't imagine who was at the door this time of day. She was doing laundry and not expecting anybody, so she was dressed very casually and hadn't taken the rollers out of her hair. She was totally surprised to see the flowers and wondered why Lee would be sending flowers today. The man gave her the big basket of cut flowers and a card in a yellow envelope. She walked back into the den, sat the basket down, and opened the card. It was a handwritten note from Sterling.

Kathy was packing her clothes; she had everything else pretty organized. She was moving the furniture from the guest room and the high top table and bar stools from the kitchen. She was going to buy a desk and love seat for the living room once she got to New York. She was moving into a one-bedroom apartment, so her living room would have to double as her study. She had been thinking about Sterling. She liked him a lot, but she couldn't take her eyes off the prize: her PhD. Not even for him.

The doorbell startled Kathy. She went to the door and there was a man there holding a beautiful bouquet of yellow roses. There were two lavender roses right in the middle of the bouquet. Lavender was her favorite color. The man gave her the flowers and a card in a lavender envelope.

Sterling's note to Katherine said he had done his best but Kathy "wants her life to take a different course." He thanked her for supporting him and told her he is moving on and wished

Kathy the best. Katherine sat and reread the note. She knew it was a long shot, but deep in her heart, she hoped Kathy would reconsider. At least not move so far away. Sterling ended his note by saying he would keep in touch. She hoped he would.

Kathy opened the envelope slowly. She recognized Sterling's writing on the envelope. Her hands were trembling. The note was handwritten.

"Kathy, I understand that yellow roses represent friendship. I hope you accept these as a sign of ours. If being friends is the best I can do, I accept that—I just don't want you out of my life." When she read that line, the tears came. After a minute, she continued to read, *"I am proud of you for pursuing your dream. As I stated before, I disagree with the method but it's not up to me. I get that now. Do well in school. I expect straight As! Take care of yourself and if you need anything let me know. I'm moving on like you have. Maybe one day our paths will cross again. Your friend, SC."*

Kathy stood there motionless and completely quiet. When she gathered herself she went through several emotions. She was sad, angry, hurt, and happy. She wiped tears. She was sad because she knew Sterling was hurt; she didn't realize he liked her so much. She was angry. How dare he believe he could get her to change her mind. She was hurt because he didn't support her dreams. But she was happy that he was moving on, so she could too. Two weeks from tomorrow she would move to New York City and to her new life.

CHAPTER SIXTY-THREE

The vacation week went quickly. Ben and Belinda and Kirby and Enoch had three more days. The rest of the family was leaving the next day. Ben and Belinda were going to share their news tonight. Everybody was meeting back at the house for dinner. Enoch and Ben were going to grill. They had taken the boys to the beach. Grammy, Auntie, and Belinda went to a movie, and Kirby and the girls went to an amusement park.

After dinner and after the kitchen had been cleaned—Grammy's rule—Ben called the kids and Auntie in from the porch.

"Are we going to play charades?" Brittani asked.

"We can in a few minutes," Ben answered. "I have another birthday gift for Grammy," he said handing her a long, flat gift box with two small yellow bows on it. Everybody was quiet watching her take the top off the box. There was an ultrasound picture, and because it was three dimensional, the picture of the two babies was very clear. There was a note that simply said, *"We both love you, Grammy. Your two new great grands!"*

"What is it, Gram?" Brianna asked. Kirby and Belinda's eyes met just for a second.

"Lord, have mercy . . . twins" was all she said.

Enoch, Kirby, and Auntie gasped. The girls said "twins" in unison. Ben and Belinda laughed.

"Lord, have mercy!" Grammy said again.

Auntie walked over to Belinda and hugged her and then hugged Ben. Brittani and Brianna were completely quiet and completely still.

Finally, Belinda said to Brianna, "So what do you think, Bree?"

"I'm really not sure, Mommy. I was okay with one brother or sister but two is a lot." She turned her attention to Grammy. "I sure am glad you're moving in."

"Me too," Brittani chimed in.

"Do we know if they are boys or girls, one of each?" Auntie asked.

Ben answered, saying they were identical and they hoped to know at the next visit. Belinda was concerned about Brittani and Brianna's reaction. She expected them to be excited. Grammy could see on Belinda's face that she was concerned.

"Probably be two boys, mischievous like Benji was!" Grammy said laughing.

"Yes, he was something!" Auntie added.

Grammy started telling stories about Ben when he was a little boy. "One evening, I went in the laundry room and he was standing on the washing machine. I asked what he was doing. He said, 'I want to see if I can fly.' So I told him to go ahead. He jumped off and fell about three feet from the machine. I asked him if he could fly, and he said no. I told him not to try it again."

"Well, Grammy, why didn't you make him get down?" Brianna asked.

"Because I'd rather him jump off while I was looking than when I wasn't and get hurt."

"Makes sense," Brianna said.

"Maybe having two would be kinda fun," Brittani said. "If they are boys, then it would be like Nicholas and Blake." She shrugged.

As the conversation moved on, Brittani, Brianna and the boys went in the kitchen, not really concerned about the logistics of having two more people in their home.

The ride back to Hattiesville was fine and, truthfully, Auntie and Grammy were glad Enoch hired the young man to drive them.

Natalia showed up about an hour after they were home, but the boys were asleep. She gave her number to Auntie and said she would come back the next day if they needed her. She hoped they would. As soon as she could, she wanted to make a way for Chloe to see Nicholas.

On the way back to Hattiesville from the Outer Banks, Ben was surprised to get a call from Lee Robinson. He asked Ben if he could rearrange his schedule a little and meet him on Monday.

"Are you okay, Sir?" Ben asked him.

"Yes, I'm fine. I have something very, very important—very private and personal—to talk over with you."

Ben didn't say much more. He didn't want the others to detect that something was really wrong. He had to put on his poker face, but he had a sinking feeling in his heart. He hadn't ever heard that level of stress in Bishop Robinson's voice.

CHAPTER SIXTY-FOUR

When Ben pulled into the parking lot at the church, he saw Hampton Josephs's car. He was puzzled on one hand and a little relieved at the same time. If the private, personal thing Bishop Robinson needed to talk to him about concerned the new church that meant nobody was sick or dying. If it was money, they would work it out. A lot of "what ifs" ran through his mind as he went up the elevator.

He smelled coffee as soon as he walked into the office. Lee and Hampton were seated in the sitting area of Lee's office. There was coffee, pastry, and fruit on a tray at the center of the coffee table. Ben hoped the chef was preparing breakfast. Both men stood as Ben walked toward them. They exchanged pleasantries. Ben poured a cup of coffee and had a couple of pastries while he told them about the Outer Banks and recommended they go. He also told them about Belinda expecting twins. They congratulated him in the midst of their laughter and teasing him.

"Hampton, I didn't know you would be here, so obviously there's a problem with my church," Ben said looking directly at Hampton. Hampton looked at Lee. His eyes were sad. Lee cleared his throat.

"Son, my reason for calling you here has nothing to do with the church. That project is going very well. If everything I'm involved in was in good shape like that, my life would be easier!

This is personal, and Hamp is here because he brought it to my attention," Lee leaned up and rested his forearms on his thighs. He looked at Ben without moving his head. Lee continued.

"Remember the conversation we had about the private investigator investigating Belinda?"

"Yeah."

"Well, Hamp hired him." Ben looked at Hampton.

"Why did you hire somebody to investigate my wife?" Ben asked with a very puzzled look on his face. "Ben, I knew Belinda at another time in my life." Hampton cleared his throat. "It appears that I am her biological father."

"How and why do you know that?" Ben's body language became tense and confrontational. The bishop spoke up. He told Ben that part of the story starting with Hampton thinking he knew Belinda and hiring the private investigator. He stopped short of telling him the result of the investigation. Lee knew he had to tell him, but he had to say it right.

"The PI got a copy of your mother's death certificate and Belinda's mother's death certificate. They died on the same day in the same accident." Ben's eyes widened. He was staring at Hampton.

Bishop Robinson continued, "I'm sorry to tell you this, but Shona . . . uh . . . Belinda's mother caused the accident that killed your mother."

"You don't know what you're talking about!" Ben was on his feet. Tears were in his eyes. Bishop Robinson stood and put his hand on Ben's shoulder.

"It's true, son. I checked it out myself." Hampton looked at Lee. He was offended, but he shouldn't have been. He should have expected a man like Lee Robinson to substantiate any kind of claim that affected so many people.

"Ben, Shona was my high school girlfriend, and she got pregnant my sophomore year in college." Hampton recounted the rest of the story. Ben had not really said anything, but he was obviously upset.

After a few minutes, Ben stopped pacing the room and sat down. Very calmly and quietly, he asked a few questions. "So according to what you know, the woman I love more than life itself—my wife, the mother of my children—is your daughter?" Hampton looked Ben in the eyes.

"Yes, I'm almost 100 percent sure she is."

"But you're basing that on what somebody told you thirty-plus years ago."

"That and the timing—it all adds up," Hampton said.

Ben turned his attention to Lee. "And you want me to believe that my mother was killed by my wife's mother."

"As farfetched as it sounds, it's true," Lee said.

"Why couldn't you two just keep this to yourself? This information doesn't serve any good purpose," Ben said as he looked disgusted and distraught.

"Ben, I hope we can work through this, and I can have a relationship with my daughter, son-in-law, and grandchildren."

"You cannot be serious! A relationship! No way! Stay away from my family. Our lives are great, and I intend for it to stay that way."

"Son, your grandmother and Belinda need to know about this," Bishop Robinson interjected.

"Why?" Ben asked.

"They should have the information and make their own decisions about what to do with it."

"Hell no! Grammy nor Belinda will ever know about any of this." He looked at Hampton.

"You are not gon' mess up my family 'cause you weren't about your situation and didn't handle business when you had a chance."

The three of them went back and forth, but Ben was relentless. He had to go home. He knew Belinda was waiting for him; he knew Grammy would have something for him to do. He wanted to talk to Enoch; he wanted to hug his daughters. His head was spinning. He had not heard the last couple of things Lee or Hampton said. "I've spent as much time on this as I am going to. This information does not leave this room," Ben said as he prepared to leave.

"Ben, I think we should come up with a plan." Hampton was trying to get Ben to stay awhile longer.

"The plan is you stay away from my family."

Ben looked at Bishop Robinson. "Sir, thank you for running interference on this, but I'm going to get my family. We're going back to Landridge and back to business as usual."

CHAPTER SIXTY-FIVE

Anderson was pretty amused that Jackson had been home the last two Thursdays right after his haircut. He didn't know if their talk prompted the change, and he didn't care. He only cared that Jacksa and Min were happy. Jackson noticed that Anderson had been around a lot. One evening, he came in, and Anderson was there without Jacksa. He wasn't sure what Anderson was up to, but Min and Jacksa were totally impressed with him.

The Friday JJ came home from school on break, Jackson got off a little early. He called Min to tell her to get ready so they could all go out to eat.

"Oh, honey, the guys went shopping, and they have planned to grill."

"What guys?" Jackson asked somewhat annoyed.

"JJ and Anderson!" Min said cheerfully.

"He's there again? Why?"

Min laughed. "He is a part of our family Jack."

"No, he's not. I told you I don't want the guy around my daughter."

"And I told you, that's not your decision," Min said matter-of-factly. "Now stop and get a bottle of wine for me and Jacksa."

Jackson was really ticked off. He truthfully didn't want Jacksa to be with a police officer, now FBI agent. But he was even more uncomfortable because he knew Anderson had something to hold over his head. He would make sure JJ knew how he felt.

He couldn't say much to Jacksa. He didn't want her to be angry with him, and he definitely didn't want Anderson to confirm her suspicions.

Jackson got an e-mail at work reminding him "they" needed to talk about the plans for the birthday trip. He didn't respond for a couple of days, and when he did, the response simply said, "I'll call you."

He didn't intend to call, and he didn't intend to go on the trip. The truth was he was through. He did miss her. She was fun, she was accommodating, and she was a distraction from his regular routine. She wasn't dependent; he didn't have to care for her. For those few hours a week they were together, she cared for him. She wasn't fragile, and he liked the way she made him feel.

When Jackson got home, JJ and Anderson were in the backyard playing basketball. Min was sitting on the deck watching. Jacksa wasn't there yet. Min was glowing. She was laughing, and she looked so beautiful. JJ being home always made her better, but he hadn't seen her like this in a while.

She noticed him watching her and motioned for him to join her. He leaned down and kissed her and took a seat beside her.

"How was your day?" she asked.

"Pretty good. How about you?"

"Wonderful! JJ got here about eleven o'clock, so we had lunch and talked and started his laundry."

"Min, he will be here for a week. He can do his own laundry between now and then."

"Don't be jealous; I'll do your laundry too," she replied laughing and patting his face. He laughed too. They chatted, and Jackson relaxed a bit. She asked about a project at work, and he told her about it. She told him she received her contract from DavisTown College for the next academic year.

"Are you going to teach next year?" he asked.

"Sure. Why not? I have one class to teach—twice a week, online. No biggie."

"Sounds good to me." Jackson knew trying to talk her out of it was fruitless, so he didn't try. But if she said she wasn't going to teach next year, it would be fine with him. As long as she was happy, that was all that mattered to him.

As Min and Jackson were talking, Jacksa came through the kitchen and out onto the deck. She waved to Anderson and JJ, hugged her parents and took a seat beside her dad.

"Glad you're here early, Daddy. I wanted the family together."

"Well, there's one person here who's not family."

"Daddy, don't start. Anderson is welcome here; and if things go according to plan, he'll always be here," Jacksa said to her dad but looking at her mom for support.

"And I second the motion," Min said, winking at her daughter.

Jackson mumbled something they didn't hear, got up from his seat, and went inside. The ladies laughed.

To add to Jackson's displeasure, when the basketball game was over, Anderson came in with his gym bag and went to the bathroom in Jacksa's old room. Jackson went back outside and made it clear to his wife and daughter that he disliked Anderson being so familiar with their home. Min just looked at him.

"Daddy, relax. Anderson is a perfect gentleman. I like him, and you need to get used to it. He isn't going anywhere, not if I can help it." Min chuckled and looked at Jackson with an I-told-you-so look.

Before Jackson could respond, JJ came out the door, being his lively, loud self. He kissed his mother and sister on their foreheads and turned to his dad in a boxing stance. JJ started a conversation with Jacksa about food preparation, and they walked away from their parents.

"You know, Dad doesn't like Anderson."

"Why?" JJ asked.

"He says it's because Anderson is a police officer."

"Well, he got no game on the court, but being a cop ain't a reason to dislike him."

"Will you please tell Daddy that?"

"Yep, no problem." Before he could continue, Anderson came out, spoke to Mr. and Mrs. Baye, and joined JJ and Jacksa.

The guys cooked under Jacksa's supervision, and dinner on the deck turned out to be a nice evening. "Man, if I get you on the court a little more, you would be a decent baller," JJ was talking to Anderson.

"Dude, you play ball for a living; I'm a humble public servant," Anderson replied. Everybody laughed. "Nobody who carries a gun for a living is humble," Jackson said. Jacksa cut her eyes at her brother. "Frankly, I'm good with the whole gun thing. I figure if my sister's hangin' out with a man and his gun, I don't have to worry about her."

"No, don't worry about her. She is in good hands," Anderson said as he touched Jacksa on her cheek. JJ continued.

"I don't usually like too many people, well, men friends of Jacksa's, but Thorn, you good people. I'm feelin' you with my sis." Jackson looked at Jacksa, and she was smiling. He had lost the battle with Min, but he thought JJ was his ally. It seemed that he had just lost the war.

Finally, Anderson and Jacksa were left on the deck alone. They were discussing JJ.

"Since your brother likes me, are you ready to meet my family?" Anderson asked smiling.

Jacksa smiled. "Yes, I am." She took a deep breath, "I am ready to meet the other women in your life."

Mrs. Rajagopal finally admitted to her husband that she made a mistake in trying to force Raja's hand. She knew she needed to fix it. She wasn't sure how without looking totally foolish.

Jill was pleasantly surprised to get Grant's call but had mixed emotions about his wanting her to meet Sunny. He told her that they were engaged. Jill agreed to see them, but her heart hurt. The call from Grant also reminded Jill she needed to get moving on awarding the proceeds from the scholarship she and Grant created in Jill's memory. After talking over the situation with her mother, they decided to have a reception and award the scholarships while Grant was in town. Mrs. Strauss offered to have it at their home, and she told Jill she would take care of the details. Jill and Grant needed to look at the scholarship application and decide who should receive the awards.

The guests would be the recipients and their families, the director of the nursing school, the foundation board, the Robinsons, the Sturdivants and the Strausses. "We can kill two birds with one stone; meet Sunny without any pressure on anybody and cover the deserving students' education," Ellen said to Jill. "Mom, you always make things so easy. Thank you."

Jill didn't want to meet Sunny for the first time at the reception, so she invited her and Grant to dinner. Grant needed to see LaLa anyway.

CHAPTER SIXTY-SIX

Hampton was back in Landridge, but he was not totally satisfied with the result in Hattiesville. His expectations had been somewhat unrealistic, thinking Ben would just accept him. He was in denial that Ben wouldn't be upset about his mother. He didn't really consider what emotions would be dredged up; especially the massive emotion to find out your wife's mother killed your mother. Hampton's thought process was very selfish. Lee Robinson advised Hampton to give Ben some time, and he promised to talk with him in a few days.

Hampton didn't go to church the Sunday following their meeting, but he couldn't just avoid Ben. So he would go this Sunday. Plus, he wanted to see Belinda. He wanted to look at her. She was his daughter, and she was carrying his grandchildren; and the girls, he wanted to get to know them. They had lost enough time. But speaking of daughters, Hampton decided to tell April the whole story. He could only pray that April would embrace the news, and that one day she and Belinda would be sisters, and they would all be a family.

Hampton and April shared a home. She lived on the second floor, and he lived on the first floor. She had a private entrance from the garage. April designed the house herself. She said it was perfect for two dating adults. The formal areas were on the first floor. They entertained there especially on the holidays. Hampton was sitting in his den thinking about having Christmas there with his daughters, his grandchildren, and son-in-law. He would invite Belinda's sister, Kirby, and her family, and Ben's grandmother and aunt. But it had to start with April. In the midst of his thoughts, he heard the garage door open.

Hampton opened his door to the garage. "Hey, girl."

"Hey, Daddy."

"Can you come back down here for a few minutes after you get settled?"

"Sure. Are we working?" she asked.

Hampton chuckled. "No, not this time." About fifteen minutes later, April came downstairs and into the den. She knew something was bothering him. He was listening to jazz, his thinking music. Otherwise, its was old R&B. Motown was his favorite, and he would be singing.

April sat Indian style on the sofa, looking at Hampton sitting in his recliner. "Where are you and Mrs. Coffey on the plans for their house?" he asked casually.

"I submitted the plans to the contractor for review day before yesterday. I expect them back by the end of the week. Why, I thought we weren't working."

"No, we're not. I just asked. I need to tell you about a situation that involves them." He took a deep breath and blew it out slowly.

"When I first met the Coffeys, I was totally intrigued by Belinda. There was something familiar about her. I just couldn't take my eyes off her."

"Daddy! Do I really want to hear this?"

Hampton didn't respond to April's question; he just kept talking. "I thought about her constantly." April put both feet on the floor and was staring at her dad with her arms folded. "So I hired a private investigator to find out who she is and find out some stuff about her and Ben. What he told me stunned me." She unfolded her arms and had both hands under her chin, but she didn't take her eyes off her dad. Hampton let the footrest down on the recliner. He leaned forward, looked at the floor, and then looked up at April without moving his head. He told her about the birth certificate and the death certificates. April was perfectly still, and her eyes were widening with each word.

She interrupted him. "So what are you saying exactly?"

"April, Belinda Coffey is my daughter. She's your sister."

Hampton went on to tell April everything he knew about Belinda and his relationship with Shona. April listened without interrupting him, but a dozen questions were running through her mind. Hampton told her about his and Lee's conversation with Ben and how he reacted. "This situation has consumed my thoughts since I found out."

"That's why you've been so distracted?" April finally said something.

"Yeah, I guess so," Hampton said quietly.

"So I guess Belinda doesn't know."

"I doubt it," Hampton answered.

"Ben was adamant about not telling her or his grandmother, well, not telling them Shona caused the accident that killed his mother."

"Daddy, do you know how insane this is?" April got up and walked around the sofa. "Oh my god! This is unbelievable! What are you going to do?" She sat in a chair closer to him.

"I don't know, baby. I just don't know."

"Belinda Coffey is my sister. That is absolutely amazing." She was shaking her head. "Our family has grown tremendously in a short period," April said to her dad.

"I just hope Belinda wants to be family," Hampton said quietly.

"How can she not?" April asked. "Once she knows all the details, she will love you, Daddy. Don't worry, she's a reasonable person."

"Yeah, but is she going to take on her mother's part in all this? How is this situation going to affect her relationship with Ben?" Hampton asked her.

"You have to let them work that out. You can be supportive, but you can't fix that for them."

"How do you really feel about having a sister after all these years?"

"Daddy, to be perfectly honest, I'm feelin' some kinda way about it! I haven't ever had to share you. Now there's a sister and grandchildren. I'm not sure how I feel, but I'm sure I'll adjust. I have to. You know me, I play the hand I'm dealt."

CHAPTER SIXTY-SEVEN

Cicely and Clay had a long talk about the sleeping arrangements when Sunny and Grant got there. Clay was sure they would stay at Gretchen's house, and they wouldn't have to worry about it. Cicely and Clay weren't going to spend a night at their new house until they were married, and Cicely wasn't particular about anybody else staying there either.

Sunny was a little uneasy about the visit. She was fine with meeting Grant's parents and his twin sister Gretchen but not so much the extended family and the whole scholarship presentation for Leah. She had to suck it up. She was going to marry Grant, and they all needed to put Leah to rest and embrace her.

Sunny carefully chose everything she planned to wear while she was there, even down to the accessories. She wasn't Leah; she wasn't competing with Leah. This would be the last hoorah for Leah. She hoped.

They were greeted at the airport by Gretchen and Clay. Sunny was glad Clay was there; he lessened the tension. Gretchen did greet her with a hug, so that was a good start. The thirty-minute ride from the Charlotte airport to Hattiesville left Sunny out of the conversation for the most part, but she was fine with that.

After getting settled at Gretchen's house, their first stop was Grant's parents' home. They were having dinner with Jill and Raja afterward. Paul and Grace Sturdivant were wonderful. They both greeted Sunny with a hug. "Mr. and Mrs. Sturdivant, it is my pleasure to meet you," Sunny said smiling.

"It's our pleasure darling. Welcome to our home and our family," Paul said.

Grace took Sunny into the den to show her pictures of Grant when he was young. The first picture she saw was an eleven-by-seventeen-inch picture of a beautiful bride. It had to be Leah. Sunny realized at that moment she had never seen a picture of Leah. She looked nothing like Sunny pictured her. Grace was talking, but Sunny's eyes were fixed on Leah's picture. The sound of Grant's voice brought her out of her trance.

"Ma, did you show her my picture in mid-air over the hurdle?" Grant asked as he came in behind his father in the wheelchair. Sunny turned around and focused on Grant.

"Oh Lord! Here Sunny. This is what he's talking about." Grace handed Sunny a picture in a frame.

They walked around and looked at pictures as Grant and Paul told stories. None of them seemed to notice the many pictures of Leah; nobody but Sunny. It was a good visit, but the ghost of Leah was lingering.

By the time they arrived at Raja and Jill's townhome, Sunny had recovered. She was looking forward to meeting Jill. Raja and LaLa answered the door. Jill was a few feet behind them just standing there. When Grant walked in, he lifted Jill off her feet and spun her around. She laughed like a little girl. And because she was laughing, LaLa laughed and clapped her hands. When Grant put her down and introduced Jill to Sunny, they shook hands. As they walked from the foyer to the great room, Sunny noticed a picture of Jill and Leah on the credenza and a smaller version of the same picture she saw at the Sturdivant's—Leah in her wedding gown. The Leah ghost was everywhere.

LaLa and Raja were dancing so the conversation turned to her. "She's so pretty, Jillie," Grant said. Jill told him that LaLa was starting preschool two or three days a week "depending on my schedule."

"Yeah, Jill was torn up the first day because LaLa didn't cry!" Raja laughed.

"I don't blame Jill. I would want my baby to be a little unhappy that I was leaving her," Sunny said, needing to join the conversation.

"I know the very independent Jillian Strauss didn't expect to have a daughter that would be a crybaby,"

Grant said mockingly. Raja handed Sunny a glass of wine and said, "You're right, and Leah Rajagopal is her mother's child."

"Leah!" Sunny didn't realize she said it out loud until they all looked at her. "I didn't know her name was Leah. I thought it was Lola."

"It's Leah Lola. My brother gave her the nickname LaLa," Jill explained.

Sunny was embarrassed and ready to go home. She didn't know how much more Leah she could take.

Just as Jill sat some appetizers on the table Sunny's phone rang. It was Cicely. She walked away from the others long enough to tell Cicely about all the pictures of Leah. "Remember, Sunny, he was with her for years. Those pictures have been there for years; they probably don't even notice them anymore."

"But the baby's name is Leah!" Sunny whispered.

"Oh, I don't think I knew that!" Cicely said. Grant walked into the hall where Sunny was standing. "It's Cicely," Sunny said to him.

"Okay. Tell Clay we'll hook up with them in the morning." Sunny took that as her signal she needed to get off the phone.

She took a deep breath and walked back in to the dining room. As the evening progressed Sunny relaxed a bit. Jill was cordial, Raja was engaging, LaLa was entertaining, and Grant was his attentive, loving self. He wasn't any different toward her because Jill was there. Sunny felt guilty for thinking he would be.

After they ate and talked for a few minutes, LaLa got restless, so Raja left the room to get her ready for bed. Jill and Grant were talking and he showed her Sunny's engagement ring. "It's very pretty Sunny. Congratulations," Jill said to her.

"Thank you Jill." Grant was still holding Sunny's hand.

"Have you set a date?" Jill asked looking at Grant.

"Not a firm date, but we should be able to while we're here," he answered. Raja called Jill from down the hall. When she left the room, Sunny looked at Grant with a sadness in her eyes.

"What is it, babe?"

"We'll talk later." She smiled a little. He kissed her just as Jill walked back into the room.

"Oh get a room!" Jill said smiling. They all laughed.

"Tell me about this 'soiree' tomorrow night," Grant said to Jill.

"Me too," Raja said as he rejoined them.

"It doesn't take long to put her down," Sunny said to Raja.

"Depending on the day," he said. She was hoping the conversation would move to the baby, but it didn't. Jill went on to explain the plan for the evening.

"My mom is going to make the presentation" Jill said as she got up from the sofa. She went to the desk, got a folder, and gave it to Grant. They talked over the applications and decided to award smaller scholarships to all four applicants rather than choosing just two.

"Why is your mom making the presentation rather than you?" Grant asked Jill. Sunny swallowed hard. "I can't do it. I'm not ready."

"Jillie, what would Leah say?" She didn't say anything. Sunny noticed Raja rubbing her back. "Jill, it's been three years. I want you to make the presentation, and I know that's what Leah would want too. You were her best friend." Tears were rolling down her face, but she still didn't say anything.

"Why don't you do it together?" Sunny said to Grant.

"I will if you will," he said to Jill.

"Okay," she whispered.

Sunny and Grant left a few minutes later. Sunny was glad. She was so over the emotion. She got it— Jill and Leah were best friends; that Leah and Grant were together for years and had been engaged; and that he had loved her deeply. What she didn't get was why after all this time Jill was still crying and she wasn't sure how Grant really felt. And she had to deal with this for two more days: the scholarship presentation the next evening, church on Sunday, and meeting Leah's parents.

CHAPTER SIXTY-EIGHT

Ben had purposely not spoken with Bishop Robinson since their meeting with Hampton Josephs. But he knew that couldn't go on much longer. Belinda was working. He was going to drop the girls at the library for their summer book club, then go to his office, bite the bullet, and make the call.

Ben didn't know what he was going to say to Bishop Robinson. He replayed their meeting in his mind over and over. When he was back in Landridge, he kept his family close and didn't deal with the change orders for the new church. He told Juan to handle what he could handle, and he would deal with the rest of it later. Ben knew he was prolonging the inevitable with Hampton Josephs too.

"Hello, son. How are you?"

"Hey, sir. I'm okay. How are you?"

The sound of the bishop's voice gave Ben some comfort. Lee asked about Belinda, the twins, and the "new twins." They talked about the progress on the church, but they both knew there was an elephant in the room. Lee took the lead.

"I know our last meeting has been on your mind. Have you changed how you feel?"

"No, I haven't. Not for now. I may tell Belinda one day, after the babies come, but I just don't know how this will affect her, and I'm not willing to take that chance."

"You're right, and it's understandable why you feel that way. But is it fair for you to make that decision for her?"

"Yeah, I think it is. It's my job to protect my wife, and that's what I intend to do." They talked a few more minutes, and Lee tried to make the case for Ben to tell Belinda and Grammy what he knew, but Ben's answer was an emphatic "no."

Lee sighed when his phone rang again, and he saw Hampton Josephs name on the screen. He got right to the point and told Hampton that Ben was still in the same place. He had no intention of telling Belinda. Hampton argued that she deserved to know, and while Lee agreed, he intended to honor Ben's decision.

"Lee, she's my daughter. I have her best interest at heart too."

"That may be true, Hamp, but she's been your daughter for a couple of months. She's been his wife for some years. She knows him, trusts him, and he knows her. Neither of them knows you."

"That's why I need her to know. I want—I need to tell Belinda my side of the story."

"Man, do you really expect her to embrace you, look over the situation, and have Sunday dinner?" Hampton hesitated, so Lee continued. "That's not realistic."

"Lee, I told April." Lee didn't immediately respond so Hampton kept talking. "She is a little stunned to have a sister after all these years, and she's also like the rest of us, shocked by the situation but saddened by it also."

"Does she think Belinda should know?" Lee asked.

"We didn't talk about that specifically, but she did say she expects Belinda will be okay with all this in time." They talked a few minutes more, and then Hampton told Lee he was seriously considering telling Belinda himself.

"Hamp, I respectfully ask you not to do that. Not for me but for yourself."

"For me, what—" Hampton interrupted him, but Lee kept talking.

"If you ever want to have a relationship with Belinda, don't cross Ben. She will never forgive you. They absolutely adore each other. What is it the kids say: ride or die? That's them. If you tell her and she knows Ben didn't want you to, you can forget it."

"I am her father!" Hampton said.

"And your point is what?" Lee shot back.

Hampton was silent. "One piece of advice: if you have a chance to form a relationship with her, be her friend. You're thirty years too late to be her daddy."

CHAPTER SIXTY-NINE

A friend of Janis's sent her a text message that she read three times before she believed it was real. *Grant is in town:) Saw him at the beauty shop w/ sis. Call me.* Since the whole scene in DC, Janis hadn't figured out what her next step would be. Grant being in town would certainly make that easier. She sat for a minute to decide what to do. She replied to her friend's text, saying thank you and she would call her later. One thing was for sure, she had to leave work and get her daughter settled so she could look for Grant.

She called her manager to tell him she wanted to leave a little early, and then she called her niece to see if she would watch Carmen. With that taken care of, she just had to decide how to find Grant and how to approach him when she found him.

As Janis was driving along, it dawned on her that Sunny may be in Hattiesville with Grant. She hoped not. That would cause an obstacle she didn't need. But if Sunny was there, she would just have to deal with her. "I owe Ms. Sunny anyway," she said out loud.

By the time Janis was situated, she didn't expect Grant to still be at Gretchen's beauty shop. She also didn't know if he drove to Hattiesville, so she had to just look for cars with DC tags and look for any other sign of him. She put an overnight bag in the car just in case.

Just as Janis was headed in the direction of the beauty shop, her phone rang. It was her friend with more news. "What does Grant's girlfriend look like?"

"Why?" Janis asked annoyed.

"I just saw Clay and his girlfriend and another tall, dark-skinned, very attractive lady."

Janis's heart dropped. "That's her." Janis had told her friend about her run-in with Sunny and Grant in DC. She left out the part about Sunny slapping her.

"Where were they?" Janis asked as she pulled into a store parking lot.

"Walking downtown by the courthouse."

"The courthouse! Oh my god. I hope they weren't getting a marriage license."

"Well, Grant wasn't with them. So if they were getting a license, it had to be Clay and that nurse."

"Okay, that's right."

"What are you going to do?" the friend asked.

"I'm going by the shop to see if Gretchen is there. Let me go, I'll call you back."

Janis pulled into a parking space and turned off the engine. With Sunny being in town, she would be meeting the family. That meant Grant was really serious about her.

When Janis talked to her friend again, she didn't have any more information, so Janis decided to drive by Grant's parents' house. She hit pay dirt, so she thought. As soon as she came around the corner she saw the Sturdivant's, Grant, and of course, Sunny, getting into a specially equipped van. She pulled over and stopped a few houses down the street. They were all dressed up. Janis slowly backed up so she could get away without being seen. When the van came by she was down the street. She followed the van at what she thought was a safe distance. As they were driving, Janis had a flashback of the last time she followed Grant. She and Grant had struggled over her gun. She ended up shot and spent months recuperating. But this time she didn't have a gun, but she didn't have a plan either. She would have to wing it.

She allowed a car to get between her car and the van. They traveled about twenty minutes toward DavisTown. She didn't know much about the area. The van made a right turn into a gated community, and the car in front of her did, too. They showed some kind of card to the man at the gate. Janis had to think fast.

"Good evening, ma'am. May I see your permit?" the guard asked nicely.

"I don't have one. I work for the caterer."

"For which event, ma'am?"

"I don't remember the name. They called me at the last minute to substitute for somebody." As she was talking, she watched the van make a left turn at the first street.

"If you let me in the gate, I will call to get the address."

"You will need to make the call from here. I can't let you in without the proper credentials. Ma'am, please move over there." He pointed to the other side of the entrance. When Janis looked in her rearview mirror, there were several cars behind her. She pulled over, out of the way of the other cars. She called her friend and told her where she was. She couldn't help. While she was sitting there, she saw Clay's car go through the gate, and then she saw Bishop Robinson's car go through the gate.

The security guard was not going to let her in, so she just pulled away and decided to ride around to see if there was another way to get in. A golf course and club house surrounded the sides and back of the community. Janis was crushed. She was so close but so far away.

She thought about her next move. Any event they all would attend was going to be at least two hours, especially since they were all dressed up. Grant looked so handsome in his suit. She couldn't just sit there for two hours so she decided to go to the mall. It would be very easy to spend two hours there.

CHAPTER SEVENTY

Everybody that was expected to be there was there. The caterers were serving hors d' oeuvres and beverages, and the guests were mingling. As usual, Ellen left no stone unturned. Kirby and Enoch Casebier were there to represent Belinda and Ben. Belinda and Leah were been good friends. Leah taught at the nursing school during the time Belinda was there. Ben didn't want Belinda and the girls to make the trip without him, but he couldn't get away. Tara and Robert were there too, mainly to support Jill. Sunny was glad Cicely was there. Grant had been pretty quiet all afternoon, so she just let him be. The Sturdivants were very cordial to her. So had everyone else she'd met. Grant introduced her to several people as his fiancée, and they all congratulated them.

After dinner, Jill asked for everybody's attention. She thanked them for being there and explained why they had gathered. "As you all know, Leah Robinson was my very best friend. We met in middle school and were like sisters. I was absolutely devastated when she passed, and it has taken me every minute of the last three years to make peace with it. When Grant presented the idea to me to do something special to honor her memory through the foundation, and gave me the check to get it started, my emotions were mixed. I wanted to honor my sister-friend, but I didn't want to deal with the reality of the situation." She got choked up as she was talking. "But God is so wonderful, and I relied on Him to get me through those rough days." An echo of "amen," "yes," and "that's right" went through the room.

"So we are here tonight to present the first Leah Robinson Scholarship to the nursing school at Charlotte Memorial Hospital School of Nursing." Everyone clapped as she cleared her throat.

"I want to ask Grant Sturdivant to join me." He moved from beside Sunny to stand beside Jill. She handed him the microphone. He just stood there for a few seconds. Sunny's heart was pounding.

"Good evening everybody. When I asked Jill to create a memorial for Leah, I didn't intend to have to say anything. I wanted her to handle it!" The guests laughed. "Jill said she was devastated; well I was triple that. I couldn't imagine living without Leah. I didn't want to live without her." Grant looked up and saw his mother and Leah's mother holding hands, and both were wiping tears. He knew they needed to get this over with. "I moved to Washington DC, as Leah and I planned, to my dream job, but without the love of my life. I went brokenhearted and barely able to put one foot in front of the other. But like Jill said, God is wonderful. I walked into an office for a lady to help me do some paperwork, and she became a good friend. Who would have thought lightning would strike twice in the same place in my heart." He patted his chest. "Now that friend is my true love." He pointed to Sunny. All eyes were on her. She smiled. He winked at her. "Thank you Sunny for being here to support me." She nodded and smiled slightly. "And she agreed to marry me, so I'm feeling pretty good about myself." They all laughed. He gave the microphone back to Jill.

She told how they arrived at the decisions they made, gave each of the four recipients letters indicating how much money was going to the nursing school on their behalf, and had each of them make brief comments. Then Ellen joined the two of them to tell the guests how they could contribute to the fund to increase the scholarships for next year.

The evening went well, even better than Jill expected. Sunny was pleasantly surprised at how it turned out. Jill was cordial to her, but still a little cool. All the other people she met were warm and friendly. Much to Sunny's surprise, meeting Leah's family went extremely well. Her parents and sister hugged Sunny and congratulated her on the engagement and told her what a great guy Grant was.

Paul was getting tired, so Grace was ready to leave, but she knew Grant couldn't leave until all the guests were gone. Clay told his aunt that he would see about Grant and Sunny, and he and Cicely helped them to the van. When they pulled away, Cicely and Clay walked back up the driveway holding hands. He stopped walking and pulled her into his arms. They held each other tight and then kissed. Cicely knew what he was getting ready to say, but she didn't want to hear it.

"Cicely, if something happens to me . . ."

"Clay, please don't . . ."

"No, listen to me. I want you to fall in love again, get married, and move on."

"Clayton Sturdivant, I love you with my whole heart. I cannot imagine being in love with anyone else."

"But, baby, you deserve to be loved, so promise me you will."

"If you promise me the same thing," she said.

"You first," Clay said, looking directly in his eyes.

"I promise," she said.

"I promise too." Clay said.

CHAPTER SEVENTY-ONE

The two hours seemed to pass quickly, and Janis headed back to the neighborhood where she followed Grant and his family. It was quiet. The guard was in the booth, but no cars were coming or going. She parked across the street from the entrance and waited. After about thirty minutes, cars started coming out, but none of which she recognized. A few more minutes passed, and she decided she had missed them. Very disappointed, she started her car and pulled away. Just as she pulled into traffic, she saw Bishop Robinson's car, but she couldn't turn around for about fifty yards. She made the U-turn, but she didn't see anybody else she knew. She gave up after about ten minutes and decided to go home. As she drove down the interstate and passed the exit to the home of Grant's parents, she decided to drive by. When she did, there was nothing to see. The van was in the driveway, and the house looked quiet. She had missed them.

As she rode home, she had an idea. She called her friend. "Let's go to Hattiesville Community Church on Sunday."

"You can't be serious."

"Yes, I am," Janis said and told her friend about the evening. "I know Grant is going to go to church," she said.

"You're probably right. But can you go to that church?"

"What?"

"The restraining order," the friend said.

Janis had forgotten about that. "Do you think it's still in effect?" Janis asked.

"I don't know. But are you willing to take that chance?"

Janis was willing to take the chance. If anybody stopped her, she would tell the she thought the order had expired. "Yeah, I am willing to take that chance."

CHAPTER SEVENTY-TWO

Of all days for Grammy and Auntie to have "other plans," they weren't available to watch Blake and Nicholas. Enoch said he wouldn't go; he would stay with the boys and let her go.

"No, Enoch, I want you to go too. I'll call Natalia." Kirby was sure that was a good solution.

"K, you know how I feel about that. She's a great kid and all, but she's friends with Chloe Matthews."

"Enoch, she works for the firm. I don't know if they're really friends." Enoch looked at her but didn't say anything.

"Can you trust me on this please?" Kirby asked him.

"Okay, Kirby, if you say so," Enoch said.

"Plus, sweetie, we haven't had a date night in a while. It will be good for us to be out without the boys, and I want both of us to be there to support Grant. You know how important this is to Belinda." Kirby put her arms around Enoch's waist as she talked.

"Oh, you tryin' to seduce me to get what you want!"

"Is it working?" she asked with a smile.

Natalia was glad Kirby called. She needed the money, she wasn't busy, but the best thing was she had gained Kirby's confidence. Pretty soon she would ask if she could take the boys for an outing to the park. That's when she would let Chloe know to come see them; come see Nicholas for herself. Natalia noticed Chloe hadn't said much about him lately. *Maybe she has given up on seeing him*, Natalia was thinking, *but not if I can help it*.

When Chloe's phone alert sounded, she just glanced at it. She brought work home and was right in the middle of it. She noticed a picture so she picked it up. When she saw Natalia's name she unlocked the screen. Natalia sent a video. It was Nicholas and Blake. The video was a full minute. Most of it was Nicholas. Chloe watched it twice and then texted Natalia to say thank you. She went back to her work for a few minutes before the tears clouded her eyes. One, two tears dropped on to her laptop keys. She pushed herself away from the desk and allowed herself to cry. She had been strong as long as she could.

Chloe worked hard to keep her promise to Campbell. She stopped going to the school to watch Nicholas play, and she put away the research she was doing to try to take him away from the Casebiers. She resigned herself to the fact that they made the best decision they could at the time. And as soon as they were out of school they would be married and have more children, lots of children. She knew she would never replace Nicholas, but she could fill the hole in her heart.

CHAPTER SEVENTY-THREE

Kathy shipped most of her things, and now she was finally on the road to New York. Her mother offered to drive up with her and fly back, but Kathy wanted to do this on her own. A friend told her she wouldn't need her car, but she wanted to have it, and she paid a small fortune for a parking space.

The drive was long but not hard. For the first time in a long time, Kathy felt free. She felt independent. She was an adult on her own again . . . finally. She had plenty of time to think. She thought about Leah and Grant and how Grant had moved on. That's all she wanted for herself, and she was a few hours from what she wanted.

Kathy also thought about Sterling. He was a great guy, just not the guy for her. Or maybe he was the guy for her but not now. She had to work her plan. Once she becomes Dr. Kathy Robinson, she would think about getting back together with him.

Things at the Coffey home were normal, and that's the way Ben intended to keep it. The girls were busy. Belinda was working a few days per week and seemed to be getting bigger day by day. Thelma was there almost every day helping around the house, helping with the girls. She had organized everything for Grammy's move and was starting to rearrange things in the house. With the plan changes to the new house, they wouldn't get to move before the babies came, so it was going to be a lot of work with four children, two of them infants.

Ben was busier than ever at the church, with the day-to-day things plus staying on top of the renovations at the new building and preparing to move. He wanted to be busy; he wanted to keep his mind off Hampton Josephs and his news. He wanted to keep his mind off the fact that his mother's fatal car crash was caused by his wife's mother. Neither of them had anything to do with any of that, but it was disturbing. His grandmother had lived without that knowledge for fifty years, why would she need it now? As far as Ben was concerned, Hampton Josephs was being selfish. He wanted to walk into Belinda's life and play daddy. "Not on my watch," Ben was thinking. "I'm not having any part of that."

As he was sitting at his desk doing more thinking than actually working, the phone rang. It was Enoch. "What's up, man?"

"Ain't much," Enoch answered Ben.

"You got a line on the tickets to the Falcons and Cowboys game?" Enoch asked.

Ben laughed. "Yeah, man. As a matter of fact, I'm waiting for a callback now. Don't sweat it. I got this."

They both laughed. "It's a one o'clock game so you coming for the weekend? You bringin' the family?" "I'm coming early Sunday morning, going back Monday, and coming solo," Enoch answered.

"How you manage that?" Ben asked.

"That will be my weekend away."

"Belinda will have a fit if you come without her sister and nephews."

"My pregnant sister-in-law will be just fine."

"I am not gon' be the one to tell her what you doin'." Ben wanted to tell Enoch what was going on but he wasn't sure he could even say it out loud. He decided right then he would tell Enoch when they went to the game.

Enoch told Ben about Grant and Sunny. "How did that go over?"

"It was all right, man. She's gorgeous and personable and smart. She's real bubbly. You know how much everybody loved Leah, you feel kinda guilty liking Sunny, but you can't help it."

How was Grant?" Enoch laughed.

"Man, dude is in love. For real in love. It's funny and different. I can see the change in him. Clay told me, but I saw it for myself and they live together."

"Grant and Sunny live together!" Ben said.

"Yep, have been for months. He did propose, so now they're getting married."

When Ben and Enoch ended their conversation, Ben realized he felt better than he had in weeks. For those few minutes his mind was off the dilemma his family was in.

CHAPTER SEVENTY-FOUR

Mrs. Rajagopal decided to write Raja a letter. She had come to the realization that having a long-distance relationship with her son and granddaughter was better than not having one at all. They only had one picture of LaLa, when she was a few weeks old. She discussed the situation with her husband and with Tara's mother. They both advised her to make peace with Raja, and her husband reminded her she had to make peace with Jill also. Mrs. Rajagopal reminded her sister-in-law that she should take her own advice and make peace with Tara too.

She worked on the letter for a week before she mailed it. It was handwritten in her perfect penmanship on her pale pink stationary.

Dear Manavendra,

How are you, my dear son? How are Jillian and Leah? Please tell Jillian I said hello, and please give Leah a hug for me. I know you are surprised to receive this letter, as we have not spoken since your father and I visited you.

I have given much thought to this, and it is important to your father and me to have a good relationship with you and your family. We want to be able to see our granddaughter, and hope, when she is older, she can come here to visit us and travel home to India with us on holiday. We shall also visit you again.

Please understand I meant no ill will toward any of you. It is just very important that our culture and heritage is maintained. The decisions you made have put that in jeopardy. You are our only child. How can your father and I have serenity in our later years unless we know our family values are intact?

I appreciate you sending pictures of your family. We have only one picture of our granddaughter. Your cousin, Yash, also says he can get you on the computer so we can see her. I hope that is acceptable to you.

Please respond to my letter. I will accept your call. I know Leah is too young to know the value of the tea set enclosed, but I want to start a collection for her. Your father also wants her to have these earrings. We hope she is enjoying her bangles and the teddy bear. I await your call.

Very truly yours,
Mother

When Delia looked at her phone and saw Clay's name on the ID, she decided not to answer. She blocked him from her cell phone; so today he was calling her at work. She snatched the phone off the hook. "Clay, what do you want?"

"Is that any way to greet an old friend?" Clay said.

"We are not friends!" Delia responded.

"Dee, why do you keep running away from me?"

"Clay, I am in love with Javier. Why can't you get that through your pathetic head?"

"Delia, you would've had sex with me if you hadn't seen Cicely's picture and realized that was her apartment. So are you really in love with him, or do you just want to be married?"

"I could ask you the same question," she responded.

"Ask me whatever you want to. I love Cicely. We are getting married in a few weeks . . ."

"Yeah, but you were going to screw around on her two weeks ago," she interrupted.

"No, I wasn't. I had no intention of having sex with you. I was trying to make a point."

Delia was fuming. "Make what kind of point?" she asked.

"That you're not ready."

"And I guess you are," Delia said. Before he could respond, she continued. "Clay, I am ready, and I am going to marry Javier. We are going to have a family together in our new home and live happily ever after. I wish the same for you. Please don't call me ever again, and I hope I never see you again. Goodbye, Clay, forever."

Clay held his phone in his hand for a minute. He was somewhat taken aback. Delia sounded like she meant what she was saying. At some point over the last few years, she had changed or grown up or something. By now, he should have been able to talk her into doing what he said.

I guess I've lost my touch, he thought to himself. *Oh well*. He shrugged.

Delia left her desk and went to the restroom. She was shaking. She was glad she stood up to Clay, but she felt guilty. Javier asked her if she heard from Clay again, and she told him no. If she really was ready to get married, why didn't she tell him the truth? Why didn't she tell Javier about the incident at the apartment? Delia was holding back tears. Maybe Clay was right. Maybe she didn't need to get married. But everything was fine until Clay started trying to distract her. Delia did cry a little. Then she looked in the mirror and took a deep breath. She wiped her face, got herself together, went back to her desk and back to work.

CHAPTER SEVENTY-FIVE

Jackson had ignored voice mail messages, text messages, and e-mails. But he was going to face the music today. After his haircut this evening, he was going to call and tell her he wasn't going away for her birthday. He hoped he wouldn't have to be mean to her. He cared for her greatly, but he loved Min, and he wouldn't put his marriage in jeopardy anymore. He knew the conversation wouldn't be easy, but they had to have it.

"Jack, that's not fair. You promised me a birthday trip. I can't believe you would renege on me. What is going on with you?"

He sighed deeply. "What's going on with me is I don't want this double life anymore. I need to make things better at home. Being away for a weekend, lying to my family about where I am, I don't like it, not gon' do it." Jackson was firm.

"Why are we having this conversation on the phone? You should come over here so we can talk about this in person," she said.

"No."

"No? Jackson!"

"No, I'm not coming over there," Jackson said. "Because you know just like I do that we won't talk; we will end up in bed. I'm going home, home to my wife."

"Jack, please don't go." Her voice was just above a whisper. "I need you, and you need me." Jackson was sitting in his car in the parking lot of a grocery store. He leaned back against the headrest, and closed his eyes. He was trying to gather his strength, but his body was betraying him. They were both silent for a minute.

"Look, I gotta go," he finally said. She didn't respond. "Are you there?"

"Yes, I'm here. Don't treat me like this. We agreed the trip would be our last time together. I made peace with that. Please don't disappoint me. I'm only going to have one fiftieth birthday."

He was melting. "For tonight, I'm going on in, but . . .,"Jackson said.

"But what?" she asked.

"But I'll reconsider the trip."

Jackson drove home disgusted with himself that he didn't stand his ground, and because he just lied again. He wasn't going to reconsider the trip, he wasn't going to call her again and he wasn't going to respond to her contact. But he still felt bad.

When Jackson got home, the house was quiet. He didn't think Min was there, but she didn't usually go anywhere without letting him know. As he walked down the hall toward the bedroom, he could see the television flicker but there was no light on.

"Min, hey, sweetie." She didn't respond. He shook her shoulder slightly. She stirred a little. He shook her again. "Honey, what's wrong?" he asked her anxiously. She tried to pull herself up in the bed, but she was too weak. Jackson turned on the light, lifted Min up and propped her against some pillows. She still hadn't said anything. "Can I get you something? What's wrong?" She wasn't responding. He decided he needed to get help. Her eyes were open, but she wasn't talking, and it appeared she couldn't focus. He didn't know whether to call 911 or take her to the hospital himself. He decided he shouldn't move her.

The paramedics arrived in about six minutes. The only change: she had closed her eyes. She appeared to be asleep again. Jackson answered all their questions, gathered her medicine, and locked the door as they put Min in the ambulance. He climbed in his heart beating rapidly. When they arrived at the hospital, they took Min into an exam room immediately. The nurse told Jackson to wait. He called Jacksa.

When Jacksa arrived, she was able to add some information. Her mom told her she had a headache and was going to take some medicine and go to bed. Based on the timeline, she was asleep at least three hours. The doctor told them he would do an MRI and a CAT scan, and would talk to them when he had the results.

While they were waiting Jacksa got a phone call. As Jackson sat there alone, he thought how much more serious this would be if he hadn't come home. At that moment, he decided to never go back to the other situation.

Anderson walked in about the same time the doctor called them into a conference room. He hung back not wanting to interfere, but Jacksa motioned for him to join them. The doctor wanted to keep Min for a couple of days for observation, but he felt sure she was experiencing an exacerbation of the multiple sclerosis.

"I did see a few new lesions on her brain," the doctor said. She had been well for so long. The doctor also wanted to know if there were any changes in her life and reminded them that stress was a negative in her situation. Anderson didn't look at either Jacksa or her father. Jacksa spoke up.

"My mom has been really happy at home, but I think she's teaching too many classes."

"She told me she only plans to teach one class next semester," Jackson added.

"That may or may not be it," the doctor said. Jackson tried to swallow the lump in his throat.

They talked a little more, and the doctor told Jackson he could see Min for a few minutes. He was anxious to see her, and so thankful he went home when he did.

CHAPTER SEVENTY-SIX

On Sunday morning, Janis and her friend arrived at Hattiesville Community Church a little late to assure they would be directed to the balcony. They were able to sit where they had a pretty good view of the lower sanctuary. Janis saw Grant. He was sitting with his family, and of course, Sunny was with him. Now that Janis saw Grant, she didn't know what she was going to do. She simply wanted a private moment with him. Everybody was there—Grant's parents, his sister, Clay, and Cicely. It was going to be hard to get him alone. She had to though. There was no way she could let him marry Sunny.

It seemed to Janis the service was really long. When it was finally over, she and her friend stayed in their seats until they could see which way Grant was going. There were a dozen people waiting to speak to him. He introduced many of them to Sunny, and she noticed a couple of them looking at her hand. "Oh, my god. She's wearing an engagement ring!" Janis felt sick. Finally, Sunny and Cicely walked away with Gretchen and Grant's mom. Grace had her arm around Sunny. Clay and Grant went out a different way behind his father in the wheelchair. Janis and her friend walked downstairs to the side of the building, where the wheelchair vans were parked. Her friend stood back, and Janis slowly approached the men.

"Grant, how are you?"

He turned around. His smile faded when he saw her standing a few feet away.

"Janis, where did you come from?" He was annoyed, and it showed.

"I want to talk to you for a minute," she said.

Clay also turned around to see her standing there. "You just like getting your butt kicked, don't you?" Clay said. "Sunny 'bout gave you a beat down already. Don't you learn?"

She was embarrassed that Clay knew what happened in Sunny's office. Before she could respond, the ladies came out the door. There she stood, looking at Gretchen and Grace Sturdivant, Cicely, and the icing on the cake—Sunny.

Sunny's and Janis's eyes met. Sunny's first instinct was to approach her. But she thought better of it. She didn't want to act up in front of Grant's parents. Clay knew he needed to handle this. As if Gretchen was reading his mind, she took her mother's hand and led her to the van. Cicely walked over to Clay, looked at Sunny, and nodded toward Grant. Sunny walked over to Grant took his hand and walked to the van. Cicely and Clay walked toward Janis.

"I'm not here to see you, Clay I came to see Grant," she yelled.

"Janis, let's not do this. Not here, not now. You know Grant is going to marry Sunny. He doesn't want you! You have made a complete fool of yourself by showing up here like this. Have a little bit of dignity and leave," Cicely insisted earnestly.

"I don't know you, you don't know me, and you don't know what you're talking about!" Janis was still screaming.

"Yes, I do, and so do all the people in this parking lot." Janis looked around. There were lots of people just standing and watching. Cicely was holding Clay's hand. She knew her cooler head needed to prevail. Janis felt totally exposed. "All I wanted was to have a conversation with Grant. We have some unfinished business."

"Janis, I know you and Grant talked. I know he told you he is moving on and advised you to do the same. I also know you can be arrested for even being on this church property," Cicely continued.

"Now like Cicely said, have some scruples; leave without being escorted away," Clay added. She turned and walked away. Her car was on the other side of the building. As she practically ran to the car, people were looking at her, some staring, some laughing and pointing. Cicely was right. She made an absolute fool of herself, and she knew it. Her friend was driving up by the time she reached the front of the church. She jumped in the car, and they drove away quickly.

Janis screamed when she was in the car. "I can't believe Grant told Clay, and now Cicely knows all our business! I hate him!"

"Janis, you brought all this on yourself! I told you this wasn't a good idea, but you said you were willing to take the chance. You took it and blew it. Ain't no need in you hatin' Grant," her friend responded. "You don't understand. I love Grant, and he treats me like dirt."

"Grant treats you the way you want to be treated, like you crazy! The man told you a hundred times he don't want you. You tried to shoot him. But he forgave you; he didn't even press charges."

"He didn't press charges because he understands I didn't want to shoot him. I was just trying to get his attention," Janis said innocently.

"Janis, please get a grip. You need to get over Grant Sturdivant. You did it today. You humiliated yourself in front of half this town, including his whole family. And you know what, I'm done. Count me out of anymore of your Grant Sturdivant foolishness!"

CHAPTER SEVENTY-SEVEN

Kathy was walking back to her car. She was hungry. The orientation went well, but she didn't expect it to be four hours. She picked up her books and, after getting a bite to eat, intended to start previewing the books and the syllabi.

Since she moved to New York, she had talked to her mother every day and to her dad almost every day. She talked to Campbell and a few friends, but she hadn't heard from Sterling. She thought he would call to make sure she was settled.

On her way into the apartment, Kathy checked the mail. She wasn't expecting anything, she just decided to look. There was a *Sports Illustrated* magazine addressed to someone she guessed was the previous tenant. On the cover of the magazine, one of the feature headlines said, "College Football Preview." She opened the magazine to see if there was any mention of DavisTown College. She didn't really expect them on the list; she was just looking for fun. To her amazement, DavisTown College was listed and projected at preseason to be number two in their conference. She was surprised. But not only was DavisTown listed in the top ten, there was an article about the head coach, Sterling Chance.

There was a picture of Sterling dressed in a red, black and white DavisTown T-shirt, a baseball cap, and his whistle around his neck. He was so handsome. Kathy read the article twice. It talked about him being an all-American at DavisTown and his time in the pros. The article talked about his statistics in college and at the pro level. And that the expectation was for him to coach at the professional level one day.

She sat and looked at his picture for a while. She thought about when they first met, and when they reconnected, and the time they spent together. Then she thought about how she left things between them. She missed Sterling. She really missed him.

Jill took the mail from the box and saw the package from London. She laid it on the desk for Raja to open. It was addressed to him. He told her he was going to be late. She planned to put LaLa to bed before he came in, and have a late dinner with him. They needed to talk about buying another house. They had put it off long enough. He wanted to have another baby, but there was no way they could bring another child and all the necessities that went with a baby into their townhouse. She didn't think they could endure building a house from the ground up, so she would make a couple suggestions of areas where they could look.

Trey wanted her to sell the townhouse to him, and he suggested she ask their parents to sell their home to her and Raja so they would downsize and Dr. Strauss would retire. Jill's only question to her big brother was why he wanted the townhouse. Didn't he intend to have a family one day?

"You have some important mail on the desk," Jill said to Raja after they finished dinner.

Raja walked over and picked up the box. He held it for several minutes. When he finally opened the box, he took out the tea set and earrings that were carefully wrapped so they wouldn't be damaged, and then he handed the letter to Jill.

"What do you want me to do with this?" she asked.

"You open it, you read it, and then tell me about it," Raja answered her.

Jill read the one-page letter. She was quite amused but was careful with her body language. "It's from your mom. She apologized and wants to have a 'good relationship' with your family," Jill said, moving her fingers in the quotation sign. "She wants pictures, and she wants you to call her."

"She wants me to call her?" he asked sarcastically.

Jill was quiet. She wasn't really sure how to respond. Jill didn't trust her mother-in-law, so she was unimpressed with the letter. She couldn't wait to talk to Tara.

"What are you going to do?" Jill asked Raja.

"I don't know; think about it for a couple of days." He changed the subject. "Did you ask your mom about selling the house?"

"No, should I have?" Jill responded.

Raja laughed. "I thought you and Trey had decided . . ."

"Me and Trey! That was Trey making decisions for everybody." They both laughed.

"Are you seriously interested in buying my parents' home?"

"I like it. I like the location, and it's a real house, well built and all that."

"Okay, I'll talk to them tomorrow," Jill said smiling.

"Now can we talk about having another baby?" Raja asked her smiling.

Later that night, when Jill was asleep, Raja lay in bed thinking about the letter from his mother. He didn't know what to do. He wanted to believe she was sincere, but he didn't know if he should trust her. He had a great life without his parents, and he just didn't want the tension of having to deal with them. The letter didn't say anything about them moving to North Carolina, which he never believed anyway. He knew there was no way Jill would agree to let LaLa go to London or to India with them unless she was old enough to get on a plane and come home if her grandmother changed the plan. He totally understood his parents' desire for LaLa to know about her Indian heritage, the fact was she looked like his family more than she did Jill's family.

I guess I should do a better job of making sure she knows both sides of her family, he thought to himself. *And it's up to me, not my parents, to raise my children.*

He decided to call his mother, thank her for the gifts, and accept her apology, but decline her direct involvement in the life of his family. He decided to tell her that he would take the lead on the depth of their relationship. It was settled. He went to sleep.

CHAPTER SEVENTY-EIGHT

Anderson was more excited than he had been in a long time. His grandmother, mother, aunt, and sisters were on their way to visit him and to meet Jacksa. He wasn't able to work out Jacksa meeting his sisters first. So they would all meet her at the same time. He wanted them to meet Min too, if she was up to it. She had been home from the hospital for a few days, and he visited her every day. He took her lunch and flowers and put two books on her nook.

He knew the stress of Jackson's affair made her sick. He couldn't tell Jacksa, but he could help care for her mother. They didn't tell JJ about Min being sick until she was out of the woods and he was headed home for the weekend. Jacksa was coming to Anderson's house for dinner on Saturday, and he hoped they could all go to see Min and have dinner with the Baye family on Sunday.

Anderson flipped through the mail as he was thinking. He opened the letter from the FBI. The decision was made. He would be assigned to the field office in Charlotte! "YES!" He was ecstatic. That was the best news ever. He was so sure he would have to move. He couldn't wait to tell his family, and Jacksa. Now he could do what he wanted to do—talk to Jacksa about getting married. This was amazing. Nobody started in the Charlotte office. But he definitely planned to take full advantage of the incredible opportunity.

Jackson took some time off from work to be home with Min. He was perturbed that Anderson stopped by every day, but he didn't say anything. Min was pretty quiet, but it was obvious she was better. The nurse came daily to give her intravenous steroid treatments. She hated the needles, but tolerated it so she could get stronger. The following week, the physical therapist would come for a few sessions.

Min wanted Jackson to go back to work. He was hovering. She knew he felt guilty about her getting sick and she was sure he thought his affair was the reason. In a way, she wanted him to feel guilty, but it wasn't his fault she wasn't a wife to him.

When Jackson walked in the room, Min was on the phone and she was laughing. "I don't know about that. I'll have to talk with Jackson, but I'll think about it for sure." He was hoping that wasn't Anderson and another of his bright ideas. He was getting really sick of Detective Thorn. Jackson hoped he was going to be assigned a long way away so he would be out of Jacksa's life for good, and Min's life too, for that matter.

"What's so funny?" Jackson asked her. He sat down beside her, pulled her into his arms and kissed her forehead.

"That was my friend who volunteers at the animal shelter. She was telling me she received a call about a dog she thinks we should adopt."

"A dog?" Jackson repeated.

"That's what I said," Min laughed.

"It's a three-year-old German shepherd 'with special skills,' she tells me."

"What does that mean?" he asked. Min went on to tell Jackson the dog is owned by a family with a special needs child. "She says the dog is specially trained to be an attendant."

"Hmmm," was Jackson's response. "Why are they getting rid of him?"

"She said it was confidential, but she assured me there isn't a problem with the dog." He knew Min's friend had good intentions. She was one of the few people who knew what happened the night Min went to the hospital. They talked about it, and Jackson actually thought it was a good idea. After a little more discussion, they decided to bring the dog home for a trial.

CHAPTER SEVENTY-NINE

Jill left Raja and LaLa at the kitchen table eating oatmeal. He was going to take her to day care. He tried to do that at least once a week. Jill was good with having another baby. Raja did his share around the house and with their daughter.

As soon as Jill was out of the garage, she called Tara.

"She did what?" Tara was laughing. "Oh my god, she has lost her mind! What did Raja say?"

Jill told Tara about their conversation. "But I think he'll accept her apology," Jill told Tara.

"He probably will, but he won't have anything to do with her. He knows he can't trust her," Tara replied.

"Hello, Mother."

"Manavendra, oh my, I am so glad to hear from you!" Mrs. Rajagopal said loud enough for her husband to hear her. He put down his newspaper and came close to the telephone.

"Thank you for LaLa's gifts. Jill put the tea set in the china cabinet and the earrings in the jewelry box. We'll let her wear them on a special occasion."

"I am really happy you like the gifts and glad you called," his mother said.

"Mother, I read your letter and I appreciate you sending it."

"My dear son, I hope you . . ."

"Mother, please allow me to finish. I accept your apology, but I need you to follow my lead on your relationship with my family."

"What do you mean?"

"You can't expect Jill to just warm up to you based on our history. Just let me handle this, and you respond." She let out a heavy sigh and gave the telephone to her husband.

"Hello, son."

"Father, how are you? I know Mother gave you the telephone so you can try to change my mind." "What did you tell her?" Mr. Rajagopal asked.

Raja repeated what he said to his mother. His father agreed with him, thanked him for accepting the apology, and ended the conversation.

"Why did you agree with him?" Mrs. Rajagopal was very unhappy with her husband.

"Because doing things your way is how we ended up in this situation in the first place. We must be glad he called at all."

After Jill and Tara talked about Tara and Robert coming to Hattiesville for the Labor Day weekend, they hung up, and Jill called her mother to see if she was free for lunch. Ellen was available, so they made a date.

When she arrived at the office, there was a bouquet of flowers and a card. It was from Grant and Sunny. The note thanked her for a "beautiful event to honor Leah." Jill held the note for a minute and fixed her eyes on the signature. *How dare he sign the card with her name*, she thought and then felt bad as soon as it crossed her mind. Leah died three years ago, and everybody had moved on, except her. Even Leah's parents were cordial, actually friendly, to Sunny. Jill knew she needed to let it go and honor Leah's memory and not be angry with Grant. He wasn't doing anything he shouldn't do. By all accounts, Sunny was a great person. There was just something about her that Jill didn't like.

When Ellen and Jill met for lunch, she told her mother about the flowers and about how she felt.

"Jill, honey, that bitterness doesn't serve any purpose. You have to move on."

"I know, Mom, but it still hurts."

"How do you think Leah would feel if she knew how you're acting?"

"Glad to know I was protecting her interest."

Ellen looked at her daughter very seriously. "Jillie, you need to talk to somebody if you are still holding on to this. It's been long enough."

Jill didn't like what her mother said, so she changed the subject.

"Would you and Dad consider selling Raja and me your house?" Ellen looked puzzled, and then she smiled.

"What makes you think we want to sell our house?"

"Trey told me you were talking about downsizing."

Ellen laughed. "You sound like you did when you were growing up—believing what your brother told you! But this time it's true. We're considering it, and if you're serious, I will talk to your dad, and we will let you know."

"I'm serious. We are finally going to buy another house," Jill said to her mother rolling her eyes.

"What made Raja finally decide?" Ellen asked.

"He wants to have another baby, and I told him we couldn't seriously talk about it unless we had more space."

"Another baby, how exciting!"

"Not yet, Mom. I want a house first."

"I will talk to your dad tonight!" After a few minutes of talking about other things, Jill told her mother about the gifts and the letter from Raja's mother. Ellen was pretty amused, but she advised Jill to stay out of it, and let Raja and his parents work it out.

CHAPTER EIGHTY

When Clay and Cicely arrived at Lola's Restaurant for dinner with the family, everybody wanted to know what happened at the church with Janis.

"My baby handled it!" Clay said, putting his arm around Cicely's waist. When they had a private moment, Clay told Grant and Sunny what he and Cicely said to Janis and that she left without incident.

As the family started to leave, Cicely and Clay decided to have dessert. They finished and left the restaurant after everybody else. As they walked to the car, they practically walked into Delia.

"Hello, Clay. How are you? You must be Cicely," Delia said smiling.

"Cicely, this is Delia."

"Hi, Delia," Cicely said.

"Clay, I've seen so much of you lately—at Jeremy's game, at lunch, and oh yeah, at Cicely's apartment."

Cicely looked at Clay but didn't say anything. Clay looked at Cicely.

"The day I moved your stuff, Delia and some friends were in the complex too," Clay said casually.

Cicely's body language relaxed just a bit. "Right, we went out to celebrate my cousin's birthday, and then I accepted Clay's invitation to come back."

Cicely was looking at Delia. So was Clay. He wanted her to stop talking. He put his hands on Cicely's back to move her past Delia. But she didn't move. Delia kept talking.

"I know I shouldn't have come back, but I did. There's something about your fiancée I can't resist." Delia was smiling.

"Dee, let it go. Why you want to start some mess?"

"I'm not starting anything, Clay. But I intend to stop something. I want you to stop calling me, stop showing up at my job."

"Delia, why are you doing this?"

"Doing what? Telling Cicely who the man she's going to marry really is!"

"Delia, why would you lie?"

At that point, Delia got angry. She hadn't intended to say anything else, but Clay saying she was a liar was too much.

"Clay Sturdivant, you know I am not lying! Cicely, he asked me to come back. I said no, but I went back to set him straight."

For a minute, Clay and Delia were trying to out talk each other. Delia was talking directly to Cicely, and she was listening. "He started pulling my pants down, and then I saw the picture of you and him in the white outfits, and I stopped him and left."

Cicely's heart was pounding, and she was about to cry. Delia said enough for Cicely to believe her. The life she had, the life she thought she would have, was over. She felt like she was going to throw up. Cicely walked toward the car. She heard Clay saying something to Delia, and then he called her name. She reached the car first. He came to her door to open it. She got in without saying anything. As soon as he closed his door, he said something, but Cicely didn't hear what he said.

"Take me to my car please."

"Baby, please look at me. Let's talk about this. I made a bad . . ."

"Take me to my car, Clay. Now!" she screamed at him, and the tears came at that moment. She was looking straight ahead. He was still talking, but she tuned him out.

Her car was at his house. When he pulled into the driveway, she got out of the car before he turned off the ignition. He jumped out and tried to stop her. She got in her car and blew the horn so he would back out of the driveway. He moved his car, and she sped away.

CHAPTER EIGHTY-ONE

JJ couldn't believe his eyes. Standing in his mother's kitchen was a dog, a beautiful German shepherd but a dog nonetheless. That was a big surprise. The woman who made him take his shoes off before coming into her house had an animal in the house. My, how things had changed!

The dog, whose name was King, had perfect posture, standing or sitting. JJ was pretty amused. Min and Jackson brought the dog home on a trial basis three days before, and Min was pretty sure she wanted to keep him. Jackson liked him because he growled at Anderson.

The house was abuzz because JJ was home, and Anderson told them that he is being assigned to the Charlotte FBI office. Jackson couldn't believe it. He thought this new job would be the way to get Anderson out of their lives. Anderson also asked Min about bringing his family to visit her on Sunday. "Yes, of course," Min said. She gave JJ and Jacksa instructions for the things she wanted done around the house. Anderson insisted his family would prepare the meal. JJ was "all in" and told Anderson he was especially looking forward to meeting his sisters!

It was Thursday, and Jackson ignored her phone calls all day. He went to the barber shop and decided to return the call when he finished.

"Hi, Jack. Thank you for calling me back."

"What's up?" His response was dry.

"I really miss you, and I need to see you," she said.

"Look, we've been through this. I'm not coming over."

She was quiet. "Okay, Jackson. Bye." She hung up.

He felt good about standing his ground.

Ben actually took his Monday off. Belinda went to work and the girls slept over at Carlotta's house. It was seldom he was home alone. There were some things he needed to do around the house, and he wanted to have a talk with his ladies when they got in.

He had a productive day and was looking at the church calendar and their family calendar when Juan and Carlotta dropped off Brianna and Brittani. They brought in the mail, and there was a packet of information addressed to each of them from their school. It was their class schedules, reading lists, writing lists, a script for Brianna, and music for Brittani. There was information about the Parent Volunteer Association and the sixth grade class trip in the spring. The tuition invoice was in another envelope addressed to Ben and Belinda. Ben opened it and braced himself. It wasn't quite as bad as he thought. Then it occurred to him that in a few years, they would be in college, and the younger twins would be in school. Thank God for Grammy. That thought reminded him; he and Belinda had another ultrasound appointment the next day. *Maybe we'll know if we're having boys or girls*, he thought to himself.

Later in the evening, they went over their respective calendars. Ben added his portion to the discussion. The renovations on the building for the new church were almost done. The move-in date was the end of September. "God is so awesome!" Ben said. The girls were cheering, and Belinda looked toward heaven and said thank You. She knew how hard Ben had worked, and now he could see the fruit. Brittani was on the computer dealing with the master calendar. She and Brianna color-coded each entity—school, church, Mommy, Daddy, Grammy, and the two of them. She quickly added the church move-in date. When they were done, she would print a copy for the bulletin board and one for Thelma. Brianna told her to put one in Grammy's room; she would be there to stay in a few weeks.

Among the entries Belinda needed to add to the calendar was an appointment with April Josephs. When she mentioned April's name, Ben swallowed hard. He hadn't thought about the Josephs much in the past week or so. He and Bishop Robinson talked and it hadn't come up, so as far as Ben was concerned, it would stay between the three of them.

"Ben, I can't confirm the appointment with April unless you can be there," Belinda said.

"I'm good. Go ahead and confirm it," Ben responded. Unknowingly to the other, they were both thinking they hoped Hampton wouldn't be at the meeting.

"Mommy, can Britt and I go with you to the doctor's appointment to see the babies?" The twins were smiling, looking at their parents. Belinda hadn't considered they would want to go. She quickly looked at Ben. He smiled and shrugged slightly.

"Sure, girls. That will be fine."

"What do we have to do?" Brianna asked.

"You don't have to do anything. Any guesses on boys or girls?" Ben asked them. One said boys, one said girls.

"I think boys," Ben said.

"You hope boys!" Belinda said laughing.

When the Coffey family arrived at the doctor's office, everybody was amused including the other patients that they were expecting a second set of twins. Belinda went in for her exam first, and then the girls and Ben joined her for the ultrasound. They heard the heartbeats first, and then they saw the two little people on the screen. The girls squealed in unison. Then they were perfectly quiet, almost like they weren't even breathing.

"Well, ladies, there are your little . . . brothers!"

"Yes!" Ben said and pumped his fist.

Brianna and Brittani clapped their hands and cheered. Belinda lay there quiet, closed her eyes, and let the tears roll down her cheeks. *Thank you, God*, she said to herself. She knew Ben wanted sons, and now he would have them.

The doctor and the ultrasound technician continued to point out things to Brittani and Brianna. They asked a few questions, and then the technician printed each of them a picture. Brianna said she couldn't wait to show Grammy, and Brittani said she couldn't wait to show her friend, Carlotta.

The tech and the girls left the room while the doctor talked to Ben and Belinda. "Everything looks fine, Belinda. You are twenty-eight weeks, so I want you to carry the boys at least six more weeks. There's not a lot of space left in there for them to grow so you have to be careful." Belinda was nodding her head and smiling until the doctor made his next statement.

"You need to consider you may be off your feet for a few weeks toward the end." That was the last thing Belinda wanted to hear, but she knew it was true.

CHAPTER EIGHTY-TWO

Janis cried for two days. She called out sick on Monday. She went to work Tuesday but basically just sat in her office and did nothing. She went home and lay across the bed to watch the news. There was a live report from the airport. As the reporter was talking, the camera scanned the crowd, and there was Grant and Sunny standing in the check-in line. Janis stopped breathing. She couldn't believe, of the hundreds of people in the airport, the camera would spot them. She cried again for hours.

Grant and Sunny stayed in Hattiesville a day longer, trying to help Clay find Cicely. After a few hours of calling and riding around and not finding her, Clay called Grant to tell him what happened. Sunny called Cicely, but she didn't answer. Eventually, she did send Sunny a text message to say she was okay. Clay was a wreck. He sent a dozen texts, left a dozen messages, and kept calling. He absolutely could not believe Delia told Cicely what happened between them. He felt sick . . . literally. He knew calling Delia was a mistake and kissing her was an even bigger mistake. He really wasn't going to have sex with her. He wanted to prove to her she shouldn't marry Javier. Now it had backfired, and he was paying with his heart and with his life. He crisscrossed Wyndham where he lived and Hattiesville where the new house was. Where in the world could she be?

Cicely left Clay's house and got on the interstate. It would be easy to lose him if he was following her. She went south toward

Charlotte but got off an exit and doubled back. She went back to the house, quickly gathered some things, and left again. She drove to the traveling nurse's residence hall at the hospital in Charlotte. She didn't know if Clay would think of looking for her there, but even if he did, he couldn't get in. She wanted to turn her phone off, but she was expecting a call from her brother.

She left the bags in the trunk of the car and took only an overnight bag into the residence hall. She didn't want anybody to question her being there. She would head somewhere tomorrow; somewhere away from Clayton Sturdivant.

Cicely was numb. She hadn't really cried, but she was shaking all over. Her heart was racing. She could hear her pulse in her ears. She went in the room and closed the door. She was barely inside before she had to throw up, then the diarrhea came, then the tears. When she finally left the bathroom, she cried into her pillow for over an hour. Her phone ringing got her attention. It was finally her brother.

"Clay and I broke up, and I need you to come here to help me get my things."

"Are you okay?"

"No, and I probably won't ever be again," Cicely told her brother.

She didn't tell him the whole story, just that she found out Clay had "been seeing" his ex-girlfriend. Her brother didn't care what happened. His sister needed him—that was the only thing that mattered.

"I need to get some sleep before I get on the road. Are you good for the night?" her brother asked.

"Yes, he can't find me here. I'm going to turn my phone off, so leave me a message when you get on the road. I'll call you back."

"Okay sis, but call me back if you need to talk."

"I will. Thank you."

"No problem. You know that. Love you."

"I love you too."

Cicely's brother asked if she called their other brother. She told him no and asked him not to call either. "I will call him when we're together, and he'll l know I'm fine."

They both knew he wouldn't be rational at all about Cicely. While Cicely and her brother were talking, Clay called and texted again. Before she could turn the phone off, there was another text from Sunny. It read *Please call me. We can talk privately. I promise.* She texted back: *Not tonight!*

Clay told Grant and Sunny the whole story. "Damn man," Grant said.

"You are a fool, Clay!" Sunny told him.

"I know that Sunny. I know that." They were yelling at each other. Sunny got right in Clay's face and told him how crazy he was, called him a whore, and told him she didn't blame Cicely for leaving. Her accent kicked in, and Grant saw her other side again, like he did that day with Janis. He wasn't sure he liked that Sunny.

CHAPTER EIGHTY-THREE

Natalia was doing such a good job with the boys; she became their regular sitter. But she knew they were moving soon, and Aunt Avis would be living with them, so they may not need her as often. She needed to go ahead and set up a time for Chloe to see Nicholas. She debated whether to tell Chloe or let it be a real surprise.

"That's a game-time decision," she said to herself and laughed. That was a phrase Chloe's dad used in the office a lot.

Natalia liked knowing American jargon. She liked that she fit in. Other than her French accent, nobody knew she was from Haiti. She wore an American-girl hairstyle, clothes, and shoes like Chloe. She learned how to bargain shop, to shop at thrift stores, and she took good care of her things, especially the things Chloe gave her.

School was going to start in a few weeks. Her senior year in high school! Natalia thought a lot about going to college. The reality was that she would have to go to a local school. She wasn't a United States citizen yet so she didn't qualify for any financial aid. The Matthews were going to help her, and she was applying for scholarships, but there was no way financially that she could go away to school. Her host family was fine with her continuing to live with them, and the Matthews would let her keep her job, particularly because Chloe was going back to Atlanta for her senior year in college.

Sandra Matthews admonished Chloe and Natalia to make lists and assign timelines for what they had to do to get in law school and college, respectively. Natalia created an Excel spreadsheet right away and added a column for budget. Chloe didn't bother to do any of it; she had other things on her mind.

The visit with Anderson's family went really well. Jacksa was nervous, but his mother, grandmother, and aunt put her at ease. His sisters were a little cold at first, but they warmed up as the day went along.

Anderson and his grandmother had a little private time while the others prepared the meal for the next day. He told her he wanted to talk to Jacksa about getting married. She asked a few questions and was satisfied with his answers. Her advice was to do things right and ask her father for his daughter's hand in marriage.

"But he doesn't like me, Honey."

"That's fine. Most fathers don't like the man who wants his daughter. But you do the right thing."

"What if he says no?" Anderson was serious.

"Baby, it's her decision. If he does say no, you can't control that. What do I always tell you?"

"Control what I can control", he answered her.

"Right, baby. That's right. I don't know Jacksa well, but she appears to have a mind of her own. If she wants to marry you she will, and her father's answer won't influence her answer."

When Jacksa left Anderson's house, she went straight to see her mom.

"Mom, they are great people. You are going to love them!" She wanted to make sure everything was ready and to her mother's liking for their guests arrival.

"Have you talked to your husband about his behavior?" Jacksa asked her mother. Min laughed.

"Your father knows what I expect from him. He wouldn't embarrass me."

Anderson took his family and Jacksa to church. He didn't go regularly, but he always went with them to Hattiesville Community Church when his family was visiting, and he always went to church with them when he was home in Catawba. They went to the early service, back to his house to pick up the food, and on to the Baye residence. Anderson was like a kid in a candy store. He was in the midst of the people he loved, and who are the most important to him.

CHAPTER EIGHTY-FOUR

Delia thought it was funny she ran into Clay and Cicely. She knew Cicely was upset, and Delia was glad. *That's what he gets,* she thought. *After all these years, I got him back.*

She hadn't told Javier the whole story about the night she saw Clay at Cicely's apartment. She left out the part about the kiss and told him Clay asked her to have sex with him. Javier was angry that she went back, but he cooled off in a few days. When she left Lola's, she went home to tell Javier what happened. He was not impressed, and he told her so.

"You and Clay are playing games, and I am pretty sick of it. He has probably lost his fiancée, and if you're not careful, you're going to lose yours," Javier said to Delia as he walked out of the room.

Delia couldn't believe Javier was so angry and would threaten to leave her. He was a no-nonsense person, but she didn't expect that reaction. He told her she needed to mind her business and spend her time on her own family and relationships. The thought of losing Javier frightened Delia. She had most likely ruined Clay's relationship, and that's what she wanted, but not at the expense of her own. She didn't sleep that night. When she got up the next morning to go to work, Javier was still in bed. She hated to wake him, but she had to fix this. He sat up but didn't say anything.

"Please forgive me for all this mess with Clay. I just wanted to get back at him because he told me I shouldn't marry you. I own my part of it, but I love you, and I don't want to be without you. Will you accept my apology?" He didn't answer. He just looked at her.

Belinda asked April if they could meet at home again, but April said there were floor plans and a model of the house that were too big to easily move. Belinda knew going to the office increased her chance of seeing Hampton. She thought to herself, "Okay Belinda. Be a big girl, you can do this."

All of Ben's defenses were up. He didn't want to go to the office, didn't want to run into Hampton, but he hoped Hampton knew not to cross him.

The meeting went off without a hitch. They made some minor adjustments to the plans, but for the most part, Belinda and Ben were pleased with what they saw. April did a fantastic job, taking what Belinda envisioned and turning it into reality. She was actually excited now. It was a project she was working on. Now it was going to be their home, all seven of them. All of a sudden, she was totally overwhelmed.

They met with April for over an hour, and there was no sign of Hampton. April and Belinda set another appointment to talk about paint colors, counter colors, cabinet hardware, and those types of things. April said she would also be able to give them a timeline at the next meeting. The only projection she would make is they should be in their new home by spring.

As Ben was opening Belinda's door, Hampton pulled into the parking lot. He was on the phone, but ended his conversation when he saw them. He hurried to get out of his car. "Ben, Belinda. How are you?"

"We're well, Hampton. How are you?" Ben extended his hand to shake with Hampton.

"Fine, thanks."

Belinda was seated but her door was open, and Hampton got a good look at her belly. He thought she was very pretty pregnant and thought that was how Shona looked pregnant with her. Belinda knew she couldn't just ignore him. "Hello, Hampton." She sounded as pleasant as she could.

"I haven't had an opportunity to congratulate you on expecting the babies. April told me you are having twins," Hampton said.

Belinda smiled pleasantly and accepted his congratulations. Hampton was trying to make conversation.

"How do your daughters feel about two siblings?"

Ben chuckled. "They're excited about their little brothers."

"Boys?" Hampton asked.

"Yeah, found out yesterday," Ben said with a big grin.

"Awww, man. That's great. Congrats again. I know you like that!"

"Yep, I'm pretty pumped."

Grandsons, Hampton was thinking to himself.

If anybody who didn't know the situation was looking on, they would only have thought Ben and Hampton were acquaintances—pastor and parishioner, customer and businessman. Belinda looked at her watch, which made Ben look at his. He excused himself, and they left.

Hampton got his things from his car and walked into the office. He walked pass the conference room on his way to his office. April was on the telephone but motioned for him to come in. He looked at the plans for the Coffey home and noticed a few changes. When April hung up, she immediately started talking to her dad about the meeting with Ben and Belinda. She pointed out the few changes. She was pleased with the outcome. His response to her was, "Ben told me the babies are boys, two grandsons." He was staring straight ahead, like he was daydreaming. April looked at her dad; she was immediately furious. After looking at him for a long moment, she walked out of the conference room.

April closed the door to her office and sat down hard in her chair. She was getting really sick of Belinda being her "sister."

No, what she was sick of was Belinda being her dad's daughter. "I've been an only child for twenty-six years. Now all of a sudden, he finds his long lost daughter, and she became the center of the universe!" His daughter, his granddaughters, now his two new grandsons, she was saying to herself. "For goodness sake, he should just tell her, so everybody will know, and we can all move on." She said out loud, "One thing's for sure, I built this company, and he needs me to keep it going, so I hope he doesn't have any ideas about involving his "new family" in my company or in my money. If he does, I have a few ideas of my own."

Hampton stood in the conference room for a few minutes. He thought about Belinda, which made him think about Shona. His imagination got the best of him as he thought about being married to Shona and the two of them raising Belinda together, and April too. His thoughts shifted to April. She was obviously not as excited about having a sister as he was about having another daughter. She was supportive at first, but now she wasn't. They would have to talk because he wanted to make an adjustment to the house plans. He looked at the plans and decided they could build up and give his grandchildren a recreation room. His mind went back to Belinda. She had endured so much and accomplished so much. Her first husband died in Iraq during the war. She graduated from nursing school and is a sought-after surgical nurse, all without him. He could only imagine what she could have, would have done if he had raised her. April was proof. But he was proud of Belinda just the same.

CHAPTER EIGHTY-FIVE

Raja was in Chapel Hill to assist with a major surgical procedure and was gone for a couple of days. Jill and LaLa were glad he would be home that evening. After dinner, playing with LaLa, and putting her to bed three times, Raja and Jill had some time to talk.

"I talked to your dad today about the house."

Jill's eyes lit up. "What did he say?"

"He wants us to make him a 'reasonable' offer."

They talked about what they would offer Jill's parents on their house, a few other things, and then Raja mentioned his parents.

"I want to take a few pictures of LaLa to e-mail to my parents," Raja said to Jill.

"Okay. I'll take a few tomorrow," Jill responded, but she was puzzled where that came from so suddenly.

He saw the look on her face. "I'm keeping my word to my parents, so if they don't keep theirs, we won't have to discuss it."

Several days passed since Jill e-mailed the pictures to the Rajagopals, but they hadn't gotten any response. Raja didn't tell Jill, but he called his parents the day before, and there was no answer. He prayed they were not on their way to the United

States unannounced again. After two calls and no answer, Raja called his cousin Yash.

"Oh, cousin, I apologize. I thought you knew. Your father has become ill and is presently in the hospital."

"What? When did that happen, and what's the problem?" Raja asked Yash.

"We don't understand why your mother has not called. He suffered a heart attack two days ago. He is stable but very weak."

As Raja listened to Yash, he was wondering why his mother had not called. "Can you please tell me who his cardiologist is and give me the phone number so I may call myself?"

Yash gave Raja the information and promised to have his mother call.

As soon as Raja ended the conversation with Yash, he called his father's doctor. His answering service transferred Raja to him. He was glad to talk with Raja because he wasn't getting anywhere with Mrs. Rajagopal.

"Your mother is very emotional, and I'm afraid she is not facing reality."

"My mother is very dramatic, and she creates her own reality." They both laughed.

After a thorough conversation, Raja was sure he was going to have to go to London. What he wasn't sure about was how Jill would take the news.

Kathy was homesick, plain and simple. But she couldn't admit that to anybody. Her cousin Michelle was the only person she talked with every day. Taking four classes probably wasn't the best decision she made. She went to class and studied. She hadn't found a church or made any friends. The only people she saw outside her class were the people in her study groups. She was doing well in all her classes, but she was so tired. She wanted to talk to somebody. She called Campbell. He was glad to hear from her, and they talked about half an hour and caught up on each other's lives. Chloe was still in his life, much to Kathy's dismay.

She would be glad when she could get him out of DavisTown and to New York and far away from Chloe.

When Kathy and Campbell hung up, she couldn't get back to work. She couldn't concentrate. She knew her parents were out, so she couldn't call them. She decided to call Sterling. They hadn't talked in weeks and had only a couple of conversations since she left Hattiesville.

The phone rang several times before he answered. "Hey Kathy, is everything okay?"

"Yeah, I'm good, just had a few minutes, and wanted to say hi."

"Oh, okay. Studies going well?"

"Yeah, there's just so much of it," Kathy said.

"I'm sure," Sterling said. His tone was very formal, and he wasn't saying much. She asked about preseason practice and told him she saw the *Sports Illustrated* article. He gave her a short answer and then thanked her for calling and ended the call.

She was caught off guard by how abrupt he was. She couldn't believe he wouldn't talk to her! Kathy called Michelle.

"Oh my gosh! Kat, you are so naïve."

"What do you mean, Chelle?"

"Kathy, obviously, he had company, female company." Kathy's heart dropped. She didn't say anything. "Kathy, are you there?"

"Yes, I'm here." She let out a big sigh. "It didn't occur to me he was busy."

"He wasn't busy, he had a date. Busy is doing laundry."

"I can't believe Sterling!"

"Kathy! Really! Seriously! You cannot be surprised! You left him!" Michelle was screaming at Kathy. "The man told you he wanted to be with you, but you decided to move to the Big Apple. Now you surprised because he moved on. Why?"

"Michelle, it's only been a couple of months."

"What is your point, Kathy?" She didn't answer. "You don't have one. I told you not to leave Hattiesville. I think my exact words to you were 'put him back out there if you want to.' Now you're upset, but you have absolutely no right to be. Men move on. What is it your daddy used to tell us all the time when we were growing up?"

"Every decision has consequences," they said in unison.

Kathy couldn't study, so she went to bed. But she couldn't sleep. She knew Michelle was right. She was dealing with the consequences of the decision she made. But she made another decision right then, she was going home for fall break. She would work things out with Sterling. She could have a relationship and finish her degrees.

"Mrs. Robinson." Katherine turned around to see Sterling standing behind her with a young woman who looked familiar.

"Hi Sterling, how are you?" They hugged.

"I'm good. How 'bout you?"

"I am well. Thank you for asking," Katherine said smiling and looking toward the young woman. Sterling introduced them, and Katherine remembered who she was. She was the volleyball coach at DavisTown College, and she had played volleyball and won a gold medal in the Olympics. She and Katherine shared a brief hug, and Katherine turned her attention back to Sterling. "Coach Chance, I'm glad you took some time out to come to worship this morning." He laughed. She was always getting on him about his irregular church attendance.

"Yes, ma'am. That's why I wanted to make a point of letting you know I was here! The season starts in a couple of weeks, so I'll be on the road."

"I understand, but keep God first."

"Always. No worries about that. And I'll have the whole team here week after next."

Katherine thanked Sterling's guest for coming and invited her to come again. There were several other people waiting to see Katherine.

Later that day, Katherine replayed in her mind the time with Sterling. She was awfully afraid her daughter had lost him for good. Her first thought was to call Kathy and tell her she saw Sterling, but she decided against that. The more she thought about it the more she knew leaving it alone was best. Kathy made her choice between him and school. So school it was.

CHAPTER EIGHTY-SIX

Early Monday morning, Cicely turned her phone on to call her brother. There was a text message from him, two messages and four text messages from Clay, a voice mail message from Grant, and two text messages from Sunny. She let out a big sigh. She knew eventually that she would have to talk to somebody. But she wasn't ready to talk to Clay. Each time she thought about the things Delia said, her insides would hurt all over again.

As she sat there deciding what to do, the phone rang. It was her brother. They talked a few minutes, made plans for the day, and hung up. Next, Cicely called her supervisor. "I have a family emergency and need some time off." The supervisor was agreeable, asked if there was anything she could do, and told Cicely to let her know when she would be back. Cicely was so glad her supervisor didn't ask any questions.

Cicely took a deep breath and called Clay's office voice mail, she knew he wouldn't be there yet. She left a message. "The new house tonight at eight o'clock." That was all she said. She sent him a text with the same message. One minute later he called her, but she didn't answer. She sent Sunny a text. *Are you back in DC?*

Sunny texted back *No still in Hville looking for you. Pls call me.*

Let me know when you are back in your office was Cicely's response. Her phone rang. It was Sunny. She didn't answer.

Sunny texted back, *Okay, but if you want to talk before then pls call. I won't tell Clay.* Cicely trusted her not to tell Clay, but she knew Sunny would tell Grant and that was the same as telling Clay.

When her brother arrived, she told him the whole story. She cried as he tried to make sense of it for her. She told him she loves Clay, but she was so hurt she didn't think she would ever recover. He assured her she would. They made a plan for the day, and then he was going to take her home. He would take care of his big sister for a few days. He certainly owed her. She had taken care of him most of his life.

Cicely gave her brother the keys to Clay's house, and he was going to get her things. She didn't know where Clay was, and she didn't want to run into him. He assured her that if he ran into Clay, he would handle it. She just hoped her brother wouldn't leave anything.

Clay was a wreck. He hadn't slept, but at least he would see Cicely that evening. He would apologize and beg her if he had to. He had to get her to agree to still marry him. He was sitting on his bed looking at her picture. She was so beautiful, and he loved her so much.

The day went without a hitch. Cicely and her brother didn't run into Clay, Grant, or Sunny. Late that evening, at around six o'clock, Cicely's brother took her to the new house—their house, where Clay proposed to her, where she poured so much of her heart into making it a home. She gathered her things slowly. Most of them were still in boxes anyway. She wasn't going to be there when Clay arrived for their eight o'clock meeting, but he would know she had been there. She knew he would come early so she needed to execute her plan and get out of there.

As her brother was taking the last box to the car, Cicely went to the kitchen and took a champagne glass from the cabinet. The lantern was still sitting on the deck table. It was dusk, barely dark. She walked onto the deck and lit the lantern. She sat the glass in front of the lantern the way Clay did the night he proposed. She slowly slid the engagement ring off her finger and looked at it. The beautiful ring had been his mother's ring, the one he put away for the "right woman." She put the engagement ring in the glass, took a very long, very deep breath, and blew it out slowly. Then she poured water in the glass on top of the ring and walked away.

CHAPTER EIGHTY-SEVEN

Jackson decided to take the birthday trip, one last time together. Then it would be over. He made sure she understood that. They were talking on the telephone.

"Oh, Jack. I am so excited! Thank you for changing your mind."

"Just keep in mind that this will be our last time together. I don't want you to lose sight of that."

"I understand. Really, I do."

They worked out the details, and Jackson hung up and went home. It wasn't late, so he knew Min would still be awake. He could spend some time with her.

When he walked in the house, Min was sitting on the deck, and King was running around the backyard. She was on the phone. King noticed Jackson and came to the deck to see who was there with Min. He played with Jackson for a brief minute and then looked at Min as if wanting her approval. She patted his head, and he ran back into the yard. King had become very protective of Min, and Jackson was fine with that.

Jackson sat across from Min, and after a couple of minutes, realized she was talking to Mrs. Thorn, Anderson's mother. Their time together at dinner was really nice. His family was really great people and from the looks of things, Min was right—Detective Thorn wasn't going anywhere.

Anderson pulled Jackson aside the day they all had dinner to tell him he wanted to talk to Jacksa about getting married. He told Jackson he was not at the "formal proposal stage" yet, but he wanted him to know. Jackson's reply to him had been "talk to me when you get to the 'proposal stage.'"

Jackson realized he was perpetrating. He had some influence, but at the end of the day he knew he wouldn't be able to stop Jacksa from marrying Anderson.

"Absolutely, sweetheart. You have to go." Jill sounded way more supportive than she felt. She knew under the circumstances that Raja needed to manage the situation with his parents, but she didn't like it. The fact of the matter, he was their only child, so it was his responsibility.

Jill had her assistant make Raja's travel arrangements, so he could handle the necessary adjustments to his schedule. Jill asked her to leave his return open. Trey and Dr. Strauss were glad to cover what they could for him, and another colleague would also help. Raja was glad everyone was so accommodating, but he really didn't want to go.

Tara wasn't enthusiastic about Raja going, but it appeared necessary. She offered to go with him. Jill wanted her to go, and Robert was fine with it. She couldn't leave the next day, but she would join him two days later. Jill knew Tara would keep an eye on things, make sure nobody took advantage of Raja, and tell Jill what was really going on.

Raja arrived in London to find his father very ill and his mother absolutely beside herself. He never got a straight answer as to why she didn't call him. Mrs. Rajagopal was totally obsessed with the thought that her husband was going to die. Raja wasn't sure his father would survive, but he couldn't make any headway with his mother. She was more hysterical and irrational than usual. The doctors were cautiously optimistic about his father's recovery.

Once Raja had a handle on what was going on medically and he spoke to all the doctors, he called Dr. Strauss to discuss the plan with him. Dr. Strauss was agreeable with what was going on, but referred Raja to a cardiologist colleague.

When Tara arrived two days later, things quickly became more orderly. She had a way of getting things done, even though the relationship with her family was awkward. As things progressed, it became apparent to Raja and Tara that if his father survived he was going to need more care than Mrs. Rajagopal could offer. The only options were for Raja to hire someone to care for his dad and try to manage things from the United States or take his parents back to Hattiesville with him. Neither option was good.

Tara was communicating with Jill regularly, and she gave her a heads up on the latest discussion. "It's not a good situation any way we look at it, Jill." Tara was choosing her words carefully.

"No, Tara it's not. I can't imagine allowing people into my home who came here to take my child."

"I can't believe I'm saying this because you know I think they're crazy, but Jill, what else can he do?"

Jill knew Tara was right, and she felt guilty for not wanting her husband's parents to be in Hattiesville. Tara told Jill that Raja was going to call her in a few minutes, so she needed to get herself together before they talked.

"I will. I don't want him to hear anything negative in my voice," Jill replied.

As soon as they hung up, Jill called her mother. She updated her quickly, hoping her mother would offer some insight before Raja called.

"Sweetheart, I don't see what choice you have. Sometimes we have to take the bitter with the sweet." As if Ellen was reading her mind, she continued, "I know you don't have enough space for two more people, so we will just have to move more quickly on finalizing the sale. There is plenty of room here. The

Rajagopals can live downstairs, and your family can live up here, and you won't get in each other's way."

"Mom, I can't ask you and Dad to rearrange your plans. We haven't even settled on a price."

"That's okay," Ellen responded. "You didn't ask, I offered."

"You know Daddy doesn't move quickly."

Ellen laughed. "Don't worry about your dad. I'll handle him."

"I am so not looking forward to this."

Before Ellen could respond, the phone beeped. It was Raja.

"It's Raja, Mom. I'll call you back."

CHAPTER EIGHTY-EIGHT

At the Monday morning staff meeting, Roderick Matthews talked about staffing changes. Jacksa Baye would be promoted to senior paralegal. Her first order of business would be dealing with new interns. The summer interns, including Chloe, were leaving in a few weeks. As the meeting progressed, Natalia was thinking about Nicholas. She had to work out something for Chloe to see him before she went back to school. She didn't have much time.

Natalia thought all day how she could talk Kirby into letting her keep the boys for a few hours, and how she could coordinate with Chloe's schedule. She knew Chloe and Campbell would spend some time together before she left for school.

Deciding against an elaborate plan, thinking simple would be better, Natalia called Kirby to ask if she could pick up the boys from school on Friday and take them to the park for a couple of hours. Kirby told her she needed to check with Enoch to see if he had anything planned for them, and she would let her know on Thursday. That wasn't quite what Natalia wanted, but it wasn't a "no," so she would take it. She causally mentioned to Chloe she was working on a surprise and would have it figured out by Thursday. Chloe just laughed and said okay. Chloe was meeting Campbell for dinner. They were going to Charlotte. It was restaurant week, so they could go to an expensive restaurant for half price.

Over dinner, they talked about what was ahead: their senior year in college. They reflected on the last three years and talked about the next three. "I talked to Ms. Robinson, and she wants me to consider law school at Columbia," Campbell told Chloe. She was quiet for a minute.

Finally, she said, "Wow, I didn't expect you to be that far away."

"I haven't decided to apply yet. I'm still thinking about it."

She was quiet. He continued. "Until I came to school at DavisTown and started traveling with the teams, I hadn't ever been out of North Carolina, except for a school trip to Washington DC. I need to experience more. If I can get accepted, that would be awesome."

"You're right, Campbell. I'm just being selfish."

They talked a few more minutes, and then Campbell said very excitedly, "Why don't you apply to Columbia too? You know you'll get accepted."

"I never considered applying anywhere but North Carolina Central Law School. That was always my parents' plan."

"But, sugar, what is your plan? What do you want to do?"

Chloe laughed. "I don't really know, but I'll give it some thought."

"While you're thinking, think about New York City!" Campbell said as he pointed north and laughed.

On Thursday evening, Kirby called Natalia to see if they could switch to Saturday morning. "I have an appointment at the hairdresser, so if you will watch the boys that will be great."

"Sure. Are you okay with me taking them to the park?" Natalia asked.

"Yes, that's fine." They discussed the details, and then Natalia went to Chloe's desk.

"Meet me at the park Saturday morning at eleven o'clock."

"I am not running with you, Natalia." They both laughed.

"I won't be running. I told you I have a surprise for you."

"What kind of surprise?" Chloe asked folding her arms.

"If I tell you it won't be a surprise. Just trust me, sis!"

"I'm not running with you, girl!" Chloe said. Natalia walked away laughing.

CHAPTER EIGHTY-NINE

Where did this change order come from? April thought to herself. She turned the page and saw her dad's name and his initials in his handwriting. She was fuming. First, he added a second bonus room on the plans for Ben and Belinda's new house; now he was changing the plan for Belinda's suite at the church. *What was he trying to do?* she wondered And to top it all off, there was no change in cost, so she knew he did it. Neither Belinda nor Ben had asked for it.

Hampton went to the church and personally met with Juan and the contractor. He explained how he wanted to add an area in Mrs. Coffey's suite to accommodate the new babies. He wanted to create a space for two baby beds and storage, and on the other side of the room, a play area for the babies and a reading area for the girls. He explained to them the changes were a surprise and a gift to the Coffeys so he asked the men not to mention it. They agreed.

"Juan, I hired a separate decorator for these areas and I will have her see you personally."

"Si, señor. I will take good care of it," Juan said.

"Thanks, man."

Hampton felt good about what he was doing. He had so much to make up to Belinda. This was just the beginning. He headed straight to the insurance company to see the nurse practitioner. He was having an insurance physical to buy life insurance. Belinda would be the beneficiary. He also set up college savings for Brittani and Brianna, and he would do the same for the boys on their first birthday.

When he walked back into the office, April walked in his office behind him. He turned around when she slammed the door. Before he could say anything, she said, "What the hell are you doing?"

He sat down and leaned back in the chair.

"Would you like to tell me what you're so hot about?"

"Don't play with me, Dad. Did you think I wouldn't find out about the changes you made to the Coffeys' house and to the church?"

He could see the fury in her eyes. "April I wasn't hiding anything from you. I intended to tell you what I did."

She interrupted him, "Tell me; not discuss it with me!"

"If I needed to discuss the technical aspects with you, yes. Otherwise, no." Hampton was firm.

"Do you know how much that is going to cost?" April was screaming.

"April, it's not going to cost you anything. Your percentage will not change," he calmly answered her.

"Daddy, what are you trying to prove? Belinda Coffey has been your daughter, you think, for about fifteen minutes and you are giving her tens of thousands of dollars! And she doesn't even know you may be her father."

"Sit down, April. Let's talk."

"I'm fine standing."

Hampton leaned forward, put his elbows on the desk. "Have a seat, April." His voice was firm.

She sat on the edge of the chair across from him. Hampton was trying to gather himself. He couldn't believe April was acting like this. "Since you came to live with me when you were six years old, you have never wanted for anything. You have had everything you needed or wanted. If I had known about Belinda, she would have been with me too. April, Belinda grew up in foster care because I believed she died in the accident with her mother or had been put up for adoption. There are no words that can make you understand how that makes me feel. I am not trying to take anything away from you. Thanks to you, there's plenty to go around. But if I can do something to make her and her family more comfortable, I will, and when you have children, I'll do the same for you. Belinda is your sister, so get used to it."

"But, Daddy, she may not want to have a relationship with either of us. And obviously, her husband doesn't want you in her life. You can't buy her love."

Before April could continue, Hampton interrupted her. "My intention is not to buy her love. I am buying things for my grandchildren to save their parents some money. That's no more than any grandparent would do."

"But they didn't ask for a playroom at the house or nursery space at the church. You decided to give them all that. Why don't you just tell her the story and see how she reacts. She may not want you or any of your gifts," April said sarcastically.

"If it was up to me, I would. But I am respecting her husband's wishes. If the situation was reversed, I would want him to respect mine. So for now, it's out of my hands."

April was looking at her dad. For all his attempts to reason with her, she was not feeling any better about this. He went on to ask about all the technical aspects of the changes he requested. She assured him she would take care of it and walked out of his office.

"Since it's out of your hands, I guess I'll have to take matters into my hands," April said out loud as she walked down the hall toward her office. She sat down at her desk, took a few minutes to compose herself, and picked up the phone. "Belinda, hi, it's April Josephs. How are you?"

CHAPTER NINETY

Clay arrived at the house at seven thirty. Cicely's car wasn't there. He was glad; he wanted to get there first. He had a dozen roses, and he was prepared to do or say whatever he had to. He had to get her to accept his apology. He had to get her to marry him. He had to have her back. This had been the worst two days of his life.

Delia left a message apologizing to him. Of course, she didn't know how much damage she had really done. He didn't respond to her or even acknowledge her call. He wanted Delia out of his life forever. He used her and it back fired—three years later. At this moment, she had the upper hand. Her one encounter with Cicely had the potential to ruin his life forever. In his estimation, what she did to him was worse than what he did to her. He hurt her, she hurt him, but more importantly she hurt Cicely, and Cicely deserved better.

When Clay walked into the house, he knew this wasn't going to go the way he wanted. All of Cicely's things were gone. No clothes in the closet, some of the boxes were gone, her computer was gone. All the new window treatments Sunny made, and the accessories they spent hours making sure matched perfectly, were still in place. The comforters Sunny shipped were still in the boxes, waiting for the new beds to be delivered.

Clay walked back to the front of the house and on the table in the hall was the packet of information from the travel agent containing the details about their wedding and honeymoon. He stopped in his tracks and dropped his head. He stood in that spot for a full minute. When he lifted his head, the light caught his eye—it was the light from the lantern on the deck. He walked through the kitchen and out on to the deck. The view was just like the night he proposed to her. The only thing different was there were no bubbles in the glass. He picked up the glass, took a good look inside, and saw Cicely's engagement ring in water. He took the ring out of the water, held it to his lips, and let the tears roll down his cheeks. He found a chair just before the floodgates opened. He sobbed and sobbed and yelled between the gut-wrenching sobs.

CHAPTER NINETY-ONE

Natalia was playing on the sliding board with Nicholas and Blake when her phone rang. She directed Chloe through the park to where they were. In just a couple of minutes, Chloe was walking up the hill toward the three of them. She was shocked to see Nicholas. At first, she didn't smile; she was slightly angry at Natalia. She had worked so hard to put Nicholas in the back of her mind. Now there he was, close enough for her to touch him. She could hold him, hug him, kiss him, grab him, throw him in her car, and drive away with him.

She gained her composure and approached them slowly. The boys hardly noticed her. Natalia looked at Chloe with a big smile on her face. She mouthed "Surprise!" Chloe mouthed "Thank you." For the next two hours the four of them ran around the playground, walked around the lake, and walked the nature trail. Nicholas and Blake played with Chloe, but they never asked her name, and Natalia was careful not to say her name.

Natalia knew the hard part would be getting them to leave and taking them, especially Nicholas, away from Chloe. She kept an eye on the time. She wanted to have the boys' home a few minutes before she told Kirby she would.

"Let's go, guys!" Natalia said cheerfully.

"Natalia, can we get some fries?" Nicholas was asking. Blake nodded in agreement.

"Yes, get in the car and buckle up." They climbed into the backseat of her car and sat on their booster seats. As they were getting buckled in, Chloe and Natalia had a brief conversation. Chloe thanked her for "the greatest surprise ever." She walked away as Natalia checked the boys' seat belts. As they drove away, Natalia saw Chloe sitting in her car. She was looking at her phone, probably watching the video she took of Nicholas. Natalia picked up their fries and took them home.

When she left the Casebier's' home, she called Chloe. Natalia wanted to make sure she wasn't sad. Chloe invited her over. When Natalia got there, Chloe was sitting at the table in the breakfast nook, watching the video. They revisited the day and laughed at the boys. "Oh Natalia, thank you for working that out. You are so good to me. You are the best sister ever!" Natalia looked at Chloe and saw the tears.

"Please, don't cry Chloe."

"I just wish I could put him in the car and take him back to Atlanta with me."

Natalia just looked at her.

CHAPTER NINETY-TWO

Anderson and Jacksa left the gym and headed to his house. They picked up dinner from Lola's. He wanted to talk to her. He was going to the FBI training academy in Quantico, Virginia, in a few days, and he wanted to fully establish their relationship before he left. The conversation started with her telling him about her promotion to senior paralegal.

"So exactly what does that mean?" Anderson asked.

"It means I supervise all the paralegals on both sides of the office and both research staffs."

"Okay, Miss Supervisor," Anderson said laughing.

"And it means a fifteen-thousand-dollar increase to my annual salary, and my annual bonus will increase," Jacksa said wide eyed. She was still surprised about it.

"So is that enough money to pay for a wedding?" he asked very matter-of-factly.

"A wedding, whose wedding?" She looked puzzled.

"Your wedding, our wedding." Jacksa wasn't saying anything. Anderson put his arm around her. "I know we have some ground to cover, but I know you're the one for me, and I want us to start thinking about getting married."

Jacksa's mind was racing. She and Anderson had known each other a little over a year and exclusively dating for about six months. Of course, she had thought about marrying Anderson. She and her mom secretly discussed it. But Jacksa had no idea

Anderson was thinking about it. He hadn't even told her he loved her. As if he knew what she was thinking, he looked directly at her. "You know I love you."

Jacksa swallowed hard. "I love you too."

They continued to talk. He told her more about Quantico and about the part of the training he hadn't mentioned. Part two would take him out of the country to an undisclosed location. "But when I get back, we will resume this conversation."

Jacksa smiled. "I like that idea," she said.

CHAPTER NINETY-THREE

Bryce and Bradley Coffey were born seven weeks early. They were both in the neonatal intensive care unit, but they were stable. The pediatricians were concerned because their lungs were not fully developed. They told Ben that the boys would probably be in the hospital for about four weeks.

But the bigger problem—Belinda was in intensive care too. She was in critical condition. She had a heart attack. Everybody was worried about her, and April Josephs knew it was her fault.

April told Belinda she needed to see her about changes to the plans for their family's new home. "It won't take long. I can meet you for lunch," April told Belinda. Belinda agreed, and they met in the hospital cafeteria. That turned out to be a good thing.

"Mr. Josephs made a change to the house plans. He has added another bonus room." Belinda laughed that April referred to her dad as "Mr. Josephs," but cringed at the sound of Hampton's name.

"Why would he do that?" Belinda asked, frowning and shrugging.

April didn't answer her right away. She went on to show Belinda the drawings. Belinda looked puzzled.

"Did Ben ask for an additional room?"

"No," April said very sarcastically.

"Well, I don't understand. Plus, do we need another room? I'm sure this will put us over-budget."

"Oh, sister dear, there's no additional cost. Our father wants you to have the room at no additional cost, and by the way, he's giving you a nursery area in your suite at the church."

"April, what are you talking about?" Belinda was thinking about April calling her "sister" and referring to Hampton as "our father."

"I think his exact words were he was 'buying things for his grands, and that's no more than any grandparent would do.'"

"What?" Belinda screamed at April. Several people in the cafeteria looked at them. "What are you talking about, April?" Belinda's tone was sharp.

April proceeded to tell Belinda the story. She started by telling her that Hampton thought he knew her and eventually hired a private investigator. April continued by telling Belinda about the birth certificate and how Hampton determined Belinda was his daughter.

The last part of the story was when everything went terribly wrong. "So are you saying Hampton knows where my mother is?" Belinda asked April. She was crying, trembling, and breathing hard.

"Belinda, you should calm down, we can finish talking about this later."

"Answer me!" Belinda screamed at April and slammed her hand on the table.

April told Belinda about the accident, about Shona's cousin telling Hampton she believed the baby was his, about the coach telling him to come back to school. She told Belinda that Hampton told Ben the story, but he didn't want her to know. The lunch crowd had thinned considerably, and Belinda was glad. She knew she needed to go, but she had to hear the rest of what April had to say. She was so upset, though she wasn't sure she could even get up.

"Pastor Coffey didn't want you to know because the rest of the story is horrible," April told Belinda, knowing she bit off more than she could chew. Her intention in saying anything was to make Belinda angry so she would tell Hampton she didn't want the changes to the house or church plans and didn't want him in her life. She had no intention of telling Belinda the rest of the story. But she was into it now, and she couldn't walk away. Belinda had a right to know, but April knew it wasn't her place to tell her.

"The accident that killed your mother caused the death of another young mother too," April said.

Belinda wasn't saying anything. Her heart was beating fast. She was taking deep breaths, but she had a hard contraction.

"Belinda, I don't know how to tell you this. It's not my place to tell you."

"Talk . . . April." Belinda was dizzy and breathing hard.

"The lady your mother killed in the accident was Ben's mother," April said very nonchalantly.

Belinda repeated what April said. "My mother killed Ben's mother. My mother killed my husband's mother." She was trembling. "My mother . . .," she whispered.

Belinda got very hot. She started to get up, but before she could get steady on her feet, she threw up and collapsed.

A doctor in the cafeteria attended to Belinda until someone could get a stretcher and get her to the emergency room.

April admitted to Hampton what she did. He was terribly upset with her and terribly worried about Belinda. He told Ben what April told him and apologized profusely. Hampton Josephs's heart was hurting for both his daughters—for April because she was so angry she hurt her sister and for Belinda because she had yet another battle to fight. His prayer was for this situation to pass—for Belinda and her boys to be well and for April to be over her selfishness and embrace having a sister.

"God, please fix this. It has to be all right for all of us: Bradley, Bryce, Brittani, Brianna, Belinda, Ben, April, and me. Amen."

When Grammy, Auntie, and Kirby arrived in Atlanta, they went straight to the hospital. Enoch stayed in Hattiesville with the boys. There was just too much going on to try and keep them entertained. Kirby asked Natalia to be on standby if Enoch needed her. She agreed and told Kirby she would pray for Belinda.

Thelma and Lili Marcos took over everything having to do with Brittani and Brianna. Thelma was staying at the house with them. Ben was at the hospital almost around-the-clock. He only went home to take short naps, shower, and change clothes. He was grateful to have capable leadership at the church to keep things going, and Juan was on top of things with the renovation project.

The building would be ready on schedule, but they all knew the ribbon cutting and first gathering would have to be rescheduled. The church family knew the twins came early, and Belinda had a heart attack. That was all anybody knew.

Ben shared with Enoch the whole story, including April telling Belinda about her mother causing the accident that killed his mother. They agreed not to tell Grammy, Auntie, and Kirby until they were face to face.

Kirby went in to see Belinda first; Auntie and Grammy were in the waiting area with Ben. Belinda responded to Kirby, but she had a tube in her mouth so she couldn't talk. Tears streamed down her face, and she held Kirby's hand tightly. Kirby didn't cry, and she reassured Belinda that things were fine. Belinda kept shaking her head no.

"Yes, they will be. Don't worry," Kirby said to her. "I know there's something you want to tell me . . ." Belinda nodded her head yes.

"But it can wait. I'm going to the nursery to see my nephews, and let Grammy and Aunt Avis come in to see you." Belinda shook her head no and then came more tears. Kirby was puzzled. "You don't want to see Gram?" she asked. Belinda shook her head no and closed her eyes. Kirby didn't know what to do or say. She stood there for a minute, and it appeared Belinda had gone back to sleep. The nurse came in so Kirby left.

Kirby got Ben's attention before Grammy or Auntie could see her and motioned for him to come into the hall. She told him what happened. He let out a deep sigh.

"We need to talk," Ben said to Kirby.

He went back in the waiting room to get his grandmother and aunt, and the four of them went into a small private room around the corner from the waiting area. Ben called Enoch and asked him to sign on to his computer. Then he took his iPad and called Enoch on Skype.

"I need to tell you all what led to Belinda's heart attack," Ben said, looking from one of them to the other. Enoch's eyes were fixed on Kirby. "I don't really know what the beginning of the story is, so I'll start with meeting Hampton Josephs."

Kirby's heart dropped. She thought about Belinda telling her how Hampton flirted with her. As Ben talked, their body language and facial expressions changed. He was choosing his words carefully, looking at Grammy more than Kirby or Auntie.

"What are you saying, Benji?" Grammy asked.

Avis reached over and took her hand. "Gram, the person who caused the accident that killed my mother was Belinda's biological mother."

"Oh, sweet Jesus," Grammy said.

"Holy Father," Auntie said.

Kirby covered her mouth with both hands and sat perfectly still. She didn't say anything.

Ben started to cry. Auntie put her arms around him. Tears were streaming down Grammy's face too. Enoch spoke up. "April Josephs told Belinda all this and the shock of it all caused her heart attack."

"So you knew?" Kirby asked Enoch while looking at the screen.

"Not 'til yesterday," Enoch said quietly.

"So that's why Belinda doesn't want to see Grammy," Kirby said looking at Ben.

He shook his head yes. He was wiping his face with his handkerchief. He regained his composure, but Enoch answered, "As far as Ben can figure out, she feels guilty, and she's ashamed to face Grammy."

"Lord, have mercy. Why would she take that on," Grammy said more as a statement than a question. "That child is not responsible for any of what her mother did."

They talked awhile longer, and then Auntie looked at Ben and asked very seriously, "How do you feel about all this, sweetie?"

"To be honest, I was pretty angry at Hampton when he told me. Then I was really sad and hurt then really numb about the whole thing. But not until I found out that April told Belinda did I feel the full effect of how my wife would feel. But all I care about right now is Belinda getting well. We have two little boys in ICU who need their mother. She hasn't even held them, and she's only seen them briefly. We have two daughters at home who also need their mother, and I don't want them to connect their brother's birth with their mother being sick."

"The other crazy part of all this is Hampton Josephs is Belinda's dad," Kirby said.

"It appears so," Ben replied.

"Wow!" She would tell Enoch and Ben what Belinda shared with her later. "So April was jealous and that's why she told Belinda?"

"Looks that way," Enoch said.

Ben went on to tell them about Hampton making the changes to the church plans and their house plans. "And April was angry so she told Belinda, but I know she didn't intend to cause all this," Ben said.

"Have you talked to her, son?" Grammy asked.

"Yes, ma'am. We had a long talk— me, her and her dad. She was very remorseful, very apologetic, and quite upset. They both were."

"Well, let me say two things." Grammy sat up straight and sounded very firm. "I'm not going back to Hattiesville." She looked at the iPad screen. "Enoch, you make arrangements to get my things down here. Just let me know how much it costs."

"Yes, ma'am."

"Benji, you take me to see Belinda. She might not be able to talk to me, but she can listen."

CHAPTER NINETY-FOUR

The birthday weekend was here. Jackson told Min and Jacksa he was going to a baseball doubleheader between the Atlanta Braves and the Tamp Bay Rays in Tampa. He was traveling with some friends from work. Min was glad he was getting away. He seldom did anything away from the family, except his Thursday night excursion, which she had made peace with.

He parked his car in her garage. They drove her car. He had a gold and white gift bag that she was curious about. She was excited. She knew it was for her, but she hadn't expected a gift. The ride to Tampa was good. They talked, they laughed, and they were both really relaxed.

Jackson felt slightly guilty that he was enjoying himself. But she did everything he asked, accommodated all his "rules." Other than the situation with the flowers, there hadn't been any hiccups.

They checked into the hotel and actually went to that evening's baseball game. On Saturday, it would be all about her. Like she told him, she would only have one fiftieth birthday.

Min and Jacksa went to a movie and after Jacksa dropped her off, Min walked outside for a few minutes with King. She stood against the deck and thought about her conversation with Jacksa. Jacksa told her mother about the conversation with Anderson. Min was delighted. She genuinely liked Anderson. He was a good man from a good family. He was the kind of man she wanted for her daughter. She just hoped God would answer her prayer. She constantly prayed that Jacksa would not inherit the disease that would send her husband into another woman's arms.

Min heard the phone, and she expected it to be Jackson. She left him a message that she and Jacksa were going to the movie.

"Hello."

"Hey, Ma!"

"JJ, darling, how are you?"

"Good. What ya doin'?"

"I am on the deck watching King run around."

"That dog gets more love than any dog in town."

Min laughed. After a few minutes, there was a beep on the line. It was Jackson. She asked him to hold, finished with JJ, and then back to Jackson. They talked a few minutes, and then he made sure she called King in, locked the doors, and set the alarm. Min could hear a lot of noise in the background.

"Okay, babe. Talk to you tomorrow. Love you," Min said.

"Love you more. Good night, sweetie," Jackson said as he left the bar area to go back to his room.

Anderson and Jacksa spent every evening together the week before he left for Quantico. He gave her his emergency phone number and e-mail address. His mother was the only other person with that information. He explained to her that he didn't know how the training would be structured, so he didn't know how much contact he would have with her. She said she understood, but she was more nervous than she let on. She gave the whole thing a lot of thought and admitted to herself that she was afraid. This was Anderson's dream, and no matter what, she would support him. But she was afraid. There were just so many secrets. But before he came over that night, she said out loud to herself, "Put your big-girl panties on and deal with it."

Anderson was leaving on Sunday morning. He went to Catawba, took Jacksa with him, and spent Saturday with his family. When they were back in Hattiesville, he reinforced what he told her. "I love you, and when I get back, we will make some things happen." They prayed together that night, and when he left, she was smiling. As soon as he was out of the driveway, she cried.

$\mathcal{C}$HAPTER NINETY-FIVE

Ten days into Anderson's training in Quantico, things changed. He and two other new agents were told they were being sent on a special training assignment. They were not told the location, only that they should be ready to leave in one hour, and they could send one e-mail.

> As he packed his clothes, he was trying to decide if he would e-mail Jacksa or his mother. He decided to e-mail his mom and tell her to call Jacksa. He knew he couldn't say much, and the e-mail had to be sent from the bureau computer. *Hey, Ma. Being transferred today for more training in an undisclosed location. I'm doing fine, don't worry. Please call Jacksa. Love you bunches, AT.*

Not until he got there did he find out it wasn't training after all. It was an actual assignment.

CHAPTER NINETY-SIX

Chloe and Natalia had lunch the day before Chloe's last day at work. They talked about Nicholas. They replayed all the funny things he did when they were together.

"Nat, what's the possibility you can get the Casebier's to let you bring them to the park on Saturday? I would love to see Nicholas before I leave."

"I don't know. Kirby's sister is in the hospital, so they may be out of town this weekend."

"Will you please ask to see what they say?" Chloe asked.

"Sure, sis. I'll ask," Natalia said, smiling at Chloe.

Kirby agreed to let the boys go to the park with Natalia. Enoch was working. She was glad for an hour to herself. Her mind was racing. She kept thinking about everything that's been going on with Belinda. She also wasn't sure how she felt about Belinda having another sister—a biological sister. Kirby was thinking that for all their lives they only had each other. Now it appeared Belinda had a sister and a father. This was a lot to process.

Chloe was already near the train on the playground when Natalia and the boys arrived. For an hour, they played and ran around, and the boys giggled so hard Blake got the hiccups. Natalia went to the car to get him some water after trying unsuccessfully to show him how to hold his breath. The whole event was about five minutes, but that was five minutes Chloe had Nicholas to herself. She gave him a big hug. He pretended to have the hiccups too, so he could get some water.

When it was time for them to go, Natalia told Blake and Nicholas to "climb in" and opened the back doors. They hopped onto their booster seats. Natalia made sure Blake was buckled in, and Chloe made sure Nicholas was buckled in on the driver's side. When Natalia closed the door on the passenger side, Chloe closed the back door on the driver's side, and then quickly jumped into the driver's seat and drove away.

CHAPTER NINETY-SEVEN

Kathy decided she wouldn't wait until fall break to go home. She made arrangements to be home for Labor Day weekend. She was more excited than she realized she would be. Her parents were glad to see her. So were the few friends she saw while she was there.

When she arrived in town, she called Sterling. He didn't answer his office phone or mobile phone, so she called Campbell. He told her that Coach Chance was at an away game.

"When will he be back?" Kathy asked.

"The game is Saturday night. We fly back Sunday morning."

"You're with the team?"

"Yes, ma'am. My internship was extended for the school year.

"That's great, Campbell. Why are you flying?"

"We're playing Georgetown in DC," Campbell said.

Kathy's heart dropped. It didn't occur to her when she decided to come home that Sterling may be away. She didn't do her homework. Kathy wanted to know if the volleyball coach was with them, but she couldn't ask Campbell.

"Ms. Robinson, do you want me to have Coach call you?" Campbell asked.

She wanted to say yes, but it was inappropriate to ask him to deliver a message.

"No, thank you, Campbell. I'll take care of it."

After thinking about it for a few minutes, she called again and left a message. She sent the same message via text. *Hi, Sterling. It's Kathy. I am in Hattiesville for the weekend. Hope we can get together when you get back on Sunday.*

Two hours later he texted her back: *Sorry to miss you this trip. Not coming back with team.* Kathy was crushed. The intent of the trip home was to tell Sterling she made a mistake, and she wanted to work on their relationship. Too late.

CHAPTER NINETY-EIGHT

Ben walked Grammy to Belinda's room. The tube was out of her mouth, but she still had to use the oxygen face mask. The head of the bed was slightly elevated, so she didn't look so small and frail lying there.

She smiled when she saw Ben, but closed her eyes as they welled up with tears when she saw Grammy. Auntie came in last and closed the door. The tension in the room was thick. Aunt Avis spoke first. She knew somebody had to set the tone for what needed to be said. She walked to the opposite side of the bed from where Ben and Grammy were standing. She leaned down and kissed Belinda's forehead and then smiled at her.

"Belinda, sweetheart, I'm glad you're improving. I saw those boys, and they are getting along just fine. They need their mommy, though." The tears rolled down Belinda's face. Auntie looked up at Ben, and he was crying too. He cleared his throat and walked closer to the bed.

"Baby, I told Grammy and Auntie the whole story, and nobody holds you responsible for any of this."

Grammy interrupted Ben. "Belinda, honey, don't take this on. What your mother did is not a reflection on you. And I'm sure it was an accident. None of us knew. We weren't there, and what you have to keep in mind is, as awful as all this is, God allowed it. We don't know why. But we can move on, all of us."

"Avis is right. You have four children who need you; two who don't even know you. Now you need to will yourself to get better so you can take care of your family."

Belinda hadn't even tried to say anything. She just kept looking from one to the other. Finally, she whispered, "I'm so sorry."

"Sorry for what?" Ben answered her.

"For everything," she said.

Ben took her face in his hands. His kissed her lips, kissed her forehead, and kissed her lips again. "You don't have anything to be sorry for," he told her.

"Do you still love me?" Belinda asked him. Her voice was just above a whisper.

"Of course, I love you. I will always love you. The past is the past."

"But what about . . ." Belinda started, but Ben interrupted her.

"The future is what we will work on."

"She said he's my father," Belinda said quietly.

"I know, and when you get well, we will sort all that out," Ben said smiling at her.

"Belinda, are you ready to see the boys?" Aunt Avis interjected. She felt sure the babies would snap Belinda out of her depression. Belinda looked at the tubes in both arms.

"I can't hold them," she said.

"That's all right. Avis and I will hold them, they just need to see you," Grammy said. "And Benji can go get the girls. We're a family, and we need to act like it. Family is about being together."

Kirby opened the door just as Grammy was talking. She came in with a big smile, and behind her were Brittani and Brianna with bigger smiles. Thelma had dropped them off.

"Mommy!"

"Hi, Mommy!" They started talking at the same time.

"Slow down, girls," Kirby finally said.

The girls told Belinda about school and about seeing their brothers. They told her she had to get well and come home, and they promised they would help take care of her and their brothers.

After a while, Belinda dozed off and Ben asked everybody to leave the room. When they were all gone, he sat beside her and held her hand. He prayed for her, for their children, and for April and Hampton. He prayed aloud, not knowing if Belinda could hear him or not. When he finished, he just sat and watched her sleep. The nurse came in to check on her.

"Nurse, what's the chance we can take Belinda to see our boys?" Ben asked.

"I doubt the doctor will approve that, but I can probably get the pediatrician to let the boys come up here for a few minutes. I'll take care of it before my shift ends tonight."

"Thank you," Ben said smiling.

Kirby and Auntie were going back to Hattiesville the next day, so they went to Ben and Belinda's house to make sure everything was in order for the girls and Grammy. When they were all gone, the nurse who Ben talked to earlier peeped in the door. "Be right back," she said. A few minutes later, the nurse came back pushing an Isolette, and another nurse was behind her. There was a monitor, oxygen and wires, and an IV pole with medicine in two small bags. The boys were lying side by side. They wore little knit caps, T-shirts, diapers, and socks. There was a hospital bracelet on their ankles with their names so the nurses and doctors could tell them apart.

The nurse helped Ben into a gown. She lifted Bradley and placed him in his dad's arms. Ben kissed his forehead and he squirmed a little. Ben rubbed Belinda's arm. "Sweetie, look who's here. Belinda, wake up baby, you have company." She opened her eyes, looked at Ben and realized the baby was in his arms. He laid Bradley in her right arm, and then the nurse gave him Bryce. Ben kissed him on the cheek and laid him in Belinda's left arm. She looked from one to the other over and over. As best she could with the tubes in her arms, she pulled them closer to her. Ben took out his phone and took pictures of the three of them. The nurse only let the boys stay a few minutes. She laid them back in the isolette and Ben took a picture of the two of them lying there back to back. He thought to himself he always wanted his sons to have each other's back.

EPILOGUE

The birthday celebration was going nicely. At midnight, Jackson gave her part of her gift, a pair of designer gold hoop earrings. The big gold and white bag was still sitting there. The next morning he ordered room service, and they had breakfast in bed.

The sun had been up long enough for Min be up and have taken King out, but she was still in bed. King nudged Min with his wet nose. She didn't move. King nudged Min again. She still didn't move. He licked her face. She moved her head from side to side. The second time he licked her face, she opened her eyes. But she couldn't move. King barked and that kept her attention. Min tried hard to stay focused. She knew King was putting his training to work. King barked again. She made sure he knew she was engaged. The word. What was the word? Min was concentrating hard. The trainer gave them a word to say that would activate King's emergency training. Min was wearing her emergency bracelet but she couldn't move her arm. It was a German word. "Ja." That was it. It means yes in German. She looked at King and said "Ja, Ja". King barked and went to the hall and pushed the emergency button on the alarm. In a few seconds the voice on the other end called her name.

"Mrs. Baye, do you need help?" King barked again. Min couldn't speak loud enough for the speaker to pick up her voice. "Mrs. Baye, I have dispatched the medics." King kept barking. "I will stay on the line until they arrive." King kept barking.

The fire truck arrived first, then the medics, then the police. They could hear King barking inside. When the neighbor saw the emergency vehicles she came over with the key. The fireman knew to pat King's head and let him take them to Min. He ran to her room and stopped at the foot of the bed. They found Min in bed and unresponsive.

The neighbor stood beside King and told the medics about Min and the Multiple Sclerosis. She kept patting the dog's head. They quickly assessed her, loaded her on the stretcher and started out the house. "I will lock up and call her daughter," the neighbor said. King walked to the ambulance with them and when they pulled away, he used the bathroom and came back to the house.

Jacksa was working out and almost didn't hear her phone. When she saw the neighbors name on the screen she knew something was wrong. She wiped her face and started putting her things in her bag. After she spoke with the neighbor, she rushed to the hospital.

She called her dad. He didn't answer. She called JJ, told him the situation, including how King saved the day, but told him not to come home.

One day in a casual conversation, Jackson asked, and she told him she was born at twelve minutes past two in the afternoon. So at precisely that time on Saturday afternoon, he gave her the gold and white bag. It was everything she wanted, the whole designer set: chocolate brown leather blazer, boots, tote bag, pocketbook, wallet, and keychain.

"Thank you, Jack! I love it!" she said, putting her arms around his neck.

Jacksa called her dad a second time a few hours later. She left another message. "Dad, please call me right away. Mom is in the hospital."

He checked his messages Sunday morning.